THE CLASSIC CAR DISCIPLES

Subjects of propaganda

Published by Currus Press 2022

Paperback ISBN: 978-1-7391999-0-6
eBook ISBN: 978-1-7391999-1-3

Scripture quotations are from the King James (Authorised) Version, the New English Bible, and the Quran.

THE CLASSIC CAR DISCIPLES

Subjects of propaganda

PATRICK BOLTON

Contents

1
Triumph Stag

(Saffron Yellow V8 3 litre)

Nine-year-old Miles turned over in his bed and reflected on his day's religious education. With some eloquence and the instinct within his genes, his teachers instilled the certainty that God's merciful presence was all around him. An immediate need to be schooled far away in the northern countryside dictated that he pray – a prayer more along the lines of a deal. The terms to which he adhered for the rest of his life.

In the old West Riding of Yorkshire lies a valley, on the north side of which is a limestone scar of some height; the lower south side is predominantly millstone grit. Not so many years ago, the seasons used to be clear-cut here. The crystal-white snow arrived in January for a usual stay of three months. Spring brought the wind and rain, fuelling the scar with fresh-water streams to sparkle and foam, cleaning in preparation for the countryside's transposition to youthful green colours, that would gently age through the summer. A perfect place to establish a rural school for boys to mature to the highest academic standard whilst learning to appreciate the wonder of nature.

Young Miles Beaumaris was quite comfortable amusing himself, singing a pop song or two into the air rushing by the rear window of his dad's sports saloon. His elder brother, John, was privileged to occupy the passenger seat next to his father. The first port of call was the upper school to drop John off, hitherto addressed by faculty members as Beaumaris Major. Apart from a weekly five-minute walk allowed after the Sunday matins service, he was out of bounds and might as well have been on another planet. Only 300 yards distant, and at a lower level, a sweeping drive encompassing a shrubbery on a steep slope with a small waterfall on the left led to the grand façade of the preparatory school for boys. Miles could see many boys milling about from the back of the Lagonda, down the continuing incline on the right some way below. A porter was waiting for them at the imposing front door to take charge of Miles's tuck box and trunk. 'Well, this is it, Son; the first day at school,' was the best his dad could do. Dad cheerfully waved goodbye and climbed back into the car, exclaiming that it was 'no good prolonging the agony'. The nine-year-old boy standing alone, focused his eyes on the last flicker of home life as the car eased forward, steadily making its way down the long drive. At length, his dad and the vehicle disappeared back to the outside world through the baronial school gates.

Curiosity determined that the young chap should stroll back down the drive to join the listless throng, apparently waiting for the first roll call before tea. The first boy he came upon was sitting on the grass bank with tears in his eight-year-old eyes, bravely trying to listen to the Nottingham Forest V Luton Town cup final on his transistor in the afternoon sunshine. While envying the compact Philips radio pressed to his ear, Miles commented that the new boys were all in the same boat. The boy's surname turned out to be Barrow, his sobs still audible as the bell rang out for the rota before afternoon tea.

Two schoolmasters organised the boys alphabetically. Apart from Barrow, who irritatingly was adjacent to Miles, silence reigned. The roll call began . . . 'Albrecht?'

'Present, Sir.'

'Allenby?'

'Present, Sir.'

'Appleton?'

'Here, Sir.'

'Barrow?'

'P-p-p . . .'

'Louder, BARROW!'

'Per-Per present, Sir.'

'Thank you, Barrow!' the roll caller sarcastically barked. 'Next – Beaumaris Minor?'

'Present, Sir.'

As the roll call proceeded, the boys in Miles's vicinity evidenced a certain amount of mirth. Peter Barrow, however, lost control of his face as it cracked and creased from his trying to suppress the laughter erupting from deep down. 'My mum's got one of them, a Morris Minor, I mean,' he whispered.

'Well, it's an ill wind that blows nobody any good. Peter, it's probably an indication I've got a future in the motor trade!'

The school rules and discipline were explained and, in general, were not hard to follow. These were instilled into the boys in a fair and relatively modern fashion. However, it was apparent from the beginning that the regime had evolved over centuries of public school education designed to fulfil the needs of Britain's establishment and its empire.

Included in this preparation for adult life was the need for physical fitness. All pupils had to participate in exhausting long-distance runs and do their best on the playing field. The Duke of Wellington insisted that the British won the battle of Waterloo on these hallowed grounds. The curriculum and the very structure of the historic buildings seemed to be a further catalyst for moulding character to the desired goal. The shadowy passageways led to classrooms with old wooden desks, tiered up in rows to the back of the lecture rooms in Victorian style, and a ballroom that had been converted into a dining room. A formidable central staircase ascended majestically from the great hall to the dormitories above. The place's long history demonstrated the need for decency, independence, and, most essential, self-confidence.

The first lesson was French the following morning, taught in a large Victorian orangery that became extremely hot throughout the summer months. It was not the case in the winter when severe conditions hindered anyone from becoming familiar with the language.

At the age of nine and for many years to come, Miles's French teacher was an enigmatic personality replete with first-class Cambridge Honours. He was an excellent communicator with innovative teaching methods and was generally well-liked by his pupils. Miles plodded on year after year, slowly accumulating a vocabulary and understanding the language in an informal way. It would be fair to say that his rugby achievements also, were just adequate for pleasure and to get him by.

Surprisingly enough, the years passed by hardly noticed, and the time eventually came to leave this establishment. Miles would miss the reassurance of God's presence at Matins and Evensong in the school chapel on Sundays. Spiritual company would always be his constant companion, and the possibility of earning everlasting life always appealed to Miles. In these respects, he and his fellow students' mentor was the young, enigmatic Mr Lovall. A first-class honours degree in biology and physics at Jesus College Oxford. His influence was profound.

The senior masters gathered, dressed in their ceremonial university garb to wish this year's leavers well. They had done their best to prepare them for the real world with all its faults outside the baronial gates. However, would the world be ready for Miles Beaumaris if equipped with his French, a modicum of rugby talent, and a large slice of self-confidence?

In the early days and throughout the eighteenth and nineteenth centuries, a British education would never be complete without culminating in a Grand Tour of Europe. The mature student would be accompanied by a person of high moral standing on a trip that lasted months, if not years. The study of antiquities, classical ruins, and so forth is their excuse for a rollicking good time. Unfortunately for his friends, and himself, they were born some few generations later, when their opportunity to experience such a pleasant visitation had consistently shrunk from years/months to just a few days. Alas, the trip organised for them was not so much a Grand Tour, but an Easter rugby tour to the suburbs of Paris. They departed on Good Friday to return in a sorry but satisfied state on Easter Monday.

The broad framework of being chaperoned, however, has been maintained. On the modern-day tour, their esteemed guardians consisted of the club president and a few older members referred to as gentry – the remnants of long-ago legendary teams that had managed to survive the rigours of coarse rugby life and its drink-related social structure. These time-trusted men were keen to oblige the club with their presence and enjoy a few days of absence from their wives to oversee the current player's behaviour, which in most cases very much mirrored their own. The badges of honour distributed by Mother Nature herself, most evident on a chilly afternoon, revealed distinguished ruddy faces, proud purple noses, and a disciplined gait radiating a profound knowledge of all rugby matters. An impeccable judgement could be relied on after a good few pints of some wallop, thus engendering healthy respect from all the players in the travelling party.

Miles could see the single-decker bus in his mind's eye, now hired at a modest and economical cost. The actual expense would always be incurred in stocking the vehicle with more than ample alcoholic refreshments to see everyone through on the journey to Paris.

The party fondly bade farewell to their loved ones and filed on to the coach at the unsavoury time of 6.30 a.m. to catch the boat in time for the trip's second leg. The cheerful ambience and banter would generally subside a short time after their departure, the hiss of ring pulls and bottle tops diminishing by the mile. Miles was never one for the long-haul, fourteen-hour beer session and could easily join in the laugh when he felt a fitting joke would add to the general merriment.

For some reason, most Britains find themselves when aboard the cross-channel ferry, on the aft deck staring across the wake at the white cliffs of Dover, nostalgically looking back to 1940. Germany, a civilised but enigmatic country, with well-educated people enjoying substantial, economic potential but unfortunately not usually disposed to being benign imperialists, was preparing to invade Britain.

***

The Germans had managed through a weak democracy to allow their National Socialist Workers Party to gain power in 1933. The conservationists, ecologists, and even the establishment welcomed the rise to power of this fanatical right-wing regime. Born from their attachment to German romanticism, the party had constructed a framework of doctrines to bring the nation closer to nature with policies of anti-smoking, pollution control, and the regeneration of rural regions. They ruthlessly pursued the objective of a healthier lifestyle and national togetherness. They brainwashed the younger generations into a condition of contemptuous superiority. The years of regimentation, clamping down on individual freedom, and the sense of honour and duty to serve the state strengthened their zeal for political and military conquest. This hunger was quickly satisfied using a combination of diplomatic intrigue and the instruments of modern warfare. Land-based troops supported by ferocious airborne attacks overran most of mainland Europe. A non-aggression pact with the Soviet Union left Britain alone to withstand the full force of the marauding invaders. The dispossession and persecution of the Jews and other ethnic minorities now gathered pace not just in the homeland but across Europe.

Survival of the fittest and natural selection followed the Nazis' obsession with the laws of nature and the dominance and purity of the Arian race. This sacred belief was intrinsic to the party's thinking from its early formation in the twenties. Thankfully, this obsession resulted in their healthy disinterest in Nuclear Physics.

At the time of their accession to power, Professor Heisenberg was ahead of the world with his ideas on developing the nuclear bomb. However, it is evident today that he must not have shared his findings in-depth with his colleagues and did not reveal the possibilities of where his research might lead. Fortunately, it appears that he was definitely in no mind to encourage his present political masters to pursue his experimentations with any urgency.

There is no doubt that Hitler, Germany's vegetarian dictator, would temporarily have sacrificed some of his treasured green philosophies had he been advised about the unimaginable power possessing an atomic bomb would offer. He would have bankrolled a considerable investment with the usual single-minded Nazi commitment to a significant national project that would provide the unthinkable achievement of world nuclear domination by the Arian race.

The realisation of this golden chance was unknowingly within the Nazi grasp. The retreat of the allied army left 350,000 relatively unarmed soldiers trapped in a small port on the coast of northern France. The arrogant and triumphant Herman Goering, commander-in-chief of the Luftwaffe, with all the skill of a Mercedes car salesman managed to persuade his boss to abandon the overwhelmingly successful air and field attack strategy to finish off a defeated army. Hitler decided to give his air force alone the task of obliterating those stranded on the beach, seemingly unaware that this decision would set the stage for the planet's first total air battle. In fourteen days, the RAF shot down 358 enemy aircraft, damaging a further 168, for the loss of 117. Of course, the successful evacuation of 345,000 soldiers was a cause for celebration. The defeated men looked into the sky as they struggled to move off the Dunkirk beach on any vessel to hand. Many cursed the RAF for their near absence above. Completely unaware of the wrecked Stuka aircraft falling into the sea and onto the land from 10,000 feet and more above to make the soldiers' escape possible. History, or whoever writes it, placed far more importance on promoting the Dunkirk spirit than on the reality that the guardian angels fighting up to 20,000 feet above had won the first world air battle, which preceded the second and last to save the world.

The second and last great air battle of its kind commenced some two months after the first when the Germans initiated their 'all-out onslaught'. In 114 days, the RAF again shot down a staggering 1,730 enemy aircraft, albeit suffering a loss of 915. As a result, the Germans postponed Operation Sea Lion, the invasion of England, indefinitely, and once again, victory eluded them.

In a village in the north of England, there is a small fourteenth-century church in which someone has erected a stained-glass window depicting an RAF fighter pilot standing, shoulders slightly drooped, in his Sidcot flying suit, silk scarf and sheepskin boots. The figure wears a leather flying helmet. His right arm holds his parachute straps, the shute itself resting by his legs on the floor. An oxygen mask dangles from his left arm. His countenance dreamily stares forward into the future. Gone are the steely eyes glaring like gas jets searching for Luftwaffe prey.

While back in Britain, the founders of democracy were having their cities bombed to rubble in defence of freedom, however, the Statue of Liberty stood solid on the other side of the pond. As a result, Britain became an increasingly desperate customer of the neutral USA, now only too willing to oblige by the export of food and hardware. At first, these were paid for with gold, but after that cash, then securities and assets, all exchanged at knock-down prices. Finally, the USA managed to offload an obsolete fleet of warships on credit, which took until 2006 to repay.

Ninety-four per cent of the American electorate, naively oblivious to the worldwide threat, was against joining the war. They preferred life in their huge comfort zone, singing, dancing and drinking mugs of green lager on St Patrick's day, blind to the fact the band was playing 'Scotland the Brave'! Nat Burton cheerfully wrote the lyrics for the famous Battle of Britain war song 'There'll Be Bluebirds Over the White Cliffs of Dover' – unaware that the only Bluebird ever to have been near Dover appeared thirty years later, a car made by Datsun in Japan. When

Japan bombed Pearl Harbour, America's change of heart was instantaneous. Germany joined the party declaring war on the US, and by Christmas 1941, Britain (John Bull) was once again a brother in arms with Uncle Sam.

***

Be that as it may, it's time to rejoin the touring party . . . While conducive to most of the group, the bus to London, the train and the ferry experience had left some at a physical disadvantage. When alighting the vessel's gangway, the wayfarers had to rely on an athlete's instinct to put one foot in front of the other. Getting their carcasses onto the continent of Europe and into the train at Calais de Ville was now placed in the capable hands of our honoured gentry, attending to the immediate needs of the individuals concerned. That's putting it politely! Kit bags replenished with plenty of duty-free drinks boarded the train, not the Fleche D'Or but a diesel hauling those old-fashioned carriages – the ones with individual compartments and sliding doors connected by a corridor. Much harder to murder on, but ideal for a boisterous drinking party! The boys had great fun as the train pulled out of Amiens, the platform vendors waving long French breadsticks at them in the last bid to make a sale. Arms outstretched through a row of carriage windows, all grabbing at the merchandise on offer. The trader's trust in them was rewarded as they showered the necessary francs onto the now-receding platform. Typically French, the sandwich filling was to die for.

By the time they arrived, the early evening had approached, and everyone was searching for their second or third wind, so to speak. Their French counterparts gave them a joyous welcome, observing with some guile that the players were in their usual state on arrival. If the first fifteen could be entertained for a few more hours, it might enhance their chances of victory in the next day's international match. With due respect to their generous hosts and without going overboard, the lads were prepared to go along with their hosts' plan. After a good night out, everyone was comfortable, each one getting a good night's sleep as guests in individual homes in the district of Blanc Mesnil.

Match days come and go, while winning, though desirable, was not the sole objective as it seems today. From memory, over ten years of home and away honours with their friends worked out about even. The essence of their rugby was camaraderie, with support on and off the field of play. Post-match, they would assemble in the Hotel de Ville for a short speech from the elected communist mayor before departing for Paris's wonderful bars and restaurants.

On Sunday, it was the usual practice to stage a 'friendly', each player coming on for twenty minutes or so, but on many occasions switching sides. This way, everyone got a game. The sporting part of the weekend came to a close, and it was now time for the formal dinner, the 'banquet', pronounced 'le bonk hey'. The French dignitaries and our gentry sat at the top table, making speeches and proposing loyal toasts. Miles appreciated the fact that he could still understand most of the French.

The evening's proceedings generally culminated in the travelling party's obligation to sing a selection of amusing rugby songs. Of course, that would be in English to avoid offending the ladies present. The last was always 'The Red Flag' (empire version), which their French hosts seemed to like for some inexplicable political reason. With great enthusiasm, everyone joined in, singing the words to the tune of the old socialist song:

'Twas on Gibraltar Rock, so fair
I saw a maiden lying there
and as she lay in sweet repose
a gust of wind blew up her clothes
a sailor who was passing by
'e cocked his 'at and winked his eye
and then he saw to his despair
she had the red flag flying there

the working class can kiss my arse
I've got the foreman's job at last
oh, out of work and on the dole
So stick the red flag up your hole!'

The return to Blighty undid all the good physical exercise. The tourists happily accompanied their homecoming song with more beer and French wine to nourish the body and soul to extinguish exhaustion:

'Rule Britannia, marmalade, and jam
Five Chinese crackers up your arsehole
Bang, Bang, Bang, Bang, Bang
Rule Britannia, marmalade, and jam
one thousand Chinese crackers up your
Arsehole – BOOOOOOOM!'

***

In his mid-thirties, Miles's car salesman, Nigel, was of a middle-class upbringing. He stood just under six feet tall, and had curly black hair and slightly tanned skin, as though of southern European descent. His smile would reveal only one end of his modestly kept teeth and invariably left Miles wondering what was going on, but at the same time, tempted to make him laugh. He felt relatively comfortable in his presence. On returning from the tour, Nigel was waist-deep in unsold second-hand cars, chatting away to Joan, their car valet.

'Morning, Joan.'

'Morning, Nigel.'

Nigel looked up; Miles noticed his left eye had a dark shadow around it – in fact, it was black.

'Nice tour, Sir. Not too rigorous with Froggies this year?'

'Not as eventful as the weekend you seem to have had. No trouble with any of our customers, I hope?'

'Oh, nothing like that. My model aeroplane got stuck in a tree down the park on Sunday morning. Well, this young lad was skulking about nearby doing nothing useful, so I offered him a shilling to retrieve it. His dad didn't see the funny side to seeing his lad on a branch twenty feet up, so the dad came bounding along and lamped me one!'

'Well, apart from the dramatics in the park, has anything happened in these premises over the last few days?' Miles dared to ask.

'Oh, not bad. I've sold a couple of bread and butters* and that MKV Zodiac you've been smoking about in, the one you liked so much,' spoken with a smile and a look of triumph.

'Excellent! Yes, nice car. Lovely instrument panel – lots of clocks on your dash. And the long billiard-table bonnet stretched out in front. Still, better off up the road, money in the bank as it were.'

'Will this require a trip to Birmingham, Sir?' enquired Nigel, imitating Wooster's Jeeves.

'You're off tomorrow, so I'll go on Thursday and see if I can Bowler Hat** the powder-blue V4 Corsair that's been languishing at the back of the showroom for far too long. An excellent clean example drives well, but it's a hard one to sell. Not to everyone's taste; hence the need to pass it on for somebody else to have a go.'

The nation's second city greeted Miles with its busy roads and network of canals. He eventually threaded his way through the older parts to Derby St Motors, his destination once more. Jürgen, the owner of East German extraction, sat in his office ready to pounce, so he looked around. You wouldn't see anything like it today, but in this dimly lit ex-mill turned warehouse, cars that were referred to in those days as 'comics' comprising Astons, Jags, Mercs, Rolls, and Yanks were all stacked up as if on a car-transporter, maximising storage space for these mouthwatering gems.

---

*   Mass-produced, affordable cars
**   To aim a bad seller into another dealer in part exchange

Feigning indifference to any particular vehicle, Miles waited for Jürgen to make his move. He knew that, just as he would, Jürgen would try to parcel him off with one of his slow movers, which in this case was a pristine red and black '69 Mercedes Pagoda 280 SL Auto, which he was now standing beside. An exploratory glance through the off-side window revealed its drawback. The glove box in painted red metal was on the wrong side of the car. The matching console housed a neat rectangular instrument panel set between the speedo and the rev counter in front of the steering wheel, all situated on the left-hand side! They both knew the trade value of their cars. Miles had used and sold plenty of left-hooker Yanks, so he decided to give it a go and deal.

So he climbed into the driver's seat and set off back home – a great driving car, stood in at the right money with enough for three months of summer motoring and still a bit of profit to come! Miles glided through the streets of Birmingham, all smiles, making his way back to the M6. A slight wheel wobble became evident as the car gathered pace down the slip road. Not a problem – one could soon balance that out. Faster still, it felt like the universal joint on the prop shaft. Surely not on a low-mileage Merc? More speed and the car felt like it was turning itself inside out! Jürgen! Abandon ship and go straight back to the garage now.

When he described the car's performance, our esteemed trader betrayed a certain amount of irritation, protesting that it was a done deal. Mirroring his mood, Miles was not inclined to agree. At this point, he imperialistically waved him over to a corner sixty yards distant, where a dozen or so vehicles were on display, all of which were left-hookers, of course. The whole point of the day's exercise was to come away with something he could use and later sell. This did not include the likes of VW Beetles and Variants, but there in the middle was a chance of a compromise, a brand-new, pre-registered left-hand-drive Triumph Stag with only sixty kilometres on the clock. Paintwork finished in Saffron Yellow, a V8 sports car with a hard and soft top hatched from the chrysalis of the Triumph 2000 saloon by the top designer Giovanni Michelotti.

'Looks like I'll be swapping arsenic for poison here, Jürgen, so the money will have to be right,' he emphasised. To be fair to Jürgen, they got close to a realistic valuation, and for the second time, Miles made his way north to the M6.

Having dug himself out of a bit of a hole earlier in the day, he had a sense of well-being and comfort, which made up for the minor inconvenience of driving a left-hand drive. Although a little disappointed at losing the 280SL, his thought as he approached the Knutsford exit was that a small reward was well in order. So, before entering the pub, he parked it up and stood back to admire its sleek lines and twin headlights, generally appreciating its elegance now that he was the owner.

Leaning on the bar was an elderly chap about five-foot-eight inches, stocky with a round, ruddy rural face. A beer now in hand, he made Miles's acquaintance and asked the reason for his mirth. He was looking at Miles with a wry grin over his half-full pint.

'Oh, the landlord, Ronald Roulant, has just arrived back with this green Morris Mini Cooper S for Chantelle, his Missus,' he jocularly remarked.

'No way. A great car – very desirable,' Miles concurred.

'I don't think she thinks so, and she's booked on the ferry tomorrow! Going to France to stay with her mum for a few weeks, I believe.'

At this point, the double doors that adjoined the taproom opened, and Miles began to listen earnestly.

'Vous m'avez promis une voiture de sport pour mon voyage a Paris et vous revenue avec cette copie Anglais d'une Citroen Deux Chevaux.'

'Pas exactement mon amour.'

'Une voiture a bulles et je n'irai pas dedans!'

Which loosely translated means that the Cooper to her resembled a Citroen Deux Chevaux or a bubble car, and there was no way she was going to Paris in that!

Ronald was about to make the mistake of all men by cranking up an argument based on the male appreciation of the supremacy of technical engineering, which, with a woman of such sophistication and discernment, invariably leads into no-man's land.

The opportunity would be lost if Miles did not intervene now. The altercation would descend into that black shadow of human self-destruction where nobody wins.

'Is there a Ronald Roulant in the room?' He bellowed, 'I have some news of good fortune regarding a relative's legacy.'

'Good news? What good news? Who the hell are you?' replied Ronald, making himself known.

'If you would care to step outside, I will show you.'

In a moment, they were both drooling over the Saffron Yellow Triumph Stag. After a short time, Ronald re-emerged hand in hand with the lovely Chantelle Roulant, who then exclaimed, 'How have you managed this? C'est fantastique!' His strained countenance began to look less tense at the prospect of marital redemption.

She then sat in the perforated leather seat, eyes moist, staring at the neat veneer dash (derived, one might say, from many a Triumph saloon) proud of, and back in love with her husband.

The former pupil, young Beaumaris, had done many a deal sitting in the privacy of a car, and this was no exception. Having inspected Ronald's 6,000-mile Mini Cooper, Miles agreed to accept it in part exchange for the Stag at the new list price. After the trip from Birmingham, the car showed just the delivery distance of 120 kilometres on the clock. Ron thought the left hooker would be perfect for Chantelle to negotiate the roads in France while swiftly assenting to the **PX** terms; he gladly handed over the cash difference. A happy outcome for all concerned.

He was driving home in the fourth car of the day's dealings in a reflective mood, the words of Matthew with him in his mind.

Matthew 25:22: 'He also that had received two talents came and said, "Master, you did deliver to me two talents. Behold, I have gained two talents more."

Thinking of his peer's advice back in school, Miles still couldn't imagine that Latin would ever help him achieve profit. However, his French turned out to be of particular use.

Le Fin.

2
Lancia 3B Coupe

(Mirror Blue 3 Solex Double Carbs 2.8 V6)

In the fifties and sixties, most kids were state-educated and, at the very least, emerged with the ability to read and write. In the majority of cases, the standard of handwriting they achieved was infinitely higher than in today's technological age. So, back in the late sixties, it was no surprise to see Wilf's salesman, Keith, up a ladder beautifully hand-painting his boss's latest sales promotion onto the red-brick façade of the car showroom. Curiosity getting the better of Jack, he shouted to Keith, 'What's Wilf up to this time?'

'To tell you the truth, I can't see this one working, but you never know. I'll come down and have a fag and put you in the picture.'

Now beside Jack at ground level, Keith lit up and relaxed back into the conversation to get his opinion of the forthcoming ruse. Keith's long thin face decorated with a prominent nose always gave him the impression of an alert vulture. A bird with no small appetite, especially when observing his intended prey from behind the two or three rows of three to five-year-old motors displayed within the garage.

'Yes, it's a six-week campaign. Apparently, we're giving away a free turkey with every car bought between now and Christmas.'

'A hard one to refuse that one,' Jack acknowledged with a degree of scepticism.

They both laughed. 'Is Wilf about then?'

'Yes, he's in the first office to the right with his brother.'

'OK.'

With that reply, Jack left Keith to his artistry in the fading afternoon light and pushed on through the discreetly lit showroom. Out of politeness, he knocked on the office door. Wilfred's muffled tone bade him enter. The room, devoid of natural light, was tastefully illuminated by soft candlelight, complemented by a tape recorder appropriately playing funereal organ music. As Jack's eyes adjusted to the sombre light, he could make out a coffin on which stood two candelabras. Wilf sat with his chin in cupped hands a few feet back, staring sadly in Jack's direction.

'Oh, I'm so sorry, Wilf. I never met your brother.'

'You never will now!'

'Didn't even know you had one,' he replied apologetically.

Before Wilf could respond, the sound of an altercation grew louder and louder. Yes, it was Keith in dispute with a highly agitated screamer.[*]

'The engine in the Consul Capri 1300 that you sold me is on its way out!' the customer shouted.

'We did say that the 1300 engine with the three-bearing crankshaft should be nursed and not raced. We did say that! Anyhow, I've listened to the engine. There's plenty of life in it yet, treated with the respect it deserves. It's just growling a bit at the bottom end. That's all.'

'Where's that boss of yours? I'll wring his bloody neck if he doesn't do anything about it this very day!'

'I'm afraid that's not possible. Will you please calm down?' Keith advised. 'You could leave the car here, but I would not advise it in these uncertain legal circumstances. We've had a bereavement, you see.'

---

[*]   A rude client who is regretting their purchase

The unfortunate punter* then took it upon himself to burst into the office, intruding on Jack's now solitary grief beside the coffin as Wilf was nowhere to be seen. With a wistful and polite countenance, he turned to him.

'It's unfortunate, such a shock, so unexpected.'

The screamer reeled back in shock. Then returned to Keith and asked when it would be best to return and get things sorted out.

'Oh, I think in the New Year. Bring her in then.'

'The car will be out of its guarantee in January,' remonstrated the punter.

'I wouldn't worry too much about that, Sir,' said Keith as he ushered him into the driver's seat and firmly closed the door. 'We look forward to seeing you then.'

Jack joined Keith on the forecourt to witness the departure of the ailing Capri – a lovely-looking thing morphed from the American Ford Thunderbird with all its stylish lines, large boot and twin headlights. Ford's British design codenamed Sunbird produced a real looker. Shame about the engine, though.

As they returned to the showroom, they again found themselves in the enigmatic Wilf's presence. 'No point in arguing the toss with him! It works every time we enlighten them about the danger of leaving their property in the custody of a dead man. Words like probate and receivership have been bandied about here of late due to circumstances beyond our control. We don't believe that it's our fault that current manufacturers have designed world-beating, highly desirable cars with a plethora of undesirable defects. The Austin 1100 and 1300 with their subframe mountings rusted rotten after three or four years; Triumph Herald/Vitesse chassis outriggers; Ford's inner wings the same; Morris Minors jumping out of gear; Hillman Imps and Minxes all with a toxic mixture of faults. The list is endless. Purchasing good stock is a minefield today! The owners, management, designers, and trade unions all get away with it scot-free. All of this leaves dealers to restore such defective

* An optimistic purchaser

products, which sometimes requires subtle methods to keep clients on the road and at bay.'

'So, no dead brother. Just an empty coffin with candles on it.'

'No dead body, but the coffin is handy for storing unwanted paperwork.' Keith had better remember to blow the candles out before he leaves. Any slip up there, and they'd be visiting the insurance man, not the crematorium!

'All very amusing and highly ingenious. Have you got the Lancia ready, the one dad bought this morning?'

'Yes, everything's fine. Clean as a whistle and drives like a dream, one of only twelve right-hand drives imported from Italy.'

'A rare car, then. I'm not sure I like the sound of that.'

'You'll love it when you drive this truly continental sports coupé. Here are the keys. She's just round the corner, over there. Follow me. Your dad seemed to know a bit about the model. Done his homework on me, no doubt, before slotting me up* with that Zodiac convertible he's been trying to sell for months. And you are now taking possession of this lovely coupe designed by Pinin Farina with a 2.8 V6 engine; De Dion transaxle assembly with a spring-loaded four-speed manual transmission.'

Jack confessed he'd never seen this model before. He'd come across a few ugly four-door limousine versions fitted with what is known as two rear suicide doors. The ones that open in the opposite way to the front, swinging into anything or anyone moving past in a contrary direction. This car was good-looking, finished in deep dark blue with a depth of paint that mirrored the image of a human form looking into it.

The moment had arrived to bid Wilf and his establishment au revoir. Jack started the motor with a wry smile and manoeuvred her onto the road. She looked good from behind the hard, plastic wheel. The impressively shaped air scoop on the bonnet, between two typical Farina wings, accorded a sense of impending power. The early evening darkness was coming down fast. The dashboard was getting brighter. Time to collect his fiancée, drive her to her college in Ormskirk, and put the car through its paces.

* To slot-up is to purposefully sell and undesirable car

His 'Lass' had no discernment of one vehicle over another and certainly would not have known or cared that three triple-choke carburettors were under the bonnet. They delivered leaded petrol into the six cylinders, exploding and smashing down the pistons to rotate the massive-eared crankshaft, splashing oil from the sump throughout the engine. These produced the speed to complete a seventy-mile journey in good time, to take advantage of the educational establishment's visitor rules to allow Jack to enjoy additional time with her in her room.

In one's younger years, time inevitably becomes victim to selective amnesia, and before you know it, Jack had stayed way past the times allowed by the college regulations. It was past midnight when he embarked on his return trip. The roads were deadly quiet in those days, and tonight was no exception. Lancing along in the Lancia, he came off the A580 and decided to gun it up the slip road. With no other car in sight, the spring-loaded manual shift made putting her into third easy. He then changed to fourth at ninety and moved her onto the motorway. A sort of intuition compelled him to check his rear-view mirror. There, some way back was a twin-headlighter* incredibly slowly gaining on him. Glancing down at the speedo, she was more than cruising at over a ton! To be on the safe side, he eased her back to the speed limit of seventy. Soon after that, the only other lights on the road were right behind him. In no time, the other car smoothly drew level. It was a Mk 10 420 Jaguar in metallic gold – Britain's widest and most extensive sports saloon ever made. He could clearly see the driver and two passengers sitting bolt upright. They were dressed in dark but formal clothing, wearing bowler hats, which were in stark contrast to their ashen complexions. All three were transfixed, staring ahead as if he was not there.

Jack remembers the red tail light passing his front offside wing. A gap of only ten yards opened up between the two cars when, unbelievably, the Jag heeled ninety degrees and was broadside on in the full glare of his headlights. He stood on the brakes and watched her speed across his lane, then over the hard shoulder.

---

* A twinheadlighter is a car with four headlights

The great lump took off in a shower of sparks to a height of no more than ten feet. The last thing he recalled was seeing the rear wheels drop a little as her suspension relaxed in its short flight. It crashed out of sight into the dark area beyond. He was greatly relieved to survive what could have been a fatal collision. In profound shock at the near certainty of the fate of the three men, he immediately sought the next SOS phone, which, as it happened, was only a hundred yards further on. He rushed to pick up the handset and, in response to the unemotional voice at the other end, stammered out a description of the events he had just witnessed. The operator asked if he had suffered any injury.

'No, I'm OK.'

'Any damage to your vehicle?'

'No, nothing. But never mind, when are the police and emergency services due to arrive? I'll stay put and help them with their enquiries.'

'No need for that. We know who the three occupants were. Now, you must listen to what I say and proceed with your journey home.'

The voice continued . . . 'These three men amongst humanity were the product of 200,000 years of necessary evolution. All three emerged from the Industrial Revolution with a will to invent more effective weapons of destruction. They represented the negative force required to overcome the positive, so the species could progress as conceived by the original designer of life Himself. Henry Shrapnel, Alfred Nobel, and Hiram Stevens Maxim, with their ingenious, non-academic minds, passed on years ago. Their malevolent products increased the momentum of scientific advance to a fever pitch, speeding up the evolutionary process into the technological age not far off from their time. Please continue your journey home. There will be no record of tonight's incident.'

Jack felt a strange sensation that the voice seemed to know his very soul as the words fell through the night deep into his consciousness. The message to understand the knowledge of evil to fulfil his ordained destiny demanded a detailed investigation of these men. Only silence followed, so Jack replaced the handset and returned to the car, and, as instructed by the voice, he obediently continued his homeward trip for some reason.

***

Henry Shrapnel, Genteel Mankiller (1761–1842)

Henry Shrapnel was born in 1761 to a prosperous family of cloth merchants at Midway Manor, Bradford on Avon, an area famous for its wool mills. In light of his achievements in later years, various artefacts of ordnance connected with his endeavours adorned the house for future generations to admire. He became a lieutenant in the British Royal Artillery and developed a penchant for improving the efficiency of artillery ammunition. He worked out at only twenty-three years of age that having a cannonball with a range of 1,000 yards would be desirable. It would burst open mid-flight and shower a couple of hundred musket balls contained within, killing anyone unlucky enough to be below.

In 1787, he demonstrated an early version of his invention (which he now called the 'spherical case') at Gibraltar in the presence of General O'Hara and his entourage. They were all suitably impressed. But the usual reluctance to invest and spend money at that time was because most wars were colonial and not bloody enough to employ long-range artillery of this nature. They mothballed the idea as a result.

It is never a coincidence that ideas of this kind are resurrected hurriedly due to the force of circumstance. On 18 May 1803, Britain declared war on France, which began the Napoleonic War. Just sixteen days later, on 3 June 1803, a committee of artillery field officers assembled to witness and evaluate Shrapnel's exploding ball. With its long-range capability, the lethal projectile would be more effective against the Levée en masse (mass conscripted armies). The British immediately convinced those present of the weapon's potential. Within two months, his shell was in production under Henry's supervision at the Carron Iron

Works, Falkirk, Scotland. The resonance of the word 'Shrap' and '(k)nel' as in death knell seemed to appeal to the working gunners testing it at the time. They would only refer to it as Shrapnel, ensuring lasting fame bestowed on its inventor.

However, in the short term, the immediate triumph at Surinam in 1804 and, more importantly, at the Battle of Vimeiro in 1808, meant its unqualified success was kept as secret as possible. The Duke of Wellington became an enthusiastic admirer. His famous quote, ' Waterloo was won on the playing fields of Eton,' purposefully sidestepped the importance of Henry's man-killing munitions. The army honoured Henry with subsequent promotions, culminating in the rank of Lieutenant General in 1837. Also, the British government rewarded him with an income of £1,200 a year for life. But little else in national recognition was forthcoming.

Alfred Nobel, the Merchant of Death (1833–96)

Alfred Nobel was ironically the benefactor of the Nobel Peace Prize. He invented dynamite, the detonator, various fuses, and gelignite. He lodged hundreds of patents worldwide due to his experiments as an engineer, chemist, and innovator, not least of which was ballistite, a smokeless explosive propellant, in 1887. Ballistite was the predecessor of cordite, the invention of Sir Fredrick Abel and Sir James Dewar. They were both duly sued for the infringement of Alfred's ballistite patent. After several unsuccessful attempts, the House of Lords resolved the matter, favouring Abel and Dewar. The smokeless nature of both products now presents an opportunity. The world's riflemen could now shoot each other at liberty from ranges of around a mile, practically invisible to one another.

Rather than restrict his factories to domestic production in Sweden, Alfred set up what can be considered the first globalised business to manufacture explosives and related products. Being multilingual, he could speak six languages. A very astute businessman without a formal university education, Nobel exchanged patents to acquire shares and influence worldwide. He created a global cartel that guaranteed huge profits. Eventually, after years of negotiation, he persuaded his friends, colleagues, and fellow shareholders to form the Nobel Dynamite Trust in 1886. This was a multinational holding company comprising three British, four German and several independent operators. This trust would supply the capital to the industry and give a return to its international body of investors. The trust was very flexible. In the process of winning a government contract, it had the means and know-how to sidestep any inconvenient regulatory hurdles. The first two bloody years of the First World War produced an awkward situation long after Alfred's death of German and British shareholders profiting from the gruesome casualties on both sides.

Nobel claimed to know little of commerce, wishing for a quieter life in his laboratories. A few years later, in 1894, he acquired the Bofors armament factory in Sweden. He turned this former iron and steel manufacturer into a modern cannon and chemical producer while at the same time enigmatically claiming to be a pacifist!

By his death in 1896, Nobel had an interest in some ninety armaments companies and had attained great wealth. To the surprise of his family and friends, he bequeathed most of his fortune to fund the Nobel prizes still awarded to this day.

Nobel had a few monuments erected in his honour. However, in the last months of the Second World War, a massive formation of allied bombers flattened his large factory (Krummel) near Hamburg. After the dust had settled, the only object left was a bronze statue of himself standing proudly in the rubble. A monument to Nobel, an abstract form of an exploding tree, has been raised in St Petersburg. In the wake of his achievements during and after his lifetime, the international arms industry flourished.

Hiram Stevens Maxim, the Grim Reaper's Disciple (1840–1916)

Hiram Stevens Maxim was born in Sangerville, Maine, USA, in 1840, an epoch destined to be known for the abundance of privateer inventors across the planet. These creators all sought fame and fortune by inventing products that were not just improvements on previous innovations but were new in the sense of being original. The scramble for patents intensified in 1852. Intellectual property rights were successfully tailored to the capitalist system to ensure a profitable invention reward. These rights had to satisfy the growing numbers that could now afford to pay money for them, which fuelled a new monetary cycle to add to the established economic structure.

An example among many is the light bulb (Edison, 1879). At a county-town fair on an early May evening when the afternoon sun had given way to a late spring twilight, imagine the experience of the ordinary person finding himself confronted with a multitude of amusement rides and stalls for the first time. In stark contrast to the magenta night sky, hundreds of these bright incandescent bulbs of many vivid colours illuminated the various attractions. The huge steam road locomotive provided enough electricity to generate light, movement, and vibrant music.

Hiram Maxim joined the free-for-all with his first successful patent, 'the curling iron', in 1866. He lodged a further 122 US and 149 British patents ranging from an automatic mousetrap to inhalers, locomotive gas lights, steam pumps, and fire water sprinklers. In his later years, Maxim applied himself to winged flight, and in 1894 his experiments proved this to be possible but not with steam power, which was too heavy. Born of this, he designed his 'captive flying machine'. It was an amusement ride for the Earls Court Exhibition, which turned out to be extraordinarily profitable and held in high esteem by his future customers. On the face of it, all his innovations seemed beneficial to enhance human existence. His company proceeded to supply these machines to Southport, Crystal Palace, New Brighton, and Blackpool. One still operates in Blackpool's Pleasure Beach complex.

In the late 1870s, Maxim got involved in a lengthy patent dispute with Thomas Edison regarding the invention of the electric light bulb. The competition was fierce, the stakes high, and as an indirect result, he took up an offer he should probably have refused. Hiram decided to settle for an appointment as chief engineer of the United States Electric Company with a twenty-year contract at a very healthy salary. He married his first wife, Jane Budden, in 1867. But the very young girl Helen Leighton professed that Hiram had married her in 1878 and accused him of bigamy. She sued him for $25,000 but eventually settled out of court for $1,000. In 1881 he married Sarah Boston. Details of his divorce from his previous supposed spouses are shrouded in mystery. His brother Hudson, a rival, encouraged the rumours of his somewhat dubious reputation as a philanderer. However, based at its office in London, Maxim was more than ready to accept a position to oversee and safeguard the company's affairs in Europe, well away from his brother and America.

Maxim arrived in England to set up a house in West Norwood in 1881. One of his first duties for the company was to exhibit an electric pressure regulator at the Paris Exposition, a must-visit for inventors the world over, and an excellent place to socialise, exchange ideas and possibly pick up helpful information to be used to one's advantage. Such a man, Mr William Cantelo, looking to make Maxim's acquaintance and perhaps fishing for business, sought him out at his exhibition stand.

A gift horse seldom happens in a businessman's life. However, William must have enthused more than he should have about a gun he had just developed. He cheerfully advised the worst person on the continent that if he 'wanted to make a fortune, he should make a machine to help the Europeans kill one another.'

We can be sure it didn't take long for the crafty Hiram to glean enough information and promise the earth to this naive person. On his return to London, Maxim established a workshop at Hatton Gardens. The cellars and tunnels underneath readily lent themselves to the testing of automatic gunnery. Maxim had patented every conceivable firing mechanism within two years – gas, recoil, and blowback – that could possibly work. With the critical patents in place, he could now admit how fortunate he had been to meet an 'Englishman' in Paris who had advised, 'Hang your chemistry and electricity! If you want to make a pile of money, invent something to enable these Europeans to cut each other's throats with greater facility.'

Hiram had made the intellectual leap to supersede the now-obsolete hand-cranked guns of the past. It was soon evident that the most straightforward and practical mechanism was using recoil to eject the spent cartridge and insert the new one. The Maxim Gun was born! Its inventor, sometimes a practical joker, devised a toy machine gun. He took great delight in showering a multitude of black beans onto a nearby outdoor band that, for some reason, seemed to cause him great annoyance when it began to play.

William Cantelo owned an engineering factory in Northam employing forty people. He was also a respected landlord of the Old Tower Inn on Bathgate St, Southampton. Underneath the latter was a long tunnel, in which alone at first and then with the help of his two sons perfected his passion for producing an automatic rifle. Locals often heard the sound of gunfire emanating from below! On completing his enterprise in 1881, he announced his intention to take a three-month working holiday with the idea of selling his conception.

William was a keen musician, The Old Second Hampshire's bandmaster and a home-loving family man. Consequently, he departed, gun and all. His first port of call would be Paris. Unbeknownst to his wife and children, he transferred a large amount of money while travelling. After an absence of three months with no contact, his relatives at home employed private detectives to trace him. They discovered his final whereabouts in America, but the trail went stone cold. Nobody ever saw poor William again.

An English country house at West Norwood was previously the home of the celebrated author, Mrs Beaton. Her best-selling book *Household Management* became a guide to a peaceful and practical domestic middle-class way of life. The beautiful tranquil gardens consisted of several acres stocked with many colourful flowers, surrounded by a significant number of mature trees, all complimented by vast expanses of open space laid out to formal lawns. This pastoral paradise was an ideal location for Mr Siegmund Loewe, a most ingenious and enthusiastic arms salesman, to demonstrate to and tempt clients to experience the murderous potential of the machine gun. Word of its efficiency was beginning to spread, and Hiram began to climb up to the higher echelons of the political and social order. The Chinese ambassador was always a welcome visitor. On many a sunny afternoon, he and his entourage, some dressed in brightly coloured silk attire, could be seen hauling the gun across the manicured lawns. They regularly indulged in Maxim's habit of felling trees by machine gunfire. Siegmund, using this weapon, would point out to his clients how to become proficient gunfighters in a very short time.

Another illustrious client to enter the garden was Kaiser Wilhelm, emperor of Germany, in the company of his friend and relation, the Prince of Wales. He assured him that the Duke of Cambridge (commander-in-chief of the British army) intended to order some guns, which he belatedly did in 1889. The Kaiser confirmed that a formal contract would be forthcoming. The Kaiser, well acquainted with sports guns and rifles, took the opportunity to fire the weapon. He was unaware this particular model was fitted with an automatic preset 'arc tracker'. When he proceeded to fire, he inadvertently activated it. He came close to obliterating his entire general staff, who were saved only by the prompt action of one of Sigmund's employees.

The First Matabele War (1893–4) and the Battle of Shangani (25 October 1893)

A force of 700 men of the British South African Police (BSAP) commanded by Major Patrick Forbes efficiently set up camp at the Shangani River. He positioned his wagons in a circular defence called a laager. On a clear African night, the scouts and the outer sentries managed to scramble back to the surrounded encampment and warn of an immediate attack by a 6,000-strong Matabele fighting force, mainly armed with spears and a selection of modern rifles.

The night air was filled with urgent commands, and bugles blared as the men hurried to their positions to save their skins, knowing that survival against these odds was unlikely. As the black tide of well-disciplined warriors advanced, the soft night light revealed their silver-tipped spears and the reflections from gun barrels purposed to slaughter the trespassing white men. As the horde pushed forward relentlessly into range, five Maxim guns supported by 200 riflemen opened fire. The evil spirits of the night welcomed the '3,000 bullets per minute' into the advancing ranks. Crazy black shapes danced chaotically from one foot to the other as they crumbled down to irrigate their home soil with blood. Their rifles and spears clattered down at awkward angles onto the severed, motionless, dead bodies below. The chiefs determined not to offer another wall of Matabele flesh and blood to the deadly storm before them and judiciously ordered a full retreat. The battle was over. After a few minutes, some of the headmen committed suicide in disbelief.

The Battle of Bembezi (1 November 1893)

Lobengula, the ruler of the Matabele, was not present at the Shangani River and remained convinced of his infallibility. He ordered 2,000 riflemen and 4,000 warriors to engage Patrick Forbes at Bembezi, but with the same speedy consequence. A further 2,500 dead dispelled Lobengula's doubts, and he fled his capital, Bulawayo, razing it to the ground and leaving nothing to his victors. He died of smallpox in 1894, and the war ended. The BSAP then annexed Matabeleland and Mashonaland and gave them the title Rhodesia, with Salisbury as its capital.

The Second Matabele War (1896–7)

Leander Starr Jameson took his troops and arms from Rhodesia to the Transvaal to embark on his famous 'Jameson Raid', leaving the province defenceless. The M'limo, a mysterious spiritual leader of the Matabele, began to influence his people and the Shona that white settlers were to blame for the dire prevailing weather conditions. On 24 March 1896, 2,000 Matabele warriors began hand-to-hand savagery, driving the countryside settlers to Bulawayo. They constructed a central laager to sleep in and prepared the town for a siege. The armaments to hand consisted of a few artillery pieces and, more importantly, some machine guns. The M'limo and his priests tried to convince by way of propaganda that the spirits would turn the enemy's bullets into water and their cannon shells into eggs, but the 10,000 warriors declined to attack. Outright fear of the Maxim superseded their religion and held firm.

Fredrick Selous, scout and a big-game hunter, took no time to discover the whereabouts of the Matabele and, in late May, assisted the relief forces and their Maxims in clearing the field. 50,000 Matabele retreated into the Matobo Hills. Two adventurers, Burnham and Armstrong, found and entered the M'limo's sacred cave, who practised what he had preached and began to perform his 'dance of immunity' from the white man's bullets. Burnham shot him through the heart, and he died instantly. General Carrington picking off strongholds one at a time with his unopposed Maxims, continued the fight into the Matobo Hills and effectively ended the war by October 1897.

The Battle of Omdurman (2 September 1898)

The statistics: 8,000 British plus 17,000 Egyptians versus 50,000 Muslim Mahdists.

When you face a head-on attack, as in the First Matabele War, there can be no doubt about the efficiency of the Maxim gun. According to most historical reports, artillery accounted for most of the dead at the battle of Omdurman. The evidence does not support this, as eyewitness accounts confirmed that the corpses and wounded lay not in piled up heaps but each one in its own space in rows – rifle fire, as before, had supported the Maxims. The vast numbers of Muslim Mahdists using rifles could have been decimated only by the forty Maxims present that day.

British and Muslim Mahdist's Losses

The statistics: British losses, 47 dead and 382 wounded; Muslim Mahdist losses, 12,000 killed and 13,000 wounded.

In 1884, Maxim launched his first production company in Crayford, Kent. He had the backing of Edward Vickers. Four years later, he merged with Nordenfelt to form the Maxim Nordenfelt Ammunition Company. He also retained the expensive services of their super salesman, Basil Zaharoff, known in the trade as ZZ. The Maxim gun gained a fearsome reputation in the next few years. After several unethical criminal attempts to sabotage the initial international trials of the weapon, the devious and resourceful ZZ persuaded Nordenfelt to accept £200,000 for his share of the company. Nordenfelt was squeezed out, leaving Maxim and ZZ to benefit from a substantial buyout of shares and cash by Vickers, the armament giant.

Zaharoff received the informal training that early life offers an ambitious salesman and dealer. After graduating from lesser products, he emerged as the most successful international arms and shipping dealer. ZZ, a philanderer with aristocratic looks and connections, could charm his way in and out of any situation with consummate ease. He had the instinct to play on the victim's envy and curiosity, which created the aura of mystique and magnified his power, which was born of natural talent. He established banking and international finance control to allow everyone to acquire his essential products. Through his ownership of several national newspapers, he spread the word about who had bought what and tried to create an arms race between possible belligerents.

After two Matabele wars and Omdurman, it became clear that the machine gun was a prime candidate for success. So, ZZ made it his business to ensure both sides in future battles had this facility to mutilate each other on a level playing field.

The Somme, Picardy, France (1 July 1916)

The 1,500,000th shell fired at 7.28 a.m. completed a seven-day-night bombardment on the German positions, inspiring the High Command with utmost confidence. Word of this trickled down the ranks. No army and its defences could withstand such a deluge of sustained artillery fire. Now the guns fell silent, and miraculously small birds began to sing. High Command ordered 100,000 troops to advance into no-man's land across a broad front with the expectation of no significant resistance.

The high percentage of shrapnel shells proved to be practically useless. So, the German soldiers were safe from the pounding barrage in their forty-foot-deep stolen trenches built for the ultimate defence of the northern and central sectors. These men faced the main British armies. The machine gunners ate, slept and played Scat. Since Christmas 1914, larking about and engaging the enemy in interludes of friendliness in no-man's land was forbidden. However, the overlords could not prevent summer-music concerts and light-hearted banter from occasionally occurring between adversaries in this usually quiet zone. Not now! The metallic storm thundering overhead and the threat of devastating mines shaking the earth below warned of imminent action. But now, the unexpected silence above came and awakened them from their enforced hibernation. Torchlight beams shone as they urgently scaled the hewn-chalk stairways and tunnels. They dragged Maxims in tow through the darkness to the brilliant light of day, racing to occupy the parapets and rims. The sight of the battlefields before them pleased the gunners' eyes. The enemy had managed to turn large parts of no-man's land into a moonscape. There were plenty of craters to take cover in and position their machine guns to their best advantage. The British were visible through the smoke below as they emerged from the barbed wire defence line through gaps made ready for the attack. The infantry loaded down with backpacks, well in range less than a mile away, marched bravely in lines not dissimilar to an all-night queue for Wimbledon tickets. They spent the last week adjusting their weapons to perfection with years of training, and the German machine-gun detachments lost no time formulating their killing zones.

The enormous army filtered through the wire defences; each unit drilled to capture their allotted objectives. No deviation from their route as ordered was permitted. Two minutes into the offensive, everyone became aware of a strange fizzing sound, like the noise of a 1950s electricity substation – ZZUZ-ZZUZ culminating in an unceasing monotonic ZEEZ-ZEEZ. The troops fleetingly thought they were in the presence of abstract cubic volumes of air occupied by thousands of stinging ants. By mid-morning, two-way traffic of human beings was underway. Brothers in arms started to fall in the morning sun. The contorted chaotic tripping up of dying men dancing in undignified disarray announced the arrival of concentrated machine-gun fire. The broken wounded fit enough to crawl painfully back to safety and bravely sticking to orders were men walking straight into the killing zones. The mounting carpet of dead stayed put but not undisturbed as the German artillery joined the action to churn over the bodies and further dismember them.

Seven months before, in December 1915, Field Marshal Haig had announced to the world, 'The machine gun will never replace the horse as an instrument of war.' Preparing a letter two-and-a-half hours into the first Somme offensive, he informed

Lord Esher, his political spin doctor at home, that he 'had great hopes of getting some measure of success today.' Fifteen minutes later, General Rawlinson stood down the cavalry. The machine gun even paralysed logic and objective thought in its absence. By 12.30 p.m., the British had opened a three-mile gap in the German lines behind Montauban. The reserve army and even the cavalry with no machine guns to face were in an excellent position to realise Haig's dream of a breakthrough.

At 2.00 p.m., after a working lunch, both Commanders Haig and Rawlinson were aware of the success at Montauban and the current position at the Schwaben Redoubt. However, despite the success of the heavier French artillery against lighter German defences supporting the French and British advances in the south, they did nothing. The day had to run its course. It was now clear that the Battle of the Somme had no territorial objective.

There were many isolated pockets of fighting to the death in the afternoon. The British machine gunners did their part to increase the grand total of misery. They scythed down German counter-attacks with as much relish as anyone else behind such a gun on that day. The dead, dying, and wounded were unavoidably trampled on as men tried to avoid bullets and shrapnel as the turbulent, deafening afternoon wore on. Men had faces chopped away by shrapnel, and people had smashed or missing limbs but no available morphine. They were begging their comrades to shoot them to put them out of their agony. There was no shortage of sidearms to do it either. The walking wounded had an abundance of full water flasks and rations no longer needed by the fallen all around them.

Early evening slowly ushered in a slow but steady end to the day's madness, more than likely brought about by sheer exhaustion. As twilight approached, one could hear soft indistinct music through the diminishing noise of battle. At nightfall, the strains became more audible. A sound orchestrated by the wounded out there crying for help, groaning in pain. The crescendo of contrasting tones, so many that they eventually harmonised into one unbearable resonance of hell on earth.

The Aftermath of Saturday, 1 July 1916

British and empire: 19,240 dead and 38,230 wounded.

Vickers armaments: this company alone sold 71,550 machine guns, 133,000 Lewis guns, and 35,000 Hotchkiss automatics to the British armed services between July 1916 and November 1918.

British sector territorial gains: by first light on 2 July 1916, most units had evacuated back to their start positions the previous day. The only exception was Montauban.

For many nights restless in his sleep, Jack Diamond struggled to interpret the consequence of that night's vision and the reason for his presence. Perhaps war did become impossible to be replaced by the means of mutual destruction. When dreams overtake consciousness, the Scriptures proclaimed a possible explanation:

Isaiah 5:20: 'Woe to those who call evil Good and Good evil, who put darkness for Light and Light for darkness, who put bitter for Sweet and Sweet for bitter.'

John 8:34: 'Jesus answered them, "Truly truly, I say unto you, everyone who commits sin is a slave to sin.'

***

Dad would never ask his salesman Bob but would instead shout for him – he would never bully him, though. Bob was a proper gentleman, mild-mannered, a man of Cheshire with his clique of customers, most of whom hailed from that county. He stood five-foot-eight inches tall and had a round but slightly reddened face. His privately acquired spectacles concealed his soft grey eyes. He nearly always sported a brown trilby purchased in Stockport from the very best of the world's milliners.

Jack made his way in the Lancia on a wet rainy morning to see his father, an ex-officer and upstanding businessman, in the showroom.

His father looked up through those amusing but slightly irritating National Health glasses of his at a tall figure standing next to the Ford Zephyr Mk3 estate. The car had overstayed its welcome for some time. It had made itself comfortable in their possession, depreciating by the minute. A previous owner had taken it upon himself to fix the chrome horse onto the bonnet. It seemed to canter with a defiant purpose not to be sold on! The silver nag remained happily at ease when father mistook a browsing customer for a 'tyre kicker'* and let him know it. However, both Father and the inanimate steed lost a modicum of composure when the prospecting client revealed the contents of his bag. Cash! In the ensuing embarrassed silence, one could make out Bob's trilby hat above the office desk fifteen yards away.

'Well. To be treated in such a fashion is not what one expects in an establishment such as this,' admonished the deity in his shapeless, Lowry-like raincoat. He again thrust his leather bag towards the cowering ex-major.

In almost a whisper, the retired officer implored, 'The boss over there in the office has had me on the grill and griddle all morning. We've had nothing but lookers and dreamers today. Not many are in a position to afford a vehicle purchase at this time of year. I should have known that you are a man of discernment with ample means to buy and sell me before breakfast. Let alone this beautiful car before our eyes! Would you please accept my apologies and reconsider? Christmas is only a few weeks away – with a young family at home, I can't afford to lose my job due to my appalling oversight.'

'I will accept your apology and proceed with the purchase on the understanding that you knock fifty pounds off the purchase price,' the mackintosh-clad divinity replied with haughty compassion.

'Even if I have to lose my commission, I accept that such a person as you will benefit from this superb car's qualities. And will be my reward for this day's work.' He humbly rose to his feet. Still, gratefully reminded that he had survived all the Germans

---

* A tyre kicker is a time waster

could throw at him and the Eighth Army in the desert. He led the way to the office.

Even Bob had sussed what was going on by now when Dad politely enquired, 'Boss, could I have the office for a moment, please?'

Bob raised his hat to the customer and joined Jack in the showroom. Dad sat at the desk. Our numen opened his leather holdall for the second time that day and triumphantly counted out £745.00, which Dad politely put into the safe with a less deferential air.

'Well done, Dad. A hard man to please your boss, Bob.' Jack had to laugh.

'I could have sworn he was just a messer, but then he showed me the leather bag full of cash. That put me in my place.'

'Anyway, a top-class performance that just about completes my education,' he comforted him.

'You are always learning in this job, and I'm getting too old for it. The difficult aspects of life on the front line are for a younger man to negotiate.'

Bob did not hesitate to announce that Billy Connerly had been in earlier, moaning about his Morris Oxford, and said he'd be back in an hour.

'What the hell does he want now?'

'He says the knocking noise from the rear is still there,' demurred Bob.

'Not exactly the Brains of Burnley, that lad. He works hard enough and is a good payer, so we'll look after him.' Before Jack could utter another word, Bob and Dad had beaten a hasty retreat to the office.

'Good morning, Bill. Your Oxford looks as good as the day it came out of the factory. You must be very proud.'

'Top of the morning to you, but b'Jaisus, the car's driving me mad.'

'What's up, Bill? It can't be that knocking from the rear again, surely. We've double-checked the springs, mountings and shockers, and they were all OK.' Jack could see he was on his way to work. Michael O'Riley sat in the front passenger seat with Big Joe Murphy behind him in the back. The three of them are all strapping lads wearing hobnail boots ready for hard labour that I'm not strong enough or would have any care to undertake.

'Holy Mother of Mary. I can't believe it! I need the car for work every day. Without it, surely, I'll be up shit creek with no paddle.'

'Calm down, Bill. Are you sure your imagination is not working overtime here?'

'B'Jaisus, I'm not a cute hoor.* To be sure, I would not take advantage of a good man like yourself. In heaven's name, the good Lord has taken upon himself to make the noise louder when I turn the radio on, so He has.'

'Yes, Bill,' Jack replied. Billy Connerly's mastery of defying the universal laws of physics by merely turning on the mushroom-coloured five-push-button Deluxe Philips car radio was somewhat underwhelming! He reflected that maybe the highest form of human development had not been attained after four billion years of evolution.

'OK, I'll whip it around the block one more time, Bill,' he conceded.

'Morning, Joe. A hard day's work ahead, I'll be bound?'

'That there is! That there is indeed!' The voice from the back seat happily responded.

Jack took the motor around the block. He knew where all the potholes were and drove over a few to test – no sound and solid as a rock. Jack did not have a clue why he did it but instinctively leaned over to turn the radio on. It was Herman's Hermits playing their chart-topper 'I'm Into Something Good. He was astounded when the unimaginable happened – a dull knock from the rear, coincidently to the beat of the tune. Bloody hell! Too coincidently! 'Good record this, Joe.'

'B'Jaisus, I have it inside me. To be sure, I love a good tune!'

'Yes, and you with your size twelves stomping out the beat has

---

* A cute hoor is a person who revels in people trying to cheats

Billy convinced the car is knackered. The only cure that comes to mind is that you wear your slippers in future.'

The enlightened trader reached over and switched the radio off.

His dad was long gone and had left him to swap his ageing and overpriced asset into something he could sensibly use in retirement. On Friday, the last day of everyone else's working week, Jack would attend the weekly auction at Old Trafford, after which he would usually take his last chance to trade out the Lancia. A regular visit to Manny Hyman's establishment, a row of terraced houses converted to hold a stock of comic cars* brought up from the smoke, became routine.

'Good afternoon, my boy. You're here again trying to offload dear old Dad's Lancia, no doubt. Its boots** must have no tread left, traipsing up to my place every week.'

'Got anything fresh about you, Manny?' They both knew that Pater would not part with enough to come anywhere near owning one of the high-class cars on show. The Bentley continentals, Rollers, and assorted sports models were all destined for stars of stage and screen.

'Let's not turn this into a grinder.*** I'll play you a game of draughts for a quid to avoid wasting each other's time.'

'OK.' Jack warned him that he could do a good turn at board games. Manny laughingly agreed and sat down to play. During the game, Manny became quite paternal.

'I hear you're engaged to be married.'

'Not long off now, Manny.'

'Best quality in a woman is loyalty. Watch out for that. My Esther had no reservations when she burned all her precious fur coats at the end of the garden while I entertained the local CID on the threshold of our front door. That's the sort of true love a man should have.' He moved one of his pieces to threaten my flank. Good move.

---

*   Top brands which are unaffordable to most people

**   Boots are a car's tyres

***   A grinder is an endless haggle between two dealers over the terms of a deal

'I had that star of stage and screen, Melony Hassler, with her husband Toby in the gaff the other day. They left their number, but were too sensible to throw good money at these gas guzzlers. I could ring Toby and inform him that a professional board-game player, down on his luck on a losing streak playing high stake draughts in the city, is reluctantly putting his Lancia 3B coupe up for sale!' He got his pieces behind my defence and quickly finished me off.

'If you get shut of it, call it my wedding present.' He smiled and took my pound.

After two years, the Lancia had a new owner: Toby Hassler. His good lady wife hosts a popular consumer advice programme on the telly, which most retailers fail to appreciate. He was delighted with the car, and she advertised the fact in her popular newspaper column. She reminded her readers of the car's Italian pedigree and emphasised on her next broadcast that every customer should heed her advice and be aware of their rights when negotiating a purchase.

On the Friday following, the snow fell, bringing a kind of silent peace in the run-up to Christmas day. Jack's mum and dad were over for the holiday weekend, and he suggested his dad join him at the Old Trafford block for old times' sake.

'You never know – there won't be many there. A couple of cheapies may well be in the offing,' Jack proclaimed.

They could see from their approach that only a few dealers were in the auditorium, as expected. However, the auctioneer, Tony, raised his gavel and, to their surprise, began to clap. As the dealers formed a semicircle, laughing and cheering proceeded to give them what amounted to a standing ovation. It turned out that they had all read Melony's article the previous night! The Lancia was no longer part of the retired dealer's fixtures and fittings. They felt very touched, driving home through the fresh white snow-driven urban streets. Most people were now indoors, and the roads were quiet. As they passed Wilf's garage, it was plain to see that trading had long ceased, with no sign of life at all.

'How's old Wilf?' Dad asked.

'That's a long story. He had to do a runner two years ago. Things got on top of him, I'm afraid. The last anyone heard, he had disappeared to South Africa. He never lost his sense of humour, though. His last defiant act instructed Keith to handwrite his final message on the red brick façade. It stated clearly to all his loyal customers: '*No Free Turkeys This Year Due to Fowl Pest!*'

3
Aston Martin DB6

(Old English White with Chrome Wire Wheels)

'Blart Blart, Blart Blart,' the sound of the Blarter, more commonly known as the telephone, rudely replaced Miles's peaceful sleep with semi-consciousness.

'Can you get it, Lass?' he drawled.

'If I must,' she said, already halfway downstairs.

By this time, he was fully awake and sitting up. He strained to listen to the distant conversation downstairs in the lounge. At first, he could vaguely make out his wife's spoken words, but then with raised volume, she gasped, 'Are you sure? Have you got the correct number?'

Slightly flustered, she hastily scaled back upstairs with her face aghast to reveal the identity of their morning caller.

'It's the Archbishop of Canterbury on the blower. What on earth would he want with the likes of you?'

'How do I know? We'll soon see,' he retorted, grasping the handset.

'Good morning, your Grace,' Miles uttered with due reverence

'You will be rewarded with great wealth today, my son. Heed my words.'

'From which part of the Scriptures is this prophetic axiom to be found, your Worship?'

'It is written on this very day you should sally forth unto Scarborough, where riches await you at the Royal Auto Car company. Verily I say unto you they have an Aston Martin DB6 in the showroom marked up at £1,995.00, which we both know is worth a lot more in Manchester.'

'Why would this reward be bestowed upon me, with due respect to your Eminence, for thou could quickly help yourself to such easy treasure?'

'I'll accompany you in the vehicle of your choice, which no doubt you intend to launch into them by way of part-exchange, and I'll introduce you to their sales manager. The trip, of course, will allow me to be transported free of charge to a punter who urgently needs cash I intend to exchange for his not very old Lincoln Continental.'

'Ok, I'll pick you up in an hour or so at the showroom.' He put the handset back in the cradle and turned to his wife.

'Off to Canterbury for the day, are you?' she said with a knowing smile.

'Oh, nothing like that. There's a deal in the offing up at Scarborough.'

'Well, whatever next? Who would have guessed? So not the saintly Archbishop of Canterbury then?'

'Afraid not. Johnnie's just a trader from Manchester who goes by the name of Johnny One Leg. I may not make it back tonight. I'll give you a buzz later.'

An excellent choice for the trip up north would be the F-registered 67 Mercedes 250SL California, which is not the same as the 230 or 280SL. Oh no, not at all. For a start, it was worth a lot less second-hand than either of the other two, a fact lost by many traders. The car maker's lower-valuation car is that the German manufacturer decided to introduce it as a two plus two model for some unknown reason. The only way to do that at an economical cost was to remove the soft-top option and replace it with two fold-down seats just large enough for a couple of three-year-olds! Otherwise, the car had all the attractions and appearance of the other two but with an intermediate-sized engine. The object of the day's pursuit was to achieve a middle price in a swap, thus lowering the stand-in price for the DB and, of course, finding a new home for the hoodless Merc on the coast of the North Sea.

On arrival at the rendezvous, Miles's illustrious associate for the journey ahead stood in wait with his carpet bag in hand. Miles did not know him that well. Still, he had enjoyed his company several times in various car auctions. He was around thirty years old and of a thin disposition with very tanned skin, like someone who works outdoors. There was a suggestion of the legacy of a childhood affliction, as one leg appeared shorter than the other. As he approached the Mercedes, his large head tended to wobble, for he walked with a pronounced limp. He resembled a jerking marionette. Still, his sense of humour counterbalances his physical detriments. Most dealers regard him as a man of mystery with many social and business connections. A bit of a chancy lot!* Whatever happened, the day would not be dull. As an ex-public schoolboy and rugby gent, Miles, swinging his document case into the inadequate space behind the seats, was regarded by him as a suitable business companion.

'Nice car,' he opened.

'Yes, no rattles or bangs. Well made. A very tight little driver – exceedingly Germanic by nature.'

Before long, they were on the M6 motorway.

'You had the wife going with that one this morning, your Grace,' Miles added.

He turned his head and looked at him with an expansive, friendly smile across his sallow face. He answered in a genuine upper-class Etonian accent, 'I had to impress your better half that your business colleagues only come from the highest strata of society.'

'Indeed, this stratum would be the one you emanate from?' Miles asked with a bit of disbelief.

---

*   Chancy lot is a risky purchase at auction

'Without a doubt, I was born into this world, the fruit of two high-born individuals who, unfortunately for me, were not married at the time but each to someone else. Dad was of the English aristocracy, and Mum was an extremely wealthy Russian émigré. I became the secret offspring brought up by my grandad and, during holidays, parcelled off to spend them with my mum's parents.' Having got this off his chest, he sat back sort of nose in the air, satisfied that he'd convinced Miles of his pedigree.

'Amazing, this may explain your reputation as a man of many connections. We'll be dealing with the Queen's bursary next. Buck House, admit one!'

'You may jest, but a background and who you know is important, even if it's thrust upon you. We've got at least a three-hour drive ahead. Do you want me to continue with a short episode of family history that may enlighten you about events contrary to the accepted historical record?'

In those days, dealers would chat, exchange stories, fill the redundant hours and not waste them in silence.

'I'm all ears,' Miles replied, hoping to glean a little more useful info.

'My grandparents brought me up in a large Victorian red-brick house, which I can easily remember,' he continued while staring at the road ahead.

'It seemed to me even older than my grandad. The house had high ceilings with large reception rooms, cosy although dimly lit. Outside were walled kitchen gardens extending to large formal lawns affording me plenty of freedom to roam around, hiding in the shadowy nooks and crannies on the implied condition that I was not to be seen or heard, resulting in my becoming a keen listener.

'Grandfather was undoubtedly not one of those warriors reluctant to discuss the Great War. Far from it. He was an officer with Vice Admiral Beatty on HMS Lion. He would often rant and rave about the Battle of Jutland. So, I came to know every last detail of that naval conflict. The Brusilov offensive was a battle on the eastern front just days after Jutland, which enigmatically had similar characteristics and consequences. The Russian side of the family, consuming their allotted rations of champagne and vodka at various holiday visits, took great pains to augment everyone's awareness of this daring event. Although my physical condition leaves me with no taste for violence, I gained a detailed comprehension of both conflicts – Jutland and Brusilov. If you want to hear their story of human endeavour, I'll start with Jutland and the events leading to the battle if you like.'

'Why not, indeed? Carry on. I'm all ears.' So, Johnny, with his old Etonian accent, began to convey the two episodes of frivolous human folly in the early twentieth century.

'The naval arms race of the last years of the nineteenth century through to 1914 was not much different from any other in human history. The only obvious feature to note was its size and the unbelievable cost of producing relatively untried hardware. The two leading contenders were Britain and Germany. The former maintained worldwide control of the seas to protect her empire and free commercial activities. The latter gained some strength to avoid a blockade and possibly assist in its future imperial ambitions.

Fantastically, a kind of sibling rivalry fuelled some of the German desire to possess such a fleet. Both navies operated on the same lines. Germany admired Britain's and copied it in most respects. Her commander-in-chief, the Kaiser, was closely related to the royal family. Queen Victoria married a German and spoke the language fluently. The Kaiser was now an admiral in the royal navy and attended the annual Cowes Week yacht races, competing with some success on his boat *Meteor*.

Two months before the outbreak of war, Vice Admiral George Warrender, with four of the latest dreadnought battleships – one of which was HMS *Audacious* – and Commodore Goodenough with his squadron of light cruisers, attended Kiel Week. Honoured guests of the high seas fleet, they all freely socialised with their opposite German personnel, exchanging places with the British on each other's ships! These battleships boasted heavy armour and bigger-than-ever guns of enormous power and range. The sunny day's party atmosphere dictated that no one in their right mind would pitch these monsters against each other. The politicians egged on by the new sensationalist media, itself subservient to the enlarged literate electorate, were persuaded to hand over more and more public money to fill the seas with increasing amounts of heavy metal. On the declaration of war, Britain won the arms race. It achieved its ambition of being twice as powerful as the German navy, which now had to carry out plans to attack the British forces ship by ship and avoid confrontation with the entire British fleet.'

The Players

Silent Jack (Admiral John Jellicoe)

It's incredible to picture the young admiral to be, clasping his dad's hand, himself a sea captain, as they walk the coastal paths of South Devon. One day not so far in the future, this lad's destiny would be to make an on-the-spot decision that might change the course of history. On his return from many adventures, his father would regale him with numerous exciting seafarer yarns, which captured the boy's adoring attention, thus fuelling an ambition to sail the world's seas.

John's devoted mother and father sent him to Rottingdean, a private boarding school not too distant from home. He supplemented his desire for knowledge with a talent for the most popular ball games, wanting to become a reasonable all-around sportsman. He then continued his education aboard the royal navy ship for cadets, HMS *Britannia*, and moored at Dartmouth. Upon completing his training, he passed out first by over 100 marks and gained three firsts in his exams for lieutenant. He won the £80.00 gunnery prize for lieutenants at the Royal Naval College at Greenwich. Although of slight stature, he survived many life-threatening incidents during service with the navy, not the least of which was finding himself incarcerated below decks in the sick room of HMS *Victoria*, running a high temperature due to Malta fever.

On the erroneous orders of Vice-Admiral George Tyrone, HMS *Camperdown* managed to ram *Victoria* and send her down with a terrible loss of life. Executive officer Jellicoe was a fortunate survivor. The corridors of power offered no obstacle for Jack. However, he preferred to remain unnoticed in the background. He was a keen observer with a high intellect, took a flight in a Zeppelin, and had the company of high seas fleet admirals and even the Kaiser himself. At home, he mixed with the day's politicians and was a close friend of Jack Fisher. They were known as the little admiral and the big admiral in the dog-eat-dog circles of the higher admiralty. As the admiral of the grand fleet, sometimes also known as Dreadnought Jack, he possessed supreme confidence but not at the expense of recklessness on Britain's entry into the war.

David Richard Beatty

Born out of wedlock but to soon-to-be-married parents, David Beatty descended from a reasonably well-to-do Anglo-Irish family. He emerged from his traditional private Anglo-Irish education as a well-groomed gentleman equipped to be a man of action with determination. This would see him overcome all the disciplines, tests, and modern theories the senior service could throw at him. The many postings to various trouble spots overseas and his bravery in action enhanced his reputation. His first association with Winston Churchill occurred on the Nile before the Battle of Omdurman. When a young lieutenant, David Beatty, gamely threw a bottle of champagne from a gunboat for Churchill to retrieve and enjoy. In 1912, he served as Churchill's naval secretary and later gained promotion to Commander of the First Battle Cruiser Squadron. Being in the right place at the right time, his social and political connections, and his cunning intuition speeded his journey up the ranks to rear admiral at the early age of thirty-nine. He was a fine sportsman with a keen penchant for fox hunting, pursuing his quarry to the death with verve and courage. He was reasonably well off. He married a fabulously wealthy heiress, good-looking and photogenic. He always wears an oversized cap cocked in film-star fashion in his portraits. He appeared in all the day's publications and was a man always used to getting his own way! As with many stars of notoriety and fame, arrogance was a complex characteristic of his soul. Some might say that keeping it from the light of day would prove to be a bit difficult.

Admiral Reinhard Scheer (the Man with the Iron Mask)

The idea or dream of romance at sea would have been wholly lost on Reinhard Scheer. Hard work and technical training, mixed with action across the globe, are the foundation of his career. Having passed second in his final class for the sea cadets exam, he spent six months on SMS *Renown*, specialising in gunnery. However, his expertise in torpedo warfare brought him to the notice of the upper circles. Added to this, he had a passion for submarine tactics and combat. Having been given command of various warships of different sizes, he was appointed to be chief of the General Naval Department under the wing of Admiral Alfred von Tirpitz, then back at sea commanding battle squadrons comprising dreadnoughts. He was appointed in January 1916 to be commander-in-chief of the High Seas Fleet. Politically hard right-wing, Tirpitz made it his business to emphasise the honour of Germany's cause, which boosted his popularity across the ranks. The Kaiser, aware of Tirpitz's more aggressive strategies employing U-boats, and Zeppelins with ships of the fleet, readily backed Tirpitz's protégé, Scheer.

Admiral Franz von Hipper

Franz von Hipper was born in Weilheim, forty miles south of Munich, and educated at a Roman Catholic grammar school. At eighteen, he became an officer of the imperial German navy and was acknowledged as a torpedo specialist by twenty-eight. At first, he commanded a torpedo division and then a flotilla. He served in an assortment of big and small warships as a service-watch officer and navigator, among other responsibilities, and gained all-round experience as a talented career officer.

Interestingly, he served on the Kaiser's imperial yacht *Hohenzollern* when just thirty-six years of age.

During this time, Hipper was awarded several prestigious medals. No other than Czar Nicholas II of Russia presented him with the Prussian Order of the Red Eagle and the Order of Stanislaus. This was further evidence of his ability to be comfortable in the company of the elite. It was very unusual for a shopkeeper's son and ex-grammar schoolboy as most officers serving in such a vessel would usually come from the ruling classes of the day. On his tour of duty aboard the *Hohenzollern*, they sailed up the Thames to attend the funeral of the Kaiser's grandmother, Queen Victoria of England.

At the outbreak of war, Hipper was in command of the First Scouting Group. His attention to detail and leadership were unsurpassed, demonstrated when commanding a new armoured cruiser, the *Friedrich Carl*. His crew won the Kaiser's Prize for best gunnery, which did not go unnoticed by his superiors to guarantee promotion up the ranks.

First U-Boat Loss (9 August 1914)

Ironically, soon after the camaraderie of Kiel Boat week, catastrophic violence swept across Europe. Just five days after the declaration of war, HMS *Birmingham* spotted U15 in heavy fog off Fair Isle. The submarine was helplessly adrift in open water due to engine failure, a perfect target for the British gunners, who missed. She tried to dive in an attempt to evade the oncoming light cruiser, which rammed her hull, slicing her in two and sending her down with all hands.

The Battle of Heligoland Bight (28 August 1914)

The battle of Heligoland Bight, planned for 28 August 1914, was a risky enterprise devised by Commodores Roger Keyes (submarines) and Reginald Tyrwhitt (destroyer patrol) and endorsed by the First Lord of the Admiralty, Winston Churchill. They requested to bring the Grand Fleet south and introduce Goodenough's light cruiser squadron. Admiral Sturdee, chief of staff, refused and instead decided to employ lighter forces. Incredibly, Admiral of the Grand Fleet John Jellicoe was informed of the operation on 26 August 1914, only ten hours before the submarines set sail. Jellicoe was horrified at the possible consequences of this venture, so he immediately despatched his Battle Cruiser Squadron (Beatty) and First Light Cruiser Squadron (Goodenough) and set sail south with the rest of the entire Grand Fleet to be on hand if needed.

Jellicoe's message confirming his orders was stalled at the Admiralty in Harwich, leaving both commanders unaware of the oncoming reinforcements at the first sighting, which they assumed were German vessels. With a large slice of luck, no British ships suffered from friendly fire. The Germans lost three light cruisers, with three more damaged and a destroyer. They lost 712 dead, with total casualties of 1,242. The British suffered 35 killed and no losses. Had Jellicoe been consulted at the outset, he would have appropriately coordinated Beatty and Goodenough into the plan. It could have been a rout instead of a victory of doubtful consequence.

As initially planned, Jellicoe could not believe the madness of sending unsupported cruisers, miles from home virtually under the enemy's nose. It would have exposed the attacking ships to a devastating defeat had it not been for the low tide at the time preventing the High Seas Fleet from crossing the bar into the North Sea. However, it did result in the Kaiser's losing confidence. As a result, he ordered that his permission for any future combined fleet operations had to be obtained, which infuriated Tirpitz as, in his view, it would muzzle the High Command. On the British side, Jellicoe must have been bewildered at the Admiralty for not informing him until the last minute of the operation and the appalling staff work at Harwich.

An Act of the Devil (5 September 1914)

At best, HMS *Pathfinder*, a museum piece, was a light cruiser with short coal rations due to navy cutbacks. That reduced her top speed of twenty-five knots to just five on routine patrols.

Carrying ample ammunition, she sailed from Rosyth in the company of her eighth destroyer flotilla on a bright morning on 5 September 1914. By mid-afternoon, her destroyers altered course, leaving *Pathfinder* to finish her final sweep alone. Everyone aboard was utterly unaware of the presence of Captain Otto Hersing, who had been keenly observing her movements all day. She could not have been courting a worse companion on this late summer afternoon. Lieutenant Commander Favell alerted of a G6 torpedo heading straight for *Pathfinder*'s midships, gallantly attempting to turn away, but to no avail due to the hulk's lack of momentum. The darkness of death came upon them swiftly, with Favell and 261 of his crew perishing, leaving only eighteen survivors. The British author Aldous Huxley witnessed the massive explosion that scattered thousands of metal shards and human body parts towards the sky, describing the initial sight as a great white cloud with its foot in the sea.

Otto Hersing watched his torpedo's track making its way steadily towards his quarry. After years of practice and training, he was nervous that he might miss this easy target. He awaited seeing a hull punctured, resulting in a list to port – the indication of a sinking ship. When the torpedo struck, a gargantuan silver flash sent a snow-white plume of smoke upwards. At almost the exact moment, her hull blushed deep red from an explosion the like of which he'd never seen before.

Reeling back in a state of shock, he gaped at the sea and saw nothing through the smoke. His victim was no longer there. Dazed by this apocalyptic event, he altered his course for home. He now reflected on the previous day's mission on which he and his crew had bravely ventured into the Firth of Forth, sailing to the famous bridge and secretly just a few hundred yards from the First Battle Cruiser Squadron. At this point, the Carlingnose shore battery had opened fire, forcing his retreat back to the North Sea. To him, this represented warfare, as opposed to this day's work which struck him as an act of the devil.

The Live Bait Squadron (22 September 1914)

Aboukir, *Hogue* and *Cressy* were three obsolete, recommissioned armoured cruisers, part of the Southern Force deployed to protect the approaches to the English Channel. Their orders were to distance themselves from enemy torpedo boats and destroyers. They were sent on patrol with no escorting destroyers due to the previous night's stormy weather to the Broad Fourteens, an area of sea off the north coast of the Netherlands. They found themselves in the unforeseen company of Boat U9, from which Captain Otto Weddigen fired successive torpedoes and sank all three sitting ducks with the loss of 1,450 officers and men in roughly one hour.

The Admiralty's response to this action was left to Commander Dudley Pound, later to become First Sea Lord. He publicly commented that the loss of life was regrettable, but it had alerted the navy to the submarine threat. Dudley could not have been unaware that Otto Hersing had got within hundreds of yards of sinking a good deal of the First Battle Cruiser Squadron and had managed to blow up a light cruiser three weeks before this further tragedy.

HMS Audacious and SS Berlin (23 October 1914)

Hans Pfundheller, captain of the small express passenger liner converted to a minelayer, SS *Berlin*, was content to undertake mining the entrance to the Clyde. But he could not get close enough for fear of being discovered, so instead spent the time of day deploying his two hundred mines across the main shipping lane close to Tory Island, Donegal, Northern Ireland. He completed his job on 22 October and happily set sail for home after a good day's work.

The Admiralty deployed the second Battle Squadron for gunnery practice in this unusual location due to suspected submarine activity up at Scapa Flow. They were busy honing their skills when HMS *Audacious*, one of the newest super dreadnoughts built, struck one of Pfundheller's mines on 27 October. After repeated attempts to tow her ashore, the whole crew, with no loss of life, were transferred to HMS *Olympic*, the sister ship of the Titanic. All endeavours to save the enormous ship failed. She capsized at 8.45 p.m. Still afloat upside down inside the gargantuan black hull, fifteen-inch high explosive shells obeyed the laws of gravity and began to fall and ignite the cordite in store. The resulting flash blew up B Magazine, sending this monster of war in a multitude of pieces 800 yards up into the night sky. The last act of its earthly purpose was to throw down a piece of armoured plate from above to kill a petty officer aboard HMS *Liverpool*.

The Battle of Coronel (1 November 1914)

The East Asia Squadron, commanded by the excellent Vice Admiral Maximillian Von Spee, was in a great position at the outbreak of war to disrupt trade in the Pacific and challenge troop movements across that ocean. His squadron consisted of two armoured and three light cruisers, all reasonably modern vessels led by hand-picked officers. Quite clearly, Britannia did not rule the waves in this part of the world. At this time, the Admiralty back home (Churchill) indulged themselves in the politics of removing the capable First Sea Lord Prince Louis of Battenberg to satisfy the public's distaste for his German name. Half-heartedly applying themselves, they agreed on a plan to split the fourth cruiser squadron in two. Admiral Stoddard would remain on the East coast of South America if Spee slipped past into the Atlantic. Admiral Sir Christopher Craddock received the task of seeking out Spee on the West coast in the Pacific. The modern, more heavily armoured cruiser HMS *Defence* was promised as reinforcement by the Admiralty, who promptly diverted her, resulting in her arrival miles away at Montevideo two days after the battle. Sir Christopher now had a squadron comprising HMS *Canopus*, a clapped-out, fifteen-year-old pre-dreadnought battleship just reprieved from scrappage. The chief engineer (who understandably was suffering from mental illness) and his crew were battling to coax her around the Horn at nine miles per hour. This old battleship was accompanied by two recommissioned armoured cruisers, both decommissioned in 1899 and crewed by inexperienced reservists (*Good Hope* and *Monmouth*), the modern light cruiser *Glasgow* and an armoured merchantman *Otranto*.

Churchill and Craddock exchanged a few inconsequential messages. Craddock informed the Admiralty of his decision to let *Canopus* lag behind with the colliers as she was too slow. There was no comment from Churchill, who reaffirmed that his squadron possessed the force to do the job as ordered. A further catalyst to the oncoming situation was that Sir Christopher was not in a great state of mental health himself. Suffering from justified paranoia, he said in his own words that he did not intend to suffer the fate of his good friend Rear Admiral Earnest Troubridge, who was awaiting a court-martial for failing to engage with the enemy.

Glasgow rejoined the fleet at noon on 1 November 1914 after collecting messages, cables, and posts from the British Embassy at Coronel in broad daylight. Contending with the rough weather, they steamed north in search of SMS *Leipzig*, which for some reason had become detached from Spee's squadron and represented an easy kill on her own. Unbeknown to Craddock, the crafty corsair Spee used her wireless call sign, giving the impression she was alone, a ruse the British fell for again at Jutland. Craddock fell hook, line, and sinker for it and found himself head-on with Spee's entire squadron. He had no option but to turn south and run. Soon it became apparent that *Otranto* would not keep up, so, confusingly, he gave orders to turn and give battle. After some north turns to position himself, Admiral Spee obtained a total visual advantage over the British in front of the setting sun, at which point he opened fire.

On 3 November 1914, news filtered through to the Admiralty that Spee had been sighted off the coast of Chile. In response to this, the newly reappointed veteran First Sea Lord Jack Fisher gave HMS *Defence* and battleship *Canopus* strict orders to join the squadron immediately. Unfortunately, the intended recipient, Admiral Craddock, was now lying dead along with his primarily young reservist crew at the bottom of the Pacific, off the coast of Chile. Without the long-range guns of the old crate *Canopus*, Craddock had stood no chance.

Admiral Spee, not a stupid man, watched in the darkness of night in that strange silence that makes you feel utterly alone. The oily black sea, with the same remorselessness as Spee's guns, slowly extinguished the last flickering light as it lapped over the decks. The ocean was now in the business of anonymously with no conscience, claiming 1,661 of his fellow mariner adversaries with no witness but himself. He could feel no exuberance of victory.

After easily fending off the three light cruisers, Captain John Luce on HMS *Glasgow* saw no further point in hanging around for a fight. So, he turned south and advised *Canopus* to do the same, limping along at nine miles per hour, and eventually made Stanley Harbour after two breakdowns. Her mentally exhausted skipper unceremoniously beached the old girl to be used as a defence battery.

With only three wounded on board, Spee cruised north to Valparaiso. An ecstatic portion of the German population assembled to greet his triumphant return. He knew that his victory was of no great consequence to the British navy and did not get involved in the celebrations. However, when presented with a bouquet of flowers, he was reported to have said, 'These will do nicely for my grave.' He did not have to wait too long.

In the House of Commons, Winston Churchill explained that Craddock felt he could not engage the enemy impeded by the slow *Canopus*. He decided to attack with fast ships alone, believing he could inflict enough damage on the enemy – political poetry to sidestep the worst Royal Navy sea battle defeat in living memory.

The Battle of Cocos (9 November 1914)

SMS *Emden*, recently detached from the German East Asia Squadron, successfully operated as a lone commercial raider for a couple of months. She plundered the seas capturing and sinking twenty-five civilian vessels, shelled Madras and even destroyed two allied warships. Her captain decided on a further attack on Cocos Islands. The Australians received a distress call and dispatched the light cruiser HMS *Sydney* to investigate. Upon sight of each other, *Emden* opened fire, first surprising *Sydney* with her range which was longer than expected; she scored a few hits before the Australians pounded her with larger guns. Von Muller, her skipper, beached the remnants left of *Emden*. *Sydney* then pursued the collier *Burek*, which they finally scuttled. The Australians suffered four dead and sixteen wounded. The Germans suffered 138 dead, sixty-nine wounded, and 157 captured.

The Battle of the Falkland Islands (8 December 1914)

The grapevine in Valparaiso was no different from that of any other port in the Pacific. Word had spread that a newly arrived merchant steamer had seen no British presence at Port Stanley just a few days before and no reported sighting of the mystery battleship off the southwest coast of Chile. So, the victorious East Asia Squadron, reminiscent of the Flying Dutchman, now with no home port, set sail once more. Steaming south, they captured a British collier from which they refuelled at Picton Island. Furthermore, Spee decided, for whatever reason, to raid the Falkland Islands against the wishes of three of his captains.

Back in London, Jack Fisher was painfully aware of the defeat at Coronel. He ordered the battlecruisers *Invincible* and *Inflexible* under Vice-Admiral Sturdee, an old adversary of his, to rendezvous with the rest of the squadron at Abrolhos Rocks on 26 November to join Rear-Admiral Stoddard. The whole squadron reached Port Stanley on 7 December 1914.

The following morning was clear and bright. The British were busy at work refuelling and servicing their ships when they received a telephone report from the wife of a sheep station manager, Mrs Muriel Fenton, of the sighting of the German ships on the horizon.

At the same time, Admiral Spee quickly became aware that a fleet much more powerful than his was in the harbour. He immediately ordered Greienau and Nurnberg to investigate, who confirmed his suspicions.

The old battleship *Canopus* (named after the mythical ship's pilot of ancient Greece or the second brightest star in the night sky) became Spee's spiritual mentor. Still lying on its keel in the mudflats behind Port Stanley, she fired a salvo of four twelve-inch shells, one of which ricocheted off the sea to hit the base of Greienau's funnel. After a few minutes of reflection, not being suicidal and finding himself in a similar position to his former adversary Craddock, he turned southeast and fled.

After two hours, the British had closed to within firing range. Spee took the agonising decision to turn his two armoured cruisers and give battle. He signalled his three light cruisers to part company and try to escape. Now even with the foremost gunnery experts aboard, there was no chance. Just as at Heligoland, Cocos and especially Coronel seamanship was no match for heavy metal and superior force. By late afternoon the two armoured cruisers were lying at the bottom of the Atlantic. Although the fleeing light cruisers were quickly chased down and sunk, the SMS *Dresden* managed to escape. But her captain, when cornered three months later, evacuated the ship and blew up the magazine. Sensible man! Now both the Pacific and the Atlantic were free from German interference, with control back in British hands again.

In London, the now seventy-four-year-old Fisher privately and publicly criticised Admiral Sturdee for using too much ammunition with slow, ineffective gunnery. Despite the better-trained German gunners, Sturdee, like Spee at Coronel, used his technical advantage of range and power to gain victory and was rightly accorded a triumphant welcome on his return home by the public before being promoted by Churchill.

Spee, his two sons, and 2,000 German sailors went down with their ships, along with the flowers presented in Valparaiso, barely five weeks old. The British suffered only ten dead and nineteen wounded, with no more than superficial damage to their vessels.

The Raid on Scarborough, Whitby and Hartlepool

Most of the international communication cables were under the control of the British at the outbreak of hostilities in August 1914, who not surprisingly severed the German connections, leaving only wireless available, which made the introduction of secret codes necessary. The Germans issued at least one copy of the codebook to decipher orders to each ship. Fortunately, on 26 August 1914, unknown to the Germans, the Russians captured three copies from the light cruiser SMS *Magdeburg* and duly handed one to their British ally. Two other valuable codebooks were obtained and supplied to Room 40, the British codebreaker's HQ, run by civilian academics. In the early days, information was mishandled due to the academics' lack of naval experience. The Admiralty appointed Commander W. Hope to remedy this.

Getting past the usual British cliques usually resulted in further loss of time. In this case, Winston Churchill and some trusted Admiralty officers tended to censor decoded messages before handing them over to the commanders at sea. All the same, Room 40 in the Admiralty building proved an advantageous asset.

Room 40 intercepted and decoded a message successfully on the evening of 14 December 1914 instructing Hipper to leave port with his battle cruiser squadron, but with no mention of the High Seas Fleet or any dreadnoughts. In response, the Admiralty ordered Jellicoe at Scapa Flow to despatch the First Battle Cruiser Squadron (Beatty), the Second Battleship Squadron, comprising six dreadnoughts (Warrender), and the First Light Cruiser Squadron (Goodenough). And from the south, two light cruisers and forty-two destroyers covered the English Channel. Jellicoe rightly protested that with only six dreadnoughts, although a large force, it would be no match in the event of an unexpectant confrontation with the High Seas Fleet. The Admiralty added the Third Cruiser Squadron and four armoured cruisers from Rosyth, leaving the Grand Fleet at Scapa Flow.

Unbeknown to Room 40 and strictly against the Kaiser's orders, Admiral Ingenohl followed Hipper with the whole High Seas Fleet with its twenty-two dreadnoughts. Consequently, the

Germans were now in an excellent position to inflict the heaviest defeat on the Royal Navy for 300 years, if not ever.

Amazingly, after having been informed of several destroyer skirmishes in the night, which might or might not have been an advance guard of the Grand Fleet, wishing not to upset his boss, Ingenohl turned for home at 5.30 a.m. The opportunity the German High Command had been praying for was lost.

On arrival at the east coast of England, Hipper divided his fleet into two battle cruisers to shell Scarborough and Whitby, with a minelayer and two battle cruisers and an armoured cruiser to shell Hartlepool. They did as ordered and killed 122 civilians and wounded 443, causing considerable damage to the towns. The action began at 8 a.m. and ceased at 9.30 a.m. when Hipper regrouped his fleet and headed home. The raid had been fraught with danger for both sides, as the North Sea was a hive of activity, and there had been bad weather and poor visibility. But at the end of proceedings, both navies returned to port relatively unscathed.

In retrospect, confused signals drafted by Ralph Seymour Beatty's flag officer became evident. Jellicoe resolved never to let an engagement take place without the presence of the entire Grand Fleet from the start of operations. At the same time, becoming nervous of Beatty's appetite for engaging the enemy, despite this, he agreed to move the Battle Cruiser Squadron to Rosyth, nearer to any further action on the east coast.

The Battle of Dogger Bank (24 January 1915)
In light of the raid, Hipper suspected that British spies were mingling with fishing fleets at Dogger Bank and intended to remove them. Room 40 decoded a transmission on 23 January 1915, which alerted them that Hipper was planning a short sortie with three battlecruisers, one armoured cruiser, four light cruisers and eighteen destroyers for 24 January 1915. To counter this, the Admiralty, Churchill, Wilson, and Oliver despatched a superior force of five battlecruisers, seven light cruisers and thirty-five destroyers. On sighting the British, Hipper turned southeast and ran.

Beatty positioned his battle cruisers well and opened fire at 20,000 yards. The Germans could not reply at this distance because they were out of range. After a few salvos, shells started to straddle SMS *Blucher*. If Beatty had remained at this range, he could have indulged in some target practice at no risk to his fleet. As he foolishly took his ships into closer range, Beatty's overconfidence and hunger for a famous victory got the better of tactics. *Lion*, Beatty's flagship, hit battle cruiser *Seydlitz* with a 13.5-inch shell, which penetrated her aft turret, causing an ammunition fire that would have sunk her but for an officer flooding the magazine. The ever-grateful and astonished Hipper found himself in range and rained twelve-inch shells on *Lion*, one of which hit the forward turret, causing a small yet significant ammunition fire. It was immediately brought under control and extinguished. Eventually, she was put out of action with no electric supply, leaving her dependent on Flag Officer Ralph Seymour yet again. He got it incredibly wrong once more, hoisting two signals simultaneously, which resulted in the other battlecruisers breaking off the pursuit. This was not the intention of Beatty, who had now lost control of his ships. The *Blucher* sank. With great skill and courage, the remaining crew aboard the *Seydlitz* managed to return the wrecked ship to her homeport to undergo repairs. More importantly, it gave the German engineers working in the dry dock the chance to examine the vessel with a fine-tooth comb. They gained invaluable knowledge of the make-up of a battle cruiser and its fundamental characteristics and flaws.

Jan 1915–April 1916

Failing to sink *Seydlitz* proved to be catastrophic. At the behest of Lord Fisher, the British engineers undertook running repairs on HMS *Lion* without going into dry dock at Armstrong's on the Tyne. Despite being reduced almost to a write-off, no one investigated her strengths and weaknesses. Beatty stubbornly believed that rapid supply to the turrets was worth the risk of a cordite flash, as he had gotten away with this to date.

The forces at Scapa Flow focused on target practice and gunnery, with easy access to relatively safe sea areas. With not much else to do, they looked down on the men at Rosyth. Their comrades in the south could visit Edinburgh and surrounding towns on leave. Target practice was nigh impossible in the Firth of Forth, as one 13.5-inch shell could shatter more than 1,000 civilian windows. So gunnery practice was diminished.

On the other side of 'The Dead Sea', or shall we call it 'No-Man's Land', Admiral Hipper had discovered the importance of a cordite flash. SMS *Seydlitz* revealed her secrets. Gunnery practice in the confines of the Baltic now included the art of plunging shells into horizontal target rings. The Germans rigorously introduced a strict code of safety procedures on all ranks with no exceptions, admirals included! Specialist gunners were made aware that they would get only minutes of clear visibility in a battle to hit their target.

Gretna Green, March 1916 (the 'Devil's Porridge')

After a brief rainy holiday together in Morecambe, Flo, Mildred, and Ethel took up employment at Gretna. With no formal education but grounded in northern common sense and innocence, they could clearly understand the dangers of cordite.

'It's on account of my Fred, you see.'

'What's on account of your Fred?' Ethel asked.

Flo, with her round, honest face looking at the other two, knew the answer.

Mildred, dressed just like her friends in khaki smock, gaitered trousers and elasticated cloth cap designed for safety at work, continued, 'Well, it's that German chap, the one all the papers refer to as "The Baby Killer". It was 'im that blew Fred's legs off, arms too. Killed in the very house we lived in over at Hartlepool. That's why I'm here.'

'There are 10,000 girls like us going to produce 800 tons of cordite a week in the not-too-distant future here at HM Gretna, so the recruiting officer just said,' remarked Ethel.

'That Conan Doyle, the Sherlock Holmes man, said that us

mixing nitroglycerin with gun cotton with our bare arms and hands would blow us to atoms in an instant if certain small changes occurred. He called the mixture the 'Devils Porridge' Flo gossiped on.

'That's why the recruiting man said they were strict on clothing, shoes, matchboxes, and even jewellery. My wedding ring, just a curtain ring, is not allowed. No drink, of course. They send some girls to prison for disobeying the rules,' warned Mildred.

'I hope our sea captains have ordered our sailor boys to take good care with this stuff,' all three chimed together.

The Battle of Jutland (31 May–1 June 1916)

Admiral Scheer, now obsessed with his strategy of destroying a portion of the Grand Fleet, planned a raid on Sunderland for mid-May 1916 and duly despatched a fleet of U-boats to patrol the British entry points into the North Sea. Lousy weather and ship repairs enforced a delay to 31 May, the last day the U-boats could safely remain at sea. With no immediate Zeppelin involvement due to the bad weather, he abandoned the raid on Sunderland and replaced the plan with a patrol into the Skagerrak to lure Beatty out once more. Room 40 decoded Scheer's intentions but this time used his home-port wireless signal to disguise his whereabouts, as Spee had done at Coronel.

The Grand Fleet set sail immediately on receipt of this information, first to rendezvous with Admiral Jerram from Cromarty and finally with Beatty west of the Skagerrak with orders to wait for the Germans to appear. At this stage, neither Jellicoe nor Scheer knew of each other's presence in the North Sea. By 2.00 p.m. Beatty reached 260 miles east of Britain and duly turned north to rendezvous with Jellicoe as ordered. As a result of the turn, the Fifth Battle squadron (Evan-Thomas with four super dreadnoughts) was now leading five miles to the northwest. At 2.20 p.m., two British and two German destroyers investigated a neutral Danish steamer plodding its way into what was about to become the most extensive sea battle zone in history after the British fired the first shots at the Germans at 2.28 p.m.

The South Run

On Beatty's turn south at 2.32 p.m., Evan-Thomas's Fifth Battle Squadron was still steaming north because HMS *Tiger* was now leading the line too far away to make her signal visible. There was an appalling lack of coordination between Evan-Thomas and Beatty back in Rosyth in following the flagship. This culminated in the fact that now four of the world's fastest and most powerfully armed super dreadnoughts had fallen some ten miles behind. Despite the prevailing circumstance, Beatty resolved to steam at full speed towards the enemy, even with his fleet divided in two. Very brave but incredibly stupid! What reason could Beatty have had to act in this cavalier fashion? His gunner's range-finding efforts were frustrated by the vessel's vibration. The super dreadnoughts could not catch up, so Beatty threw away the priceless advantage of range precisely as at Dogger Bank. Yet there was no immediate rush to do anything, as Hipper with Scheer following, were still steaming northwest to Jellicoe.

Hipper was ecstatic as his enemy was closing range. He decided to turn southeast to lead Beatty on to Scheer, who, even at this speed, had ten more minutes in which to open fire unopposed. If Beatty had stayed that distance, the damage he could have inflicted would have been devastating. On top of all this, he had not organised his fleet into a battle formation during the chase. As a result, four of his battlecruisers were still turning, which hampered their aim when Hipper opened fire at 3.48 p.m. The opening exchanges went to the Germans with no real damage as the British began to sort themselves out.

At 4 p.m., the hour of revelation came when a twelve-inch shell fired from SMS *Lutzow* plunged straight into the Q turret amidships of HMS *Lion*, killing the gunners. The flash travelled down the supply shafts into the handling rooms to kill all within. The cordite stored there for speed of action ignited and blew the roof off the turret. Most of its energy burst upwards, but not all. A Major Harvey, mortally wounded, bravely ordered the magazine doors shut. He miraculously saved the ship and was posthumously awarded the Victoria Cross. Fortune does indeed seem to favour the brave, as both HMS *Lion* and its illustrious admiral lived to fight another day.

At 4.02 p.m., specialist gunners aboard the *Van Der Tan* were given a clear vision of HMS *Indefatigable*, last in Beatty's line, for that fraction of time their training had prepared them. From a great distance, guided by the sun's rays shining down momentarily through the cloud ceiling, they landed three eleven-inch shells on her upper aft decks, and a fourth made a direct hit on the forward A turret. The cordite flashed in a second and surged through the handling rooms into the cordite storage and magazine. The enclosed metal hull turned into a gigantic bomb that exploded, sending large and small metal parts spiralling 400 yards into the air and leaving no sign of the vaporised 1,019 men and boys.

At 4.15 p.m., Evan-Thomas finally came into range and opened fire, with his trained gunners proving to be deadly accurate.

At 4.19 p.m., HMS *Queen Mary*, doing well from the middle of the line, emerging into a pool of light through the mist and smoke of the battle, did not go unnoticed by the gunners aboard SMS *Defflinger*. Nor did it go unnoticed by SMS *Seydlitz*, from which a shell penetrated her Q turret. Once more, flash fire shot through the shafts, handling rooms, and corridors with its usual speed and efficiency. After one of those mini seconds when the world seemed to stand still, the *Queen Mary*'s midships began to glow red, freckled with white-hot spots. Then she blew apart, her bows lifting clear of the sea. The stern folded inwards, funnels and masts collapsing into the central chasm as the smoke began to conceal the last minutes of her existence. The bodies of the 1,266 crew atomised to nothingness, their souls following their comrades from the *Indefatigable*. Beatty exclaimed his off-the-cuff Nelson-like quote for posterity, 'There seems to be something wrong with our bloody ships today!' Half an hour later, the run to the south ended.

The Run to the North
With the High Seas Fleet in sight, Beatty turned 180 degrees to head north and Hipper duly obliged by giving chase. Standing on the bridge as an admiral should with his cocked oversized cap having finished quoting, even he must have felt highly embarrassed. The engines below vibrated with accelerating power to fuel his lust for action once again. Ever the master tactician, Beatty did not need his telescope to observe that Evan-Thomas, with his super dreadnoughts, had passed by in the opposite direction towards the enemy's entire fleet. Beatty gave the order to turn in succession. Again Ralph Seymour delayed executing the order, confusing the situation. Thankfully, HMS *Malay*, the trailing ship, turned early in her own sea area rather than together with the others, which would have presented Scheer's forward ships with four sitting ducks.

The Fifth Battle Squadron now acted as rear-guard as Beatty steamed north out of range, drawing the Germans to Jellicoe, who now ordered the Third Battle Cruiser Squadron (Hood) SSE to support Beatty. As yet, Jellicoe had no accurate information about Scheer's movements and was still in cruising formation but had to decide soon. He had narrowed deployment down to two choices. Turning to the west would take his force closer to Scheer and gain valuable time at the risk of the Germans arriving before the completion of the manoeuvre. Deploying to the east (port turn) would take his force away from Scheer but make the crossing of the T possible, giving his gunners a promising target against the setting sun while camouflaging his fleet against the grey northern sky. East would make a retreat to port more difficult should Scheer be put to flight.

At 6.14 p.m., Beatty was minded to respond. He furnished the imperative information just in time. With this in hand, Jellicoe decided on the east at 6.15 p.m.

British ships of all shapes and sizes were scurrying about in haste to get to their proper stations. Beatty was crossing the van of the British dreadnoughts to join Hood to distract Scheer's attention, as he still had no idea of the Grand Fleet's presence.

At 6.29 p.m., the light opened like the parting of the Red Sea, revealing a silver avenue across the water to spotlight HMS *Invincible*. SMS *Lutzow* and SMS *Deflinger*, themselves in a poor state by now, lost no time to volley shells onto the highlighted ship, one of which smashed through her midship Q turret. The cordite flashed and detonated the magazine below. The mammoth steel-armoured ship exploded, scattering its wreckage and causing dead human bodies to float in the water, the only memorial to the 1,026 crew lost instantly.

At 6.30 p.m. Scheer naively was surprised as the approaching Grand Fleet appeared before him about to cross his T as Jellicoe had planned, and he now knew he could not win the battle. The 13.5- and fifteen-inch shells began to rain down on his leading dreadnoughts, justifying Jellicoe's turn to the east. Scheer immediately ordered an about-turn to starboard 180 degrees, well-practised in training and now efficiently done, knowing that survival until the darkness of night was now his only option. It became evident that a continued stern chase would not buy enough time and would result in massive damage to his fleet, making a later escape impossible. So, he took the unwelcome but brave decision to turn about again and launch a surprise head-on attack on the enemy at 6.55 p.m. Jellicoe crossed his T once more with devastating effect.

Scheer, for the second time, ordered an about-turn at 7.17 p.m. On this occasion, his line buckled in great confusion under heavy fire. In disarray, he ordered the badly damaged First Scouting Group to draw rear-guard fire in what is now known as 'The Death Ride' to receive thirty-seven hits. Submarines, torpedo boats, and destroyers launched torpedoes head-on, forcing Jellicoe to turn away. Not one hit, but more time was lost, which gave Scheer his opportunity to slip into the night.

The flashes of light in the distance did not reveal the nature of busy naval manoeuvres in the dark five miles astern of the Grand Fleet now in night cruising order. Torpedoes, close encounters, and even ships ramming each other could only be indistinctly made out. The Germans, better equipped and trained for night fighting, seemed just as reluctant to engage as the British were in the chaotic three hours before dawn. To open fire with big guns would give one's position away and was largely avoided by both sides. Several messages confirming Scheer's position were not sent forward by a sole junior officer left in charge at the Admiralty, who did not realise their importance. The combination of German wireless jamming skills and the British inadequacies at communications combined to keep the admiral in the dark. The risk of full confrontation at night was of no interest to Jellicoe anyway. Scheer was in full retreat, crossing his wake, trying to save his battered fleet from certain destruction in the coming light. By 4.15 a.m., Jellicoe, blind to the situation no more, with the required information now to hand, knew his chance to intercept at Horns Reef was gone.

No Trafalgar! No Acclaim!

Later that morning, 'after breakfast', as Doveton Sturdee, an admiral with a bad dose of Nelsonitus would have put it, the British dinosaurs, intact and largely undamaged, returned to their home at Scapa Flow. They steamed in an orderly ten-mile line like over-tried trained elephants exiting the circus ring nose to tail, overlords of the North Sea to be fed and watered into eventual extinction.

Jellicoe, the master tactician of the battle, was not to be influenced by the media-driven desire to become a second Nelson with a Trafalgar under his belt (which he might well have had with a bit of help from his friends). Certainly not at the expense of losing the war and possibly leaving the English east coast open to invasion with the help of a German surface fleet.

Admiral Doveton Sturdee

Stimulated by the press, the British public was in a frenzy of nationalistic fervour at the outbreak of war. As far as the navy was concerned, my grandad's physician regarded this as a mental condition and gave it the medical term 'Nelsonitus', a plight from which admirals and politicians were not immune. He also formulated that the only cure for this was an outright victory or total defeat in a naval battle.

In August 1914, two possible sufferers, Admiral Sturdee, a well-trained gunnery/torpedo expert but not a particularly good chief of naval staff and the First Sea Lord Winston Churchill, failed to consult and involve the commander-in-chief of the Grand Fleet, Admiral Jellicoe, of their plans for a battle at Heligoland Bight. Sturdee and Churchill were thus hoping for a quick victory for which they would take all the credit.

Sturdee's symptoms reappeared in December when confronted with the news of Admiral Spee's arrival eight miles from Port Stanley. While still refuelling and servicing his ships, Sturdee reportedly gave the inept Nelsonic quote, 'Send the Men to Breakfast.' Luckily for him, Spee thought Sturdee's ships were up and ready. From surveillance, Spee knew they were faster than any of his. *Canopus* lobbed four shells from the mudflaps, so he turned to run. Had Spee decided to attack, our crews might well have found themselves eating 'the full English' knee-deep in seawater. To give Sturdee credit, his gunnery expertise and performance in battle far exceeded his use of the English language – he secured total victory.

Admiral Beatty

The universally liked Admiral Beatty appeared to be taking 100-year-old instructions from his mentor above during the Battle of Dogger Bank instead of following the ship's user manual. 'Our country will be more forgiving of a captain attacking an enemy than letting it go.' Everyone agreed that Sturdee should have replaced Beatty after this battle.

Jutland south run: Spee and Sturdee had demonstrated superior force used with patience and skill would always win the day. Hipper had five battle cruisers with a broadside capability of 33,000 pounds. Beatty had six battlecruisers and four super dreadnoughts with a broadside capability of 118,000 pounds, giving Beatty an advantage of over four to one. More of Nelson's words that are not in the ship's manual is, 'No captain can do very wrong if he places his ship alongside that of the enemy.'

After approximately 1 hour and ten minutes of engagement, of which three-quarters of an hour in battle took place without the stronger half of his force, Beatty (our David) turned north with his remaining three battlecruisers and one badly damaged, leaving the four dreadnoughts to fight a rear guard action against the entire German fleet. His chance of immortality gone, no Beatty's Column in a London square, he proceeded with the run to the north, drawing Scheer on to Jellicoe with some success. After a good night's sleep fifteen miles southwest of the Grand Fleet, Beatty mused over plans for his place in history and glossed over his self-inflicted defeat at the hands of Hipper.

Admiral Scheer

Scheer was late on the scene with his new aggressive ideas about North Sea warfare, which was supposed to add air reconnaissance plus the deployment of U-boats to the plans of attacking a portion of the Grand Fleet at one time. Unfortunately, his U-boats were unsuccessful, and the weather at Jutland disrupted the Zeppelins' performance. His strategy was now not much different from that of his predecessors. Facing the destruction of his fleet, history will remember him mainly for his tactical retreats.

Admiral Hipper

He executed his orders well but found himself retreating to his home port in every case. He defied the odds at Jutland, taking advantage of closer range to exploit the appalling British carelessness in their cordite safety procedures. His specialist approach of plunging shell fire into gun turrets was his best achievement of the day, at the end of which the dreadnoughts had reduced his squadron to wreckage. Still, he somehow returned them to port once again.

Silent Jack (Dreadnought Jack)-(Admiral John Jellicoe).
No one will ever know whether or not Jack was aware of Scheer's position that night. Jack was no fool and a brilliant tactician with

more knowledge and experience than anyone of that day. In the unlikely event that no signals at all reached him, his view of events unfolding astern would reveal nothing to him of any importance. He would simply have demanded to know the whereabouts of the High Seas Fleet. For the battlefield was his. We found his tactics for every outcome of enemy manoeuvres infallible when he took one minute to deploy to port when belatedly informed of the enemy's position. A very short time to make possibly the most demanding and calculated decision of the entire war! His Grand Fleet not once but twice crossed Scheer's T to reduce him to retreat. His much-criticised order to turn from what could have been 200 torpedoes, not the thirty-nine that materialised, was a masterstroke of self-control. To Scheer's credit, he knew he would have done the same if the roles had been reversed. This is precisely why he tempted Jack with a ninety-five per cent chance of everlasting fame and national deification. A bait Jack did not care to take. As the battle was already won and owing to the certainty that twenty U-boats, umpteen torpedo boats and destroyers were unaccounted for, nothing was going to persuade him to pursue a retreating, badly damaged enemy day or night into freshly laid minefields and a torpedo trap on the approach to Horns Reef. The North Sea was held tight, and the ruthless blockade of Germany would persist in bringing her down.

A quick coffee break was the order of the afternoon. Miles drew the Merc into the services. Looking with more respect at the eminent historian walking beside him, he asked if there would be time for the offensive that his mother was so proud of.

'Of course. Have you ever heard of it?'

'No.'

The Brusilov Offensive (4 June 1916)

The war of extensive movement was very quickly over, and with no regard for human lives, the land battles busied themselves in downright attrition for the best part of two years. The High Command took no interest in the thoughts of Ivan Bloch and his explanations of the technological advances in weaponry. The flawed diplomacy of 1914 was replaced by a military tunnel vision of the poorly thought out tactic to concentrate firepower in all its industrially produced forms onto a single area of attack or defence. The battlefields east and west, with no compassion or guile, had an unquenchable thirst for red blood to soak the few feet of land gained or lost at the behest of its devotees.

The only First World War general capable of winning land battles was of Russian-Polish descent. He devised a plan that deviated from localised breakthroughs and submitted it to his boss, the overall commander Mikhail Alekseyev. Not to be dismissive of its virtue, Alekseyev accepted it. After the prevarication of the Stavka – the Russian high military command – the precise particulars of the action were agreed to by General Kuropatkin (Northern Front) and General Evert, with his more significant role (Western Front). The author of this scheme was General Aleksei Brusilov (Southwestern Front), who realised the importance of attention to detail and ruthless planning. At last, the improving Russian war economy began to provide modern early twentieth-century weaponry for the imperial army. As we take notice of events in the North Sea, synchronisation of action by all subordinate commanders to stick rigidly to the battle plan was going to be imperative.

The Eastern, longer than the Western, Front runs down from the Baltic south to neutral Romania. East of the line, 1,700,000 men comprised six field armies of 102 divisions. These troops regaining strength from the previous two years' setbacks, faced 1,900,000 men of the central powers consisting of forty-eight German divisions on the North and North-central Fronts plus fifty-five Austro-Hungarian divisions positioned on the Central South-western Fronts.

The generals in Europe must have figured out that the principal killing zone before them was the vast and damaged no-man's land. Their detachment from reality, in conjunction with little knowledge of how to employ modern artillery and weaponry, fuelled their unsynchronised, repetitive, and compulsive genocide.

Brusilov's plan, not the work of a genius but born out of common sense, was to reduce this lethal area. He stretched his trench lines across the Southwestern Front to include telephone communications, forward posts, and jumping-off points for his storm troops, sometimes within fifty yards of the enemy's front lines. As a result, his adversary could not predict from where his primary attacks, even with their air superiority, would come. He positioned his heavy and light artillery to confuse, as he was in no mind to announce his forthcoming presence with a 2,000,000 shell barrage! His Southwestern Front was to be a powerful feint, with the main thrust to come from General Evert's Western Front, backed with support from Kuropatkin in the north. A short, sharp, accurate artillery barrage on 4 June 1916 (just seventy-two hours after Jutland) left the battlefield intact for his four armies to advance on a broad front as planned. By 8 June 1916, the Russians had overwhelmed Lutz and, during the process, had taken 200,000 prisoners. His troops happily going about their work in the Southwest sector sang hymns as they chased the retreating Austro-Hungarians. The pleasure of taking prisoners on a daily basis throughout June and July kept morale high.

The total defeat of Austro-Hungary seemed only a matter of time to the well-trained body of men. The tally had exceeded 380,000 prisoners, adding to the enemy's 450,000 casualties. Back-slapping congratulations from the Stavka at the news that the Germans had suspended the Verdun offensive and were planning to transfer divisions to the East hastily confirmed his worst fears.

Far away, the Romanov court, living in their fantasy world in St Petersburg, was comfortable with the aristocratic club in the Stavka to protect them. However, they were blissfully unaware that most suffered from Bonapartitus (a paranoia of attack relying on victory through retreat or inertia) and began to pervert Brusilov's plan. General Evert bombastically influenced the other overdressed, bemedaled sufferers into prevarication while he greedily stockpiled guns and ammunition to further his own cause. He delayed the agreed assault on Vilnius of 31 May 1916, designed by Brusilov to at least keep the Germans busy in the north. But more importantly, curtail rail-traffic troop movements south to Baranovichi and capture Kovel. The spiritual guidance of the mad monk Grigor Rasputin, due to his vision of a triumphant attack at Baranoviche, gave the perfect excuse to delay and eventually cancel the Vilnius operation.

Aleksei Brusilov, ever proud of his intelligence corps, was devastated to learn that after weeks of planning, Evert had not only cancelled Vilnius but changed the objective. Outraged at the moral ineptitude of his commander, Mikhail Alekseyev insisted that Brusilov should face up to Evert and Kuropatkin. In just six days, the Germans could transfer divisions (fifteen of them, as it turned out) from the Western to the Eastern Front, and time was running out. General Evert was forced to oblige at last and launched his hastily planned, ill-advised, and half-hearted attack on the new objective, Baranoviche, eight days later, on 2 July 1916.

Over the next fortnight, the Russians pushed forward in wave formation, being exposed to every form of firepower at the behest of their stubborn commanders and taking enormous casualties for little progress. Paying little attention to Brusilov's tactics, Evert and his second-in-command, Alexander Ragoza, ordered the Fourth Army to attack using three army corps to fight in the time-honoured futile way. Prince Leopold of Bavaria counter-attacked with his ninth German army to regain all lost ground on 14 July 1916. As if to prove a point, a final Russian push between 25 and 29 July predictably failed yet again, shouldering 80,000 Russian casualties against German/Austrian 13,000 in the process.

Due to ambiguous signals from GHQ Stavka in mid-June, Brusilov obeyed orders to target two important rail junctions, Vladimir-Volynsky and Kovel, splitting his armies. At the time, although not comfortable with the plan, the expected main thrust from Evert might justify letting the Austrians off the hook for a week or so. Not now, he mused!

Train whistles were blowing! The lines from the Baltic coast down to Vilnius to Baranoviche through Kovel and Vladimir-

Volynsky were open to the Romanian border. – all with direct connections to Germany herself. The aristocratic club at GHQ Stavka, with their inexhaustible wisdom, ordered Evert's troops south under Brusilov's victorious wing. Contrary to every detail in his plan, the Germans, now free to deploy divisions south at will to arrive anywhere first by train, would easily detect these troop movements. To be saddled with troops he didn't really need, with no prospect of a meaningful thrust from the Western Front, put our Russian hero in the 'last chance saloon' as far as outright victory to end the war for the Allies was concerned. They had to take the railway town! Aleksei had this forced on him by the useless Evert.

The newly arrived, highly trained Guards Army entered the equation at his disposal. This elite commando force numbering 70,000 men was under the command of General Alexander Bezobrazov and Grand Duke Paul. Both they and their field officers were products of social grace. Despite this, the Guards Army was impressed by defeating Baron von Luttwitz at Tresten and Vorochin to take 20,000 prisoners and fifty-six guns on 15 July 1916. The preceding reputation of the outfit persuaded Brusilov to take his chance. Time was of the essence. No sooner had the troops staggered back from the Baranoviche fiasco than the Guards, on 27 July 1916, marched proudly up the three causeways, each surrounded by extensive marshland and surface water, to Kovel. Basic reconnaissance revealed there would be little cover, so Brusilov insisted they approach bellies down on the flanks. That was an order from GHQ. Brought up with the inconsistencies and inaccuracies of Tolstoy's *War and Peace*, Bonapartitus's symptoms of Russian valour on the counter-attack began to emerge on the first day of the fortnight-long coming nightmare.

Flushed with the previous week's success, Bezobrazov shouldered arms and marched his men in virtual silence on the three causeways firm on foot. He deemed that none of the 3,000,000 shells Evert had managed to hoard would be required at this initial stage. Flags, standards, and colours accompanied the units as Grand Duke Paul astride his steed, inspiring the men with confidence as they advanced closer to the German defence. With the sound of Tchaikovsky's *1812 Overture* (minus the guns!) filling his head with how to achieve Russian glory, he refused the order to flank the attack.

The grand parade of well-trained, fit men focused on changing the course of the war and barely noticed the swamp as they moved on. As usual, at first, the invisible enemy just under a mile away opened fire on the assembled ranks in front of them. Corpses and the wounded piled up to shame the living around them. After two years, how could anyone not know the predictable gruesome outcome of a frontal assault on well-defended, fully-armed positions? No matter how tough, flesh and blood are no match for cold steel.

Some days into the action, utterly unaware of Grand Duke Paul's foolhardy decision, the Russian artillery opened fire on their own ranks. After an agonising period, the batteries learned of the Duke's central position and held their fire. The opportunity of free airspace afforded the Austro-German Albatross biplanes a free hand to buzz like hornets above. Their Parabellum MG-14 mounted machine guns were effectively strafing the still-advancing ground troops.

Nevertheless, incredibly they took the Austro-German trenches at Kovel with the remainder of the elite Guards Army. However, the causeways were carpeted with dead and wounded in their wake. Men desperately waded past their drowned comrades to avoid being sucked into the quagmire below. A fuse dump exploded next to a field hospital to illuminate the redness of human body parts and display the catastrophic scene. The gnarled trees splintered from ricochets stood silent amid the pitiful cries of the wounded – a horrific scene. Even the horses would not have fancied a Light Brigade charge into this devil's underworld of death. The cavalry officers, point blank, refused to support the army as planned. On 8 August 1916, the Russians ordered all units to retire across this bitterly contested ground back to base effectively to end the Brusilov Offensive.

In the beginning, with just 200,000 troops and 800 field guns, neither side (except Brusilov's) envisaged such a victory. What makes these two battles so similar in outcome is that Jellicoe suffered the same fate. However, his subordinate commanders did not stick to the plans.

The central powers eventually transferred forty divisions to the east. The attack on Verdun was aborted and committed all fronts to defence for the time being. At the very least, he had saved the allies from losing the war.

In the end, Germany, in their very own words, was shackled to a corpse, and Russia acquired the lead weight of an extra 200 miles of front line through her new ally Romania to the Black Sea.

***

'So, what's your verdict?' Johnny asked Miles, who was relaxing back to enjoy the passing Yorkshire scenery.

'Well, I suppose that if subordinate commanders had adhered strictly to plans, Brusilov would have had his lads languishing in Vienna, Budapest. Quite happy to allow the millions of prisoners of war the pleasure of tilling their smallholdings back in Russia. Jellicoe, on the other hand, with an initial battle-cruiser victory instead of a partial defeat – Admiral Sturdee would have achieved this – and a few more hours of daylight would have sent the High Seas Fleet to the bottom.'

'Two very big ifs there, Miles, but not a bad conclusion, though not entirely correct. Our unanimous family take on it was that Jellicoe retained control of the North Sea, with the similar outcome of saving the allies from losing the war. Both campaigns had similar consequences. Even if he had sunk the German fleet, it would still have been a victory. Very flattering, but that's all. The Germans enjoyed Tannenberg, the Second Battle of the Marne, and even as late as 1918, the Battle of Soissons and the Michael offensives. All victories for the media to fool their publics with old-fashioned patriotic fervour to disguise the underlying tactical failures and allow the industrialised carnage to strip the land wickedly of human life.'

Johnny happily enlightened Miles with some salient words to explain his family's conclusions.

'In August 1914, the youth of a continent found itself railroaded to war. Their superiors were eager to put the ostensibly awesome power of modern weaponry to the test. It soon became apparent that all this hardware had outpaced their ability to control it. It took away the glamour and traditional glory that had attracted hundreds of thousands to volunteer for a shorter life. Jellicoe and Brusilov, the master tacticians, understood their hardware's attacking limitations and tailored their battle plans accordingly. With the battle of Jutland behind him, Brusilov could have won the war by October 1916.

'Nevertheless, the supposed high-ranked strategists scratched their heads as it became apparent that all these artefacts of destruction and murder had severe terminal offensive defects (including the dreadnought battleships). In a masterstroke of human genius, their answer was to raise the stakes from thousands of shells, gas, and bullets to tens of millions. This, in turn, demanded the presence of millions more increasingly nervous conscripted victims forced to become a sad memory. Go to the Tate Gallery and view Mark Gertler's painting *Merry-Go-Round* (1916) – he understood. Army populations the size of cities faced each other, each supported by armoury, hospitals, food, clothing, and health-supply logistics, all top priority, miles behind their lines. Hardly surprising, with all this paraphernalia in tow moving at less than a walking pace, after a brief period in 1914, the enemy territory was getting much harder to take and hold.

'The truth of the matter is that there were no meaningful victories at all in the First World War. "One battle won doesn't win a war" comes to mind here. Nobody can get around the fact that most, if not all, modern weaponry was only really any good for anything but defence. Leon Trotsky exited the conflict a month after the Russian Revolution. His delegation representing those responsible from different social classes negotiated peace, not because of a military defeat. Still inflicting enormous casualties, the German army was not drawn to negotiation by a stunning rout and invasion. They agreed to the Armistice because the political and revolutionary social collapse at home had begun to permeate the ranks to herald the self-destruction of Germany by itself. The rank-and-file mariners of Wilhelm's High Seas Fleet mutinied and flatly refused to obey orders to set sail for a final confrontation with the British. Most of their country, reeling from deprivation and losing loved ones, was untouched by the murderous shells and bullets.'

'How did they get away with it, Johnny?'

'The early twentieth century benefited from the nineteenth's scientific advances, which European leaders failed to understand. A general strike would have stopped the trains in their tracks, but international workers' cooperation could not deliver due to media-fuelled patriotism. So invention and paranoia partnered to paper over the cracks of a war fought for no reason. The individual hunch of the many personalities buried humanity in confusion.

'Why, as usual, were the ordinary soldiers from all sides denied representation at the Armistice? Any one of whom, after suffering four years of hell on earth, might have delivered a practical solution for their ever-failing peers to consider. The same old politicians and diplomats – aren't they always guaranteed to survive intact – invite themselves to play the role of banker to end this insanity and sort out the game's winners and losers. Take this on board, Miles – a group of ordinary businessmen like us, could readily convince them that as far as our average punters are concerned, there are no winners, only losers! If we conducted ourselves in such a manner, an obligatory visit to the local magistrate would be the order of the day.'

The dignitaries duly assembled at Versailles to humiliate their perceived losers to share the armaments, most of which were obsolete and fit only to be mothballed. The losers are obliged to pay the winners money, promising more to come. They conceived newborn nation-states from the periphery of the losers to set the stage for the next bloody fixture in 1939. Everyone present agreed that the jigsaw puzzle of Europe now before them represented their perception of justice, everyone except the 20,000,000 dead, that is.

As they approached the seaside town, the sun was still relatively high in the sky behind the car to the west. Despite being mid-summer, the North Sea in front of them looked less inviting than it should, with the admiral's dreams drowned in disappointment there. English holiday resorts in the main make you feel welcome with their initial roundabouts on your arrival stocked with colourful bedding plants usually displaying the resort's name, Scarborough being no exception.

'Where to, Johnny?'

'Straight through to the centre; it's on the left.'

Miles pulled the Merc onto the forecourt on which stood a row of bread-and-butter second-hand cars; behind them stood the showroom of no great size, with enough room for ten or twelve motors.

'You go in and prepare the way. I'll follow pie-eyed in a minute,' Johnny suggested. You've got to give Johnny One Leg time to arrange things, and Miles could lip-read him now, making sure of his introductory commission.

Well, there she was. Putting on a drool was easy. The aerodynamic fastback shape is finished in pearl white, black leather interior, and absolutely mint chrome knock-on wire wheels! Plus, it was an automatic, not the undriveable pudding-stick manual.

By this time, Johnny was limping around the 250SL with the sales manager in tow, admiring this example of German engineering. Things were looking optimistic. Miles held his ground next to the thoroughbred. Johnny pulling a bit of a face with a little remonstration towards the vendor announced that Alan could only go to £1,650.00 for the Merc, but you get the wheels-off service at that price. The royal autos always performed on a vehicle of this quality.

'How about a bit more for the Merc and forget the service?' Miles politely asked, sitting down at his side of the desk.

'Are we sure you are not a motor trader?' Alan enquired.

He checked himself and gazed out of the window to gain a little time to collect his thoughts. There was a small cinema not far away.

'Oh no, but the car is not for me. I'm buying it for my dad, who lives in North Wales and owns a couple of bijou cinemas up there,' he replied, wriggling off the hook.

'That's OK, then. I'll get the paperwork sorted. Won't be a mo.' Miles duly autographed the sales invoice on Alan's return and paid the balance.

Job done! He would have to live with the inconvenience of a night in the Grand.

'How did you get on?'

'No problem, but they want to do a service on it, which means a return tomorrow. Blast it! I'll have to stay over.'

'Now we can collect your Lincoln? Where do you want to be dropped off? How on earth did you manage to find this one?'

At this, he burst out laughing.

'I am Landsburying it,' he chuckled.

'Landsburying what?'

'Well, I'm often up here for a deal with Calum. He's got a caravan site, which is where we're going next. All he has to do is deliver the milk in the morning, collect the substantial rents, and live a great life. All this and more come with a devoted wife who regularly scrutinises the accounts. Unfortunately, just like our democratically elected statesmen, monetary outgoings – in his case, gambling losses – have to be carefully massaged, laundered and even concealed to avoid unnecessary hurt to innocent parties, and that's where I come in. Today I'm buying, and next time I'll be selling bigger and better to impress the good lady. So, like Oscar Wilde, I am Landsburying it! Tonight!'

They rounded the final corner, and on the right was the entrance to Holly Tree Farm, Calum Landsbury's comfortable abode. They proceeded up the picturesque lane to the farm in the last of the evening sun.

Miles remained in the car as Johnny hopped out, carpet bag in hand. He then disappeared into the building. After a while, the Lincoln emerged gracefully from a double barn door with Johnny at the wheel sporting an American Stetson.

4
Bentley S3 Twin Headlighter

(Dark Racing Green with Magnolia Leather trim)

Benny Pickman held court over several prominent motor dealers in the far corner of the *Auctioneer* restaurant and bar. Smiling and gesticulating, he exuded supreme confidence for a man who had just completed a short sentence within an open prison situated in the lovely county of Kent. The main reason for his incarceration was his failure to mask the erroneous details he had inserted into many a hire purchase document to gain a financial reward for his good self. To his great surprise, his custodians gave him the position of overseeing the jail's accounts – by way of rehabilitation to their way of thinking, he supposed! To his credit, Benny seized the opportunity to polish out the minor literary and arithmetical faults that had landed him there in the first place. 'My further education soon taught me not to rely on information recorded by travel agents, death certificates, and especially recently erected gravestones,' laughed Benny as he stood up among the celebrated company present. At full stretch, he would be about five foot eight. His head was adorned with matted curly black hair in late sixties style, but any further growth would have rendered it scruffy and unsuitable for a businessman of his standing. His face was of a Jewish disposition that might easily attract unwanted attention from a budding Nazi of previous years. There were kindness and humour in his whole manner, evidence of his natural intuitive intelligence, cunning wisdom and the experience of human nature required to ply his trade successfully. Everyone knew Benny!

Unfortunately, he belonged to the majority of ambitious people who could make things work at considerable profit for an employer but inexplicably never for themselves. He was highly sought after and could be relied upon to 'charm the birds from the trees' in any social stratum. After his enforced absence from the motor trade, he was appointed head buyer for the South West Motor Corporation, a rapidly expanding second-hand motor dealership throughout Devon and Cornwall. His boss, the charismatic Don McDougal, knew Benny could not afford to indulge himself in any 'funny business' in this very bribable position in the company.

Miles drifted back into the auction room, which was in full flow, and vehicles were being sold on the block, one every few minutes. Tony and Arthur were adept at forcing the best price out of those at their mercy below the rostrum. Trotting the price up from the surrounding wall was common practice, all as pure comical entertainment. Tony was an expert at putting the under-bidder on the spot, in this case, selling a Rolls Corniche convertible at an astronomical price that would buy a decent semi-detached house. 'Don't miss it for the price of a round of drinks, Sir!', pointing the gavel at the aggrieved party, who was probably better off still in possession of his cash at this point. Incredibly, with a slight movement of his head, the hammer fell with a loud crack! 'Sold to the man who didn't move – that's you, Mr Bristol', he joked. He could see that today was not a time to buy, with the auctioneers in such a buoyant mood and everyone determined to pay exorbitant prices.

So, he sauntered back to the auctioneer and, pint in hand, engaged two Northern Irish judges in some light-hearted banter. They occasionally came over for a break from the situation at home to enjoy the busy hustle, sometimes buying a nice clean family car to take back home for a bit of profit. Sadly, an unknown assassin murdered one of them on his doorstep a few days later. Seeing his face on the TV sent a cold shiver down Mile's spine, putting our place in the evolutionary process into perspective.

It was some months, maybe over a year, before he next encountered Benny. It was late summer, and the picturesque town of Torquay on the Devon Riviera was busy with holiday visitors rudely referred to as Grockles. Unfairly so, as they were the locals' main source of income. The month of August was as good a time as any to buy clean stock known to northern traders as 'Devon Cars'.

Miles elected to drive down in the long-wheel-base Bentley S3 twin headlighter, his current Smoker, hoping to move it on. Everything about the car was too big, the long front wings sweeping up tsunami-style beside a straight bonnet finished in dark racing green. The luxurious magnolia leather interior with Chippendale dash emphasised this was a limousine, not a sports saloon. However, it must be said it did give one a momentary feeling of British superiority as she swept majestically to the reception area of his favourite haunt, the Imperial Hotel.

He checked in, as usual, freshened up and descended to the cosy bar with adjoining rooms that overlooked the sea. His sixth sense detecting the presence of someone else close by, he instinctively glanced over his shoulder. There he was, gin and tonic in hand, looking very much at ease but with a shade of tiredness in the five-star surroundings. 'Why Benny – how are you doing?'

'Oh, par for the course.'

'Last time I saw you was ages ago waving that chequebook Don furnished you with, practically buying everything that moves!'

'If you're on your own, come and join me over here. The table's got a sea view, and mine's a large gin and ton.'

Miles wasn't opposed to a catch-up session and might even have a few swappers to sell. So, with a pint and a large gin in hand, he joined Benny at his table.

'Cheers!' Ben raised his hand as if to stop the traffic and proclaimed, 'I'm not with the SWMC anymore. Don is kindly paying for my accommodation here until I recover my full strength and find something other than buying the odd car. We've all still got to earn the occasional dishonest shilling[*] or two for beer money, so to speak. I've got a nice MGA hardtop in old English white, red interior no wires but complete with its bandbox[**] – need bottom book for that.'

'Sounds OK to me. Hardtops are not as desirable as the rag, but I think they help to keep the car in one piece! I'm sorry to hear you've parted company with Don. What brought that about?'

'Well, I sort of diversified on account of the stress of the job.'

'Surely not, Ben. The straying-off-the-path-of-righteousness type of diversification?'

'Not on your life!' His mood lightened as he gathered steam to relate the circumstances.

'It began as a fairly cushy little number, but as time passed, the group was expanding so fast that they resorted to the bastion of professional backing, commonly known as the stocking plan. The addition of university-trained accountants and interest charges leveraged the buying ability and the need to buy even more stock, leaving my staff and yours truly scouring the whole country day and night for saleable vehicles. Getting them all delivered on time was a nightmare! The finance houses of the day were all well aware – as I of all people should know – of the need to check the existence of unsold stock before issuing more loans for future purchases to provide liquidity for the tap, which was my chequebook. Another drink?'

'Yes, mine's a pint, Ben.'

---

[*]   A dishonest shilling is a small amount earned with a little deception to make ends meet

[**]   A bandbox is a car radio

'Well, it was not long before I was required to accompany these educated halfwits every Tuesday for the group's stock check. We provided a Rolls Royce Silver Shadow to transport them from outlet to outlet. Usually starting first thing at the Gloucester branch, we'd make our way through Bristol to the A38 and south. As I politely engaged them in conversation, which was stressful enough in its own right, I felt the need to downright entertain them to divert their attention from the mini convoy of car transporters passing us on the outside lane.

'From my vantage point in the front seat, I could see young Tom, the apprentice mechanic, a fervent Bristol City fan and football hooligan with his mates from the Gloucester branch working away on the upper and lower trailer decks. They were moving about, screwdrivers and tools to hand, as fast as Gandy dancers on a push wagon. They attached new number plates to the cars at lightning speed with youthful exuberance to give the vehicles a freshness for their forthcoming location.

'With all this in mind, I turned to face my companions for the day and asked, 'Would a light lunch be in order?' To my cautious mind, this would give the cavalcade good time to unload at the Taunton showroom. As planned when we arrived, the many cars were on display with no sign of the transporters, now well on their way home. The men in suits, adequately lunched* with books and clipboards in hand, made their way around the showroom, replenished with the fresh stock on display.

'Some of these cars look very similar to the ones in the Gloucester branch this morning, especially that light green automatic Capri 2000 and the selection of Fords over there,' Crispin, the financial ogre in charge, observed in a somewhat inquisitive manner.

'Indeed, yes. Our large turnover necessitates the purchase of low-mileage vehicles from fleet operators across the country. These one-to-two-year-old vehicles are all very much alike, and without them, there would be no flat twenty-four per cent retail finance deals for your company,' I countered.'

---

*   Lunched is to make comfortable by providing lunch

'Excellent, and what were those imbeciles doing on the transporters, pray?'

'Risking life and limb to get those cars to their destination in time for our TV campaign, which starts this very night.'

'After this typical exchange, they usually did one more outlet, Plymouth or Exeter, which made it a long day. My working day was far from over, and as you can imagine, I was now eating, sleeping and breathing motor cars 24/7.'

'On top of all this, Don decided to do a Brian Epstein and try his hand at pop group management. He had apparently "discovered" a Cornish folk group, "The Kerneweks", and for strictly commercial reasons mixed with common sense, changed their name to "The Greengages". They looked and sounded like a cross between a team of clog dancers and local folk musicians. He managed to desist them from singing in their native tongue and persuaded the lads to perform several demo tapes for the recording company in the Queen's English. Under great sufferance, they did this on the condition that they could express themselves (in English). One of these was a Cornish ballad I had just adapted into a palatable pop song, "Lorna Doone". How Don induced the recording company to cut this one is anyone's guess.

'Yet again, my blarter rang. 'Don here, Ben. No one's buying our record. I've got to find a way of getting it into the charts. Any ideas?' he said with a certain amount of panic.

'As a matter of fact, I have, but it'll cost.'

'My first home was now the Imperial Hotel. I had the dubious pleasure of conversing with Jimmy Savile on several occasions. As it turned out, the famous DJ come TV personality was a fellow guest occupying a penthouse suite upstairs. Jimmy appeared in the cocktail bar on a sunny evening within a few days. He was still wearing his silver tracksuit after a bit of a jog for one of his many charities and looked like he needed a drink.

'What'll you have, Jim? I'm in the chair.'

'Goodness gracious! As it happens, a pint of water would be most acceptable,' he jauntily replied in his predictable vernacular.

'There would be no slip 'twixt cup and lip here. He reverently lit his huge Havana Ceegar – as he pronounced it – contrasting with his long shoulder-length silver hair. A pair of rose-tinted shades perched on a prominent but straight thin nose adorned his gaunt face. The whole ensemble gave the impression that his anatomy was slightly out of place. The cigar should be associated with an old Conservative. The waiter arrived with the drinks, and Jimmy turned to me with his eyes open as wide as his thin-rimmed specs and proceeded to give me a bold thumbs-up right under my nose.' 'Much obliged, much obliged.'

'In this sober environment, I would have to proceed with care to manoeuvre the conversation to the subject of my choice. There would be no other way. So, headfirst, I got started.

'Stage and screen are treating you well?' I gently prodded.

'Never better, keeping me busy, even got a bit of work down here.'

'We're the same, rushed off our feet. I'm due at Sunshine Recording Studios again this week.'

'I thought you were big in motors. I was hoping to discuss the possibility of swapping the old Silver Cloud soon.'

'No problem. But at the moment, the boss is involved with a pop band. They've just recorded their first single, but his knickers are in a twist because it's not doing the business: no airplay or chart entry.'

'You're not going to ask me to plug his record, are you? That would be unethical: the Beeb would not tolerate or like that.'

'Absolutely not, I wouldn't impose. Just a bit of friendly advice as we're new to the game.'

'Back in his showman's manner, he vaunted, 'Na then! Na then! That's different. The man you need to speak to is Tony France at Sunshine. He'll put you in the picture, and you can use me as your intro. How's about that then?'

'He then rose to his feet and swirled across the room, leaving a trail of "Ceegar" smoke to cover his exit.

'At an even earlier time, well before the crack of dawn, when my departure to Blackbush car auctions became necessary, it would give me time to bash on up to the Smoke for a progress update and listen to Tony France's ingenious plans for the future success of our group's musical composition. Although tired, I dwelt on the brash, modern, hip, and well-connected shrewd businessman's proposals while driving back to Torquay. With substantial mental and physical effort, I bought many cars that day. I was inclined to believe Tony's way of making money had some appeal, but proof of this little pie would be in the eating. Several messages awaited me at reception, including an urgent request for a phone call on my arrival to Don.

'Yes, I bought some stock, and yes, I met Tony. I'll get some sleep and enlighten you at the Argyle branch at 10 a.m. later today.'

'I retired to bed for what little was left of the night.

'The modern ceiling downlighters in the office illuminated Don's form before me. His round plump face with rosy-red cheeks blossomed with health. His well-groomed blond hair and steel-grey eyes were complemented with the sunny disposition of a man determined to hear good news.

'I don't want to hear any criticism of my Cornish protégés. Is that understood?' He firmly opened.

'As it happens . . .' I was beginning to sound like my mentor from the penthouse suite above!

'I repeat – as it happens, we only discussed the plan going forward without mentioning the group's doubted talents. You will have to get that old John Bull printing set out that your granny gave you for Christmas all those years ago!'

'How so?'

'Your initial directive to me was getting this record into the charts. That's all we are concerned about, is that right?'

'Yes.'

'OK, there will be further expense involved. Tony has agreed to supply his five-star dealers across the U.K. with any order for 500 or more copies on a sell or return basis. This, however, will require a guarantee from yourself in the likely event of the song not catching on to make good any losses incurred by his company. Nevertheless, if the disc starts to sell, it will guarantee plenty of airtime and even a TV slot. Due to the further investment, you will have to draw up a new contract much more favouring yourselves and Sunshine.'

'No problem. I'll get on to our solicitors Gridiron and Slaughter to write the contracts ASAP.'

'Mr Gridiron informed Don several days later that all the necessary arrangements were in place. Meanwhile, back in the Imperial, I encountered Jimmy Savile once more as he minced across the floor towards me, cigar in hand with a smile bordering on laughter.

BA-BOOM! 'How's about that, then? At number sixteen, The Greengages are straight in the NME with "Lorna Doone"; I'll be playing it on air for a month. It's not a bad little tune.'

'What? You're joking! I wrote that in less than ten minutes!

'My head began to swoon. I made my way to the nearest showroom and sat at a desk surrounded by cars for company. I phoned Don and informed him of the materialisation of his ambitions to be an international impresario. I felt distinctly unwell as I returned the dog to its cradle. A dull pain travelled through my arms and chest, and my eyes rolled into my head as my upper body slumped in slow motion onto the desktop. A red curtain drew over and seemed to open again, revealing a loss of external sight. Dream images moved across my mind as I saw dear Mama telling me as a child that I was the fruit of the tree of knowledge, with a perception of God assuring us of our immortality. My whole existence flickered inside me as familiar friends, relations, and sounds remorselessly became more distant. The echoes and icons of earthly beings began to recede. For a moment, a vast nuclear explosion was a momentary vision of wonder as the mushroom cloud travelled up into the sky. After that, darkness descended, and there was nothing more.'

Lighten Our Darkness

Since the Big Bang, nuclear physics has existed as the instrument of creation some 14 billion years ago. Human awareness of its properties started to evolve in relatively recent times. With their small laboratories, table-top inventors and scientists were becoming a rare breed by the early twentieth century. Scientific research fell in line with the human progression towards the dawning technological age, but the individual characters responsible for their discoveries were now beginning to be lost in history.

Ernest Rutherford, the father of nuclear physics, began to use university facilities, availing himself of the help of fellow scientists and students. He continued to build the foundations of his future work at McGill University in Montreal, where, working with radon to conduct experiments with alpha and beta radiation, he gained an understanding of radioactive half-life.

In 1907 Rutherford accepted a position at Manchester University. Under his direction, Hans Geiger and Ernest Marsden measured alpha particle beams and their behaviour. The scientists used gold foil, just a few atoms thick, to determine that atoms have a nucleus, in which most of their mass and all of their positive charge are present. The whole of which mainly consisted of empty space orbited by low-mass electrons. By 1920 he established the existence of a subatomic particle, the proton, and under his leadership, James Chadwick, in 1932, discovered his hypothesised 'neutron'. That same year, two of his students performed a successful experiment to split the nucleus. Inspired by Rutherford's efforts (regardless of his reservations), Leo Szilard conceived the nuclear chain reaction in 1933. He patented his atomic fission reactor in 1934, which ushered in a new era of big science, an enterprise affordable only to nation-states.

Inspired humans wrote the sacred texts of old to document the will of God, their creator. God's method of communication to them is diverse, but His message is clear though primarily allegorical. God granted humans dominion over all living things on earth and the ability to survive. After many years of evolution, God placed Adam and Eve in the Garden of Eden. They were put to the test because the time for human mental advancement had arrived. They succumbed to the temptation to be as wise as God put forward by the serpent and ate the forbidden fruit from the Tree of Knowledge and Evil. They admitted to disobeying God, who then altered their genetic code to include the ability to be aware of earthly existence. Humans now have reason and knowledge of their mortality. The short time to achieve the necessary changes their instincts demanded for improving the world was now apparent. The 'missing link' was performed, and they could no longer remain in the garden where the only antidote to death grew – the 'Tree of Life.

Art, science, invention, and the written word all prevail through the misery of evil and the ecstasy of good. Therefore, the mother and father of humanity were banished to the temporal world and bequeathed to thousands of future generations the commitment born of the original choice: to navigate their lives through the chaos of evolution. War through the ages became the chosen tool to strengthen the formation of nation-states, and empires came and went, their ideals smashed by nationalism and the return to ignorance, the great leveller. The last of these (British), by no means perfect, tried to educate, introduce the concept of friendly sport and did its best to build infrastructure for the benefit of its subjects. It never quite achieved its ambition of the high moral standards of international law and an attempt at human fairness. Its ethics and social values were much admired, but it began to fragment.

Jan Block, a Pole living in St Petersburg and an expert in industrial warfare, published his six-volume masterwork *Is War Now Impossible?* in 1898. There were now no excuses for politicians, monarchs and emperors not to know the consequences of modern war. Still, they chose to keep devouring God's forbidden fruit and commit humanity to bloody Armageddon. The world's nation-states turned on one another. In the aftermath, the masters' survival rates of 100 per cent compared with the near extinction of their fighting services appears to escape universal attention as usual! In 1913, a year before this catastrophe, H. G. Wells wrote his prophetic novel *The World Set Free* to explain the coming danger of atomic energy. In concurrence with the scientists of the day, of which he was one, he predicted that a handful of heavy-metal atoms could produce enough energy to heat and light a city. Or the same amount converted to nuclear weaponry can wipe out the same city.

On 6 January 1939, the world was aware of German interest in uranium fission. A report published on that date by *Die Naturwissenschaften* (a German academic journal) confirmed this. Suspicious of the German potential to develop nuclear weapons, Jewish scientific communities and others emigrated from the National Socialist axis en masse in the years preceding the Second World War. The Einstein-Szilard letter to President Roosevelt advising of the imminent danger, drafted on 2 August 1939 and signed by Albert Einstein, was eventually delivered by hand on 13 October 1939 due to the advent of war in Europe. America was still an independent, neutral country in no particular rush to invest in purchasing uranium and graphite. But word was getting out. Uranium research undertaken at the Kaiser Wilhelm Institute in Berlin culminated in the decision to cease sales of uranium ore from the recently captured mines in Czechoslovakia on the advice of the young son of the undersecretary of state, who was studying there. Investors and speculators equipped with their instinct for profit in the USA began to get wind of uranium's potential value, leaving politicians on both sides of the pond in their wake. Over the coming months, these speculators accumulated 1,200 tons from the Belgian Congo mines and stored it in a warehouse on Staten Island, New York.

The peoples of America and their elected government were out of touch with the progress made by science. Unlike the business community, the general population viewed the war in Europe as a distant rebalancing of power that did not concern them in their new-world comfort zone. The Dunkirk evacuation, the fall of Paris, and Britain's victory in the air, followed by the carpet bombing of her cities, known as the Blitz, amounted to a phenomenon not to worry about for the moment. By the end of summer 1941, the more imaginative scientists could only visualise a nightmare scenario of a merchant ship plodding up the Elbe or the Thames with a cargo of forty tons of uranium aboard needed to fuel an atomic bomb; capable of annihilating the city of Hamburg or London!

Mark Oliphant was a professor of physics at Birmingham University and head of a team developing microwave radar, a secret project of paramount national importance. He had enrolled two prominent German scientists, Rudolf Peierls and Otto Frisch, who were not allowed to work on covert war efforts because they were categorised as enemy aliens. However, research into nuclear physics was not secret, so they continued to investigate uranium enrichment and, by March 1940, produced the Frisch Peierls Memorandum. They presented the memorandum in two parts. Possibly the only two people alive who realised the implications of their findings, in the first part, they comprehensively emphasised the imperativeness of possessing this weapon first. They accurately forecast that it would eventually be used as the ultimate deterrent in a better but more dangerous world to come. The second part calculated that a bomb comprised of the isotope Uranium 235 with a critical mass of only 15 kg could produce a cataclysmic explosion, the radiation of which would linger for days, killing any survivors in the vicinity. As a result, the British establishment urgently set up the MAUD Committee and the now highly secret British Tube Alloys project.

In July 1941, Mark Oliphant was part of the MAUD Committee with a team of scientists ostensibly to discuss microwave radar, but in reality, to convince the Americans that an atomic bomb was attainable within a few years. Although Britain was months ahead in the primary research, the USA had a lead in isotope separation. To his surprise and dismay, Oliphant found that the Americans ignored MAUD's findings. He knew of the enormous expense of $25 million, and Britain was in the range of German bombers. Britain and the USA jointly needed to develop the bomb, and Roosevelt and Churchill belatedly and slowly began to understand the urgency of collaboration. Out of the blue, a chain reaction of political events removed the scales from the eyes of the unperturbed Uncle Sam.

Pearl Harbour (7 December 1941)

On 7 December 1941, at 3.18 a.m. Japanese standard time and 7.48 a.m. Hawaii local time, Japan launched a surprise attack on the American naval base at Pearl Harbour, which lasted ninety minutes. Although considered a grand strategic victory, the military consequences turned out to be of little importance to the aggressor, but the ramifications were titanic! The Japanese employed 414 aircraft, 350 of which took off from six aircraft carriers, twenty-three fleet submarines and other naval craft.

On 8 December, the USA declared war on Japan. One hour later, due to decoding problems, the Japanese reciprocated. The previous day, Japan attacked British positions in Malaya, Singapore and Hong Kong. Churchill reminded the world of his promise to declare war on Japan 'within the hour' if they attacked the USA, which he duly did.

Hitler's hatred of the 'mongrel' races, the well-off cosseted public supposedly controlled by Jewish political influence, conditioned him to think that the USA would not have the will to fight. Still, in the shadow of the potential of the atomic bomb and with his overwhelming desire to repeat the tactic of the First World War of unlimited submarine warfare, Hitler impetuously declared war on the USA on 11 December 1941. Mussolini complied and declared war on the same day. America responded almost immediately and declared war on both. Already on its way to becoming a wartime economy, America was now the arsenal of democracy. America's assistance as a full ally was now assured, and the Manhattan Project could proceed in earnest.

The Manhattan Project (on the Allies' Behalf and at America's Expense)

The advent of February 1942 saw the Germans in difficulties in Russia and was no immediate threat to Britain's or America's existence in the near future. When the worst hasn't happened, a period of indecision often occurs. A kind of void in collaboration manifested. British scientists preferred to research independently, intending to use Canada as a base. In June 1942, the United States Army Corps of Engineers (USACE) took over the project. General Leslie Groves assumed the Manhattan Engineers District (MED) command on 17 September 1942 and tightened security. The flow of information to Britain dried up. By 1943 Britain stopped sending its scientists to the USA, which needlessly slowed progress.

General Groves, a man of enormous experience, a master engineer with relentless drive who did not suffer scientists or their masters gladly, was not going to let politics or cost get in the way of achieving his objective of producing a nuclear bomb. He set the groundwork for two massive industrial facilities and relocated the few residents in these remote areas. The reward for his effort in coordination was when Churchill and Roosevelt signed the Quebec Agreement on 19 August 1943. This restored collaboration and absorbed 'Tube Alloys' into the Manhattan Project, now the only enterprise capable of producing the nuclear bomb.

Under the west stand of the football stadium at the University of Chicago, the 'Chicago Pile' or 'CP1', the squash courts met Enrico Fermi's need to conduct his nuclear experiment. The university American football team had been out of action since 1939. Some fit graduates waiting to join the army provided the muscle to lay the 40,000 graphite blocks at a rate of two layers, a shift that would enclose 19,000 slugs of uranium metal and uranium oxide. They inserted a neutron counter at the fifteenth layer, at which the reading was 390. Fermi calculated that at layer fifty-six or fifty-seven, it would reach one. A twenty-foot high by six feet wide wooden construction reinforced the now elliptical composition. They inserted cadmium rods to control the movement of uranium neutrons in the pile. As a further safety measure, they added an emergency failsafe control rod and provided a bucket of cadmium nitrate for use in an unforeseen setback. On 2 December 1942, a group of scientists straining for a better view of proceedings assembled on the viewing balcony. Fermi, at 11.25 a.m., had to abandon the morning test, which started at 9.54 a.m., when the automatic failsafe control rod tripped because its level was set too low. Fermi determined to take lunch. At 3.25 p.m., the pile went critical and achieved the world's first nuclear fuel self-sustaining chain reaction. The neutron flux alarm bells warned that preset safety levels had been exceeded, so the failsafe rod was released, rapidly shutting down the reaction. The pile had run for close to five minutes at 0.5 watts in a controlled reaction. Everyone was very pleased that Fermi's calculations had proved accurate, with no nasty accidents at a location close to the densely populated city of Chicago.

The eminent scientists present celebrated with a bottle of Bertolli Chianti Fiasco. They terminated the operation on 28 February 1943 and dismantled CP1. They reused it as CP2 for further research at a more remote location, Red Gate Woods, where the residue of the experiments was all finally buried along with other reactors used for analysis.

The death of John Hendrix's daughter and the desertion of his remaining family forced him to make peace with God. Consequently, visions of the future bestowed upon him brought him local renown as a prophet in 1903. One persistent vision was the coming of great buildings and factories to the remote Bear Creek Valley and an immense, busy metropolis between Tadlock's Farm and Joe Pyatt's place on Black Oak Ridge, Tennessee, forty years before General Groves conceived the secret city.

The newly completed Norris Dam afforded the chosen site at Oak Ridge an abundance of water and electricity. The X-10, an air-cooled graphite experimental pilot plant built there, became the blueprint for the enormous plutonium producers to be constructed at Hanford. However, the primary purpose of this vast industrial complex was to produce enough of the fissile isotope Uranium 235 from natural uranium for the gun-type fission bomb "Little Boy". A scattered local population grew from 3,500 in 1942 to about 75,000 by 1945. On completion, the K-25, the uranium gaseous diffusion separation unit, covered forty-four acres and was a mile long. Its product then proceeded to the giant Y-12 electromagnetic plant situated on eighty acres in Bear Creek Valley, southwest of Oak Ridge. Four hundred million troy ounces of silver bullion borrowed from the treasury were utilised as electrical conductors for the electromagnetic coils due to the acute shortage of copper. The alpha and beta calutrons' constant upgrading in 'racetracks' across the eighty-acre site eventually bore fruit. The frantic rush to deliver a weapons-grade beta product enriched to eighty-nine per cent Uranium 235 from Y-12 came about on 7 June 1945.

Under Japan's brutal imperial military regime, the unsuspecting city of Hiroshima was about to discover why it had been spared from recent bombing raids. The unwelcome arrival of Little Boy some weeks later would help to enlighten the world.

The army depopulated two small settlements, Hanford and White Bluffs; they also evicted all 300 residents of Richland in 1943 to make way for the top-secret industrial nuclear complex, The Hanford Site. This remote desert land, with the Priest Rapids Dam to the north and the mighty Colombia River flowing down its eastern flank, was the perfect situation for America's new space-age atomic city.

In February 1943, work started. By January 1945, 51,000 construction workers from across the land had erected this silver-coloured metropolis focused on the production of plutonium-239. Three huge water-cooled graphite-moderated atomic reactors B, D, and F, loosely based on Enrico Fermi's Chicago Pile, stood on the river's south bank in Zone 100. Their exterior design, using vast amounts of steel and concrete, resembled enormous ancient Egyptian temples facing the desert in the sun. Ten miles to the south, three chemical-separation plants called canyons processed the irradiated fuel slugs. Located in the 200 zone, they were nicknamed 'Queen Marys' because of their immense 800-foot-long solid concrete structures. By April 1945, very few people at Hanford were aware that the regular top-secret shipments of PU239 to Los Alamos were for the Trinity test and the bomb to be dropped over Nagasaki.

On 25 November 1942, the Los Alamos Ranch School and its surrounding 54,000 acres were acquired as 'eminent domain' by the War Department. It was a picturesque remote mountain-top location where scientists from the free world could work in unison and undisturbed with the sole objective of designing a nuclear bomb. A fraternity of intellect and enthusiasm began to proliferate in such an environment. Hanford and Oak Ridge could supply enough raw material to the bomb laboratories at this top-secret atomic university only to satisfy their research needs. However, as these three war institutions gathered momentum in concert, research and development advanced to produce workable models of a bomb. By 1944, three types manifested themselves as front runners. They were curiously named after two characters from the novel *The Maltese Falcon* and a short crime story, *The Thin Man*, all written by the American author Dashiell Hammett, who turned out to be a communist!

The Thin Man

In early 1943 the scientists prioritised the plutonium gun-type design over the much more complicated implosion type. A dedicated team at Los Alamos calculated that its critical mass would require high muzzle velocities. Therefore, it needed a length of no fewer than seventeen feet for a plutonium bullet to accelerate to 3,000 feet per second to avoid pre-detonation. Reactor-bred plutonium was not available for early research. Calculations and measurements using small amounts of good-quality plutonium produced by the cyclotrons confirmed its feasibility during two years of work on the bomb. Nevertheless, by April 1944 experiments at Los Alamos using the newly bred plutonium from the reactors at Hanford showed impurity of the isotope PU240, which made the gun-type plutonium design impractical. In August, they terminated the Thin Man project and concentrated their efforts for plutonium on an implosion prototype christened 'Fat Man'.

Fat Man

A long way from the Chicago University football stadium, the veteran scientists and their political and military peers reconvened to witness the first detonation of an implosion plutonium bomb, jocularly referred to as the 'Gadget'. They were granted permission for the test with reservations that ranged from complete failure to the incineration of the planet or the detachment of its atmosphere. The 500 privileged people in the desert of New Mexico nervously in position at a supposed safe distance of twenty miles looked on. Gloves, sun cream, sunglasses, and various other accoutrements deemed essential for the enrichment of the occasion were manifested among the crowd. A betting pool soon in operation gave the eager scientists an all-American opportunity to predict the result with a wager. The 'Gadget' Y1561 device sitting on top of a thirty-metre-high steel obelisk ready for the Trinity Test, a code name with Christian connotations, awaited its hour of redemption. At 5.29 a.m., 16 July 1945, the Gadget blew up in overcast but dry conditions. An incredible white light flashed across the desert and mountain ranges to herald the arrival of the planet's next master of choice. The fortunate gambling scientist won his bet with 22.1 kilotons of TNT. With a few minor technical improvements and the addition of a grotesque metal case, 'Gadget' became the transportable bomb 'Fat Man'.

Little Boy

The scientific community christened the first nuclear bomb practical for warfare, 'Little Boy'. It was a gun-type fission bomb compatible with Uranium 235, not plutonium. Due to its comparatively inefficient design, it was deemed obsolete virtually on the day of its completion. When plutonium production stalled at the Hanford reactors due to a condition called the 'Wigner Effect', Little Boy received a reprieve and was put into limited service until 1951. However, in July 1945, there had been no need for testing as was the case at Trinity because each of its many parts had undergone a thorough appraisal. All concerned were satisfied that it was fit for purpose and ready to go.

The USA employed newly occupied islands closer to mainland Japan with 100 aircraft to precision-bomb targets from high altitudes. These actions proved ineffective, so they resorted to unmitigated low-altitude incendiary operations. In one night alone, from 9 to 10 March 1945, Operation Meeting House, the firebombing of Tokyo, accounted for 100,000 dead, sixteen square miles destroyed and the loss of 267 buildings. Undoubtedly, the evidence of carpet-bombing cities in the Second World War emphasises that civilian morale is rarely dented and more often galvanised by such action. This is possible because the dead have no say, leaving grateful but guilty survivors animated with hate for their aggressors.

The estimated casualties of Operation Downfall to be inflicted on humanity would be unprecedented and terrifying. Japan was no exception. For whatever reason, their cruel, militaristic despotic regime still held sway over the indigenous population. Japan's 2.3 million ground troops were under orders to fight to the death. A civilian militia of 28 million fanatical men and women was in place, waiting for the invaders of their homeland.

Accordingly, the factory-fresh, silver-plated B29 Superfortress bomber inscribed in the contemporary American nose art style with the name of the pilot's mother, Enola Gay, was fully prepared for take-off. This beautiful silver bird was surgically modified to carry the ugly embryo of the future, Little Boy. A temporary deactivation was prudently performed should his surrogate mother miscarry at take-off. Her ladyship was safely airborne at 2 a.m. with her bomb made ready and patiently laboured six hours at 31,000 feet to her place of delivery, Hiroshima. Little Boy, rudely ejected, plunged in silence for forty-four seconds to detonate at 1,900 feet. Its flash of light and appalling sixteen-kiloton explosion heralded the city's destruction below. Having been informed of the devastation caused by a single bomb, the government was still disinclined to surrender – a view Radio Japan shared and continued to broadcast resistance to the people.

An inconvenience more symptomatic of a setback with a handover on a used-car pitch cropped up. The mirror-finished B29 bomber with 'Fat Man', the billion-dollar bomb in place, curiously developed a fuel pump problem in its 600-gallon reserve tank just before take-off. As is usual in such cases, the men on the ground in the front line had to decide. They agreed to proceed, as repairing or switching the plane would take too long before expected bad weather arrived over Japan. They had to risk that the extra weight might hamper her flying hours.

The B29 named Bockscar made three abortive bombing runs over her initial target, Kokura. Due to poor visibility, she resolved to attack Nagasaki, her secondary objective. A break in the clouds sealed this city's fate. Fat Man's plutonium detonated after a forty-seven-second fall to 1,650 feet, inflicting the equivalent energy of 21.1 kilotons of TNT on the mainly wooden, poorly designed port city below. Then the B29 diverted to Okinawa, a recently captured airbase and, with her fuel running out, was fortunate to crash land safely.

Emperor Hirohito ungraciously broadcasted his capitulation statement of surrender on 15 August. Two relatively small first-generation fission bombs comprehensively ended the Second World War. The international nature of scientific research at Los Alamos nurtured spies in the midst, so it was not long before the USSR tested its own bomb. Humankind regained its confidence and again indulged itself in another arms race. Fear, as usual, was the catalyst.

The Cuban Missile Crisis (1958–29 October 1962)

The more refined arts of world politics were played out between the two masters of the world's destiny to distribute their highest cards across the globe, each with enough destructive power to obliterate the earth twenty times over. In July 1961, a Hotel Class K19 submarine stationed off southeast Greenland ran into trouble with her reactor coolant system. Radio communication with Moscow was lost. Captain Zateyev sent a detachment of engineers to avoid a meltdown. They found a temporary solution but sadly, the team employed died from radiation exposure within a month. Moreover, the thirty-three-year-old deputy commander, Vasily Arkhipov, and the entire crew suffered irradiation.

The inhabitants of the free world were powerless, transfixed by events in the company with the peoples of the east, mostly kept in ignorance as the two principals marched on eggshells, racking up the stakes. To avoid the warlike term 'blockade,' the Americans deployed eighty per cent of their Atlantic fleet around Cuba to put her in 'quarantine'. On 27 October 1962, the aircraft carrier *Randolf* with eleven destroyers accompanied by air reconnaissance, located a B59 submarine out in international waters off Cuba. They bombarded the position with loud but unharmful, signalling depth charges to force her to surface for identification. Because of their present whereabouts deep in the ocean, trying to avoid detection, the Russians had lost radio contact with the flotilla of B59 Foxtrot diesel-electric submarines recklessly armed with T5 nuclear torpedoes.

At the most critical hour of the Cuban crisis, thousands of miles from home, running out of power and undergoing extreme conditions, three men found themselves in a position to decide the fate of humankind. The only radio contact to base their decision on was the paranoid scaremongering picked up from the radio media in Miami. Aware that the Third World War might well be in progress, captain Valentin Savitsky and his subordinate officer authorised the launch of a T5. This twenty-kiloton weapon would destroy anything within seven miles of its detonation.

Though second in command of the vessel, as commodore of the flotilla, Arkhipov had the power of veto – the order to fire had to be unanimous. After a heated argument, this quiet, unassuming, highly trained and intelligent submariner, renowned for his bravery on K19, firmly resolved to veto the launch and surface to request orders from Moscow. His action saved the world from nuclear catastrophe.

The sea air permeated the Soviet vessel to revive her and her crew, now still in the water but surrounded by US naval warships. The Americans were blissfully unaware of the Hiroshima-sized nuclear weapons present. Nearby, an enterprising US captain assembled an all-American-style welcome party consisting of a large jazz band backed by enthusing sailors dressed in white, gesticulating a cordial maritime brotherhood with their Russian counterparts.

After a short time, B59 set sail for the east, escorted but not pursued by the US navy and submerged on 29 October, followed shortly by the remaining three Foxtrots in the flotilla. It had come down to one thirty-four-year-old submariner officer alone at sea to achieve victory for humankind without the need for casualties. The Russian politicians kept his actions secret for forty years. Perhaps Admiral John Jellicoe looked down from the heavens with pride and love for Vice Admiral Vasily Arkhipov.

The Second-Generation Nuclear Bomb

The second-generation bomb is the thermonuclear fusion weapon called the H-bomb or hydrogen bomb. Fusion is the opposite of fission. Fission splits one heavy element into two smaller ones, whereas fusion joins two smaller elements into one heavier element. Fusion relies on fission to trigger a reaction between two isotopes of hydrogen (deuterium and tritium) in the first and second stages. If desired, a third-stage fusion can be employed to trigger further fission reactions, which substantially boosts the explosion.

In a relatively peaceful era, the Americans and USSR did their level best to demonstrate their capability to destroy much of our planet. Ivy Mike, a non-deliverable device tested at 10,400 kilotons of TNT on 1 November 1952. Next came Castle Bravo at Bikini with 15,000 kilotons of TNT on 1 March 1954. This deployable device exceeded expectations. It surprised its designers by polluting nearby islands and much of the Pacific. Not to be outdone, the USSR played their trump card on 31 October 1961, detonating at an altitude of 13,123 feet. 'Tsar Bomba' is the world's largest three-stage nuclear bomb to be tested at 50,000 kilotons of TNT – 3,000 times the size of 'Little Boy' at Hiroshima! A lead tamper in place of a Uranium 235 tamper managed to reduce the yield by half from a possible 100,000 kilotons of TNT to limit the fallout on its citizens. Nevertheless, this is supposedly the cleanest bomb ever concocted, yet with an unimaginable force, it fragmented window glass as far away as Finland and Sweden. Sadly, for whatever reason, the USA deemed it necessary to conduct 1,032 nuclear tests, the USSR 727, France 217, the UK 88, China 47, India 3, Pakistan 2 and North Korea 6, for a total yield of 540,849 kilotons of TNT.

The Third-Generation Nuclear Bombs

On the understanding that explosions are naturally spherical, scientists theorised that a nuclear appliance could emit a 'nuclear-shaped charge' in the form of a narrow destructive beam. The name given to this never to be built space-age contrivance is 'The Casaba Howitzer'.

The neutron bomb is an enhanced radiation weapon that can minimise its blast and maximise radiation through the emission of neutrons to kill all forms of life, leaving the infrastructure and products in its path intact. The outraged citizens of the countries most likely to be in a land war persuaded their governing bodies of this bomb's unacceptability. The USA decommissioned each one by 1992, and all were dismantled by 2011. Mercifully, the opportunity to fight a neutron-backed land battle, which would escalate into a strategic nuclear exchange, is gone.

The ' cobalt bomb ' is a popular mutually-assured-destruction deterrent for most nuclear powers. This thermonuclear H-bomb vaporises radioactive Cobalt 60, causing it to fall from the sky and contaminate the earth. However, none of any appreciable size is known to exist, but the mere threat of its existence is the cornerstone of deterrence. An example is the possible staged leak by the Russian Federation of the project 'Status 6 Multipurpose Nuclear Torpedoes' to produce a tsunami 1,800-foot wave to flood their country with Cobalt 60 contaminated seawater. So, like Silent Jack's dreadnoughts, this horrific device can be seen as the keeper of the peace.

The usefulness of the possession of third-generation nuclear weapons is wafer-thin. This device ruined the Reykjavic test-ban talks in 1986 between two relatively progressive politicians, Reagan and Gorbachev. Overconfident scientists with success at Los Alamos behind them started to believe their theories on wrongly conducted tests and results emanating from their drawing boards – the Excalibur Project was born. Based on their promising theoretical research, ever-increasing funds were easily extracted from the gullible politicians desperate for the game-changing means of defence against incoming enemy missiles. Whoever holds the sword of Excalibur would rule the kingdom. Temptation indeed to depart from the stability of Mutually Assured Destruction (MAD) for nuclear obsolescence. Under the Single Defence Initiative (SDI) umbrella, this magical, cylindrical sabre consisting of X-rays surrounding a nuclear resource was designed to destroy missiles before they could release their multiple warheads. The last sales pitch made by the respected scientist Edward Teller to the President promised a geostationary model the size of a desk that could blanket the earth with the brightest light ever known, emitting 100,000 beams to shoot down the entire Russian missile force at launch. However, the time for nuclear testing was drawing to a close. The court at Congress finally jettisoned the enchanted sword to Vivian, the beautiful lady of the lake. Vivian's slender hand pulled it down into the mystical waters of misplaced hope and, in 1992, extinguished the popularly titled 'Star Wars project.

Fourth-Generation Nuclear Bombs

The quest for a pure fusion weapon devoid of any fission stage has occupied scientists for a considerable time. The attraction of no radioactive by-products or electromagnetic pulse incorporated into an environmentally friendly nuclear bomb the size of a golf ball is intriguing to scientists still. The designing engineers concluded that only three possible methods other than fission could be employed to ignite this absurd product.

The first is the use of a powerful laser beam. After a lot of time and many unsuccessful experiments, it turns out that a power source the size of St Paul's Cathedral would be required to get the thing started.

The second way forward is to utilise isomer triggering. Nuclear Isomers are excited states of an atom's nucleus. The realisation that excited nucleons could emit much more energy in the form of energetic gamma rays than electrons could be promising. The candidate par excellence for this process is Hafnium 178/m2, which has a high-energy density and a thirty-one-year half-life. Getting this nuclear isomer to release its energy on demand has never been achieved and is unlikely to be in the foreseeable future.

The third and still theoretical way to trigger a fusion bomb is with antimatter. Antimatter is particles of mass. They are opposite to ordinary matter; when two collide, they annihilate the energy equivalent to their rest mass. Such a high energy density to catalyse their energy release makes using antimatter a very enticing proposition, with a few micrograms replacing kilograms of fission material for ignition.

Bearing in mind we are only trying to ignite a fusion bomb and would not require vast amounts of antimatter to achieve our goal. We have some considerations before us. Using today's technology, the time needed to produce a milligram is 100,000 years. Also, if inflation remained at zero, the cost of one gram would be in the region of 63 trillion dollars. Finally, as we know, antimatter would have to be confined away from ordinary matter. Any mistakes in this direction would result in a chaotic pre-detonation experience.

In a stalemate position, the two competing world powers own ninety-four per cent of the 13,865 nuclear weapons known to exist. They are the two new guardians who have saddled themselves with the responsibility for the planet's future. But is it possible humanity may no longer require them? Nevertheless, MAD and several well-intentioned treaties in place give humanity a temporary respite to perceive the next short-term threat to stability. That is the emergence of independent smaller nation-states with limited nuclear capability, equally ambitious to achieve security or dominance over imagined adversaries. A proven solution is a return to the initial deterrence strategy of mass retaliation through an alliance of the major nuclear powers.

It was time for the 560 million university graduates on the planet to successfully unearth the means to survive and evolve as intended in the Garden of Eden.

Time is also for the freedom of information, transparency, and instant communication worldwide.

Time for the ingenious 'inventions' that perfect the enjoyment of living: supplied for amusement, comfort, and convenience to open the gates of all-round salvation. The untested economic system adopted in the East appears to be embracing the concept of individual reward born of the American dream. The bearer of these benefits does not usually emanate from the academic establishment. They require the endearing character of Sancho Panza or a streetwise politician laced with humour, guile and survivability. Their importance is not noticed or appreciated, consistently underestimated but usually well remunerated. Such a person with body and soul intact on account of carers resides in Plymouth General Hospital.

***

Alone in his private ward, his darkness begins to lighten as the clouds flee to the sky, and purple rain leaves him in only peaceful sleep. Our patient dreams of a world at one through the 'brain fog' inside his consciousness. He can distinguish a humming sound in his dreams: rurr, rurr, hurr. As he turns over, his eyes focus on a nurse hastily advancing across the room. Now the familiar intrusive sound issuing from the telephone at his bedside announces the restoration of his existence: Blart! Blart! Blart!

'Who put that thing there?' he says as the nurse demonstratively cuts the caller off.

'The same person who paid for this room most likely,' replied the portly matron who was now in her wake.

'You can pull that thing's plug out, nurse, until our patient has recovered his strength.'

'I remember her standing at the end of the bed, studying my notes with a somewhat authoritarian stance.

'You can thank the cleaning staff for the swift response; also, the paramedics who brought you here. We will require a few days of cardiac rehabilitation, and then you can go.'

It seemed like an age staggering about the wards idling and chatting to other patients, with everyone forcing conversation until, at last, visitors were allowed.

'Where in the hell is that phone I paid a fortune for?' were Don's first words of comfort. There he stood large as life and probably more important. Under his right arm, a neatly folded copy of the *New Musical Express* protruded like a sergeant major's baton.

'Well, with your limited but privileged education, we never doubted your mastery of modern popular music, the best in the company; hence the need for immediate contact via the said blower.'

'What in the world are you going on about? The only music I'm worried about just at this moment in time is my heartbeat,' Benny objected.

'I knew it! I knew it! Only been here a few days, and he's come up with a great follow-up, "My Heartbeat". Brilliant! It'll give you something to work on, as I've booked you in at the Imperial for a couple of months, a working convalescence, so to speak.'

At this point, Don unfolded the journal and thrust this week's top twenty charts under my eyes. 'While you have been out cold, England has won the football world cup, and the Greengages "Lorna Doone" progressed to number seven this week.'

'An inspired composition that, Ben, all those punters emotionally drooling over your platter revolving on thousands of turntables with the song writers name on them.'

'So, I let it go at that. I had left the finer details of the deal between him and Mr Gridiron and was perfectly happy to take the credit for ten minutes work. The happy outcome of it all is that I am now on indefinite leave from the motor trade, living here in relative luxury, charged with the not-very-arduous job of stringing a few words together for their next release.'

Some weeks later, Miles returned, still in the glorious unsold twelve-miles-to-the-gallon Bentley S3. Benny, now a much-sought-after personality, agreed to meet later in the day for drinks. A much more upbeat, healthy being dressed informally in a flouncy multi-coloured shirt and tight-fitting white bell-bottomed trousers was having casual conversations at the bar. As Miles approached, he turned and threw up his arms in a friendly, welcoming gesture.

'Hey man, look who it isn't – rock on, Tommy. Great to see you way out good.'

'I beg your pardon,' Miles politely stammered.

'Come on over and meet two of our golden boys' – he had obviously taken an interest in the Greengages, seen them many times in the press and on the screen. Miles instantly recognised Kenver Diggs, the lead-guitar vocalist in company with Curnow Flow, the band's back up songbird, a rhythm guitar extraordinaire. Both were much smaller than he had imagined, dressed in more colours than Joseph was entitled to. Confident with their newfound fame and increasing spending power, they respectfully shook hands with him.

'What's with the lingo, Ben? Mine's a pint, by the way!'

'You've got to get with it, man: this is the scene; this is El Dorado.'

'Boss, the rest of the band, Enyon Banks and Cadan Salz, are fetching the Tranny with our kit. We're trucking up to Leeds tomorrow for a fill-in gig, playing to 6,000-plus,' added Kenver, desperately trying to iron out his Cornish twang. 'We're never off the road these days.'

'Is it only a couple of months ago we were playing to a handful of locals in the backroom of the Smugglers Barrel, knocking back the cider with our mates? No going back now – even a simple bloke like me can see that,' interjected Curnow as he downed his gin and tonic in one.

'Never mind that. Think of this – in a few weeks, you will be able to buy a bloody Smugglers each if anyone has the mind to, which nobody will.' Ben reassured them.

Looking at the two lads who, with their friends, had been strumming and singing 24/7 for the past two months, he thought they might have acquired a modicum of musical talent by now.

'Perhaps it is time to detach yourself from the irretrievable past and move on into the future,' Miles suggested helpfully.

'Move to a higher plane; respect the fact that with good marketing and some decent material, we might become world-famous, man. The urgent need to acquire the accoutrements that only money can provide on our destined path to stardom reveals itself. We are aware it may initially isolate us into a stratum of society not above but separate all the same,' mused Kenver.

'Yes, life will be exciting for you and not all that disagreeable. The fame and wealth are real and must be dealt with ASAP. What do you think, Ben?' Benny had been in the motor trade long enough to know where he was coming from.

'Drinks all round, everyone? Maitland do the honours, would you, on my room, of course.' Again, Ben smiled graciously. The telegraphic signal was clear not to go too far and be fair to his charges.

'The world is full of trickery and deceit, lads. I'll admit that, but come on, some of the big names in pop are performing in Leeds tomorrow. The expected grand arrival of the band currently racing up the UK charts will be somewhat diminished with the vision of four teenagers spilling out of a Ford Transit van onto the awaiting tarmac. The celestial pop music artists might have to reappraise their exalted position in their transcendent order. The risk of banishment to the temporal realms of a one-hit-wonder is not worth taking.' Continued Miles in earnest.

'Is that right, Ben?'

'No truer word said; could we persuade your racing-driver friend Charlie Watkins to wait for the S3?'

'I don't see why not. He'll be disappointed. On the other hand, he's off to the Far East. Then down under to finish the season in a week or so.

'What's an S3 when it's at home?' Kenver cautiously enquired.

'I'll tell you what it is, Kenver: it's your passport to the succour of ambrosia washed down with a good quantity of nectar. Follow me, boys; this won't take a minute. She's just a few floors down in the garage below.'

Kenver and Curlow, now languishing on the magnolia leather, began to live the dream. The twin headlight long-wheelbase super-sports saloon transformed from an enviable product designed for royalty, top politicians and captains of industry into an indispensable possession for the band. Greengages are green, after all, and the car's size dwarfed any special needs the musicians could require. It was love at first sight. The other two, Enyon and Cadan, would not need any convincing. Ben and Miles arranged the legal details after a full English breakfast early the next morning with all the band present. They prepared the car for its blue-ribbon run to Yorkshire. Phil the roadie would follow the lads in the Transit. Kenver, feigning a little reluctance, handed over the keys to his loyal servant of the past, the 57 Slug Bug,* as a guilty lover would. A car such as the Bentley can change one's personality, as it is designed to do. Four aloof noble hands bade us a formal farewell as it slipped past. Perhaps not, though! The raucous sound of 'My Generation' blasted out of the opened windows, accompanied by the obligatory V-signs. They had found the eight-track tape player and were off to influence the new world.

* A 1957 Volkswagen Beetle

5
Shadows, Clouds, Spirits and Ghosts

(The Spirits of Ecstasy)

Mark Jordan, around five foot ten, was a well-built but not athletic man in his early twenties. On close examination, you could see he was street-smart and capable of looking after himself. Mark lived with his wife in a smart bungalow misplaced between an assortment of terraced houses in the city of Chester. When in conversation with close friends, he would usually get around to the fact that he considered himself the black sheep of his family. His father was a singularly successful millionaire trading from premises in Trafford Park close to the Manchester Docks. Still, Mark always insisted on gaining no favours from him to his credit.

Nevertheless, it was Trafford Park that he would frequent on late afternoons when time allowed him to do so. Professional footballers from both sides of Manchester and various characters from radio and TV land often passed through to socialise and generally get themselves up to speed with what was going down in the town. These sessions proved popular with many people who had newly acquired money and valuable connections, and

Miles was grateful to represent the motor trade alongside Mark. He introduced Miles to a young motor dealer on one occasion and eventually got to know him quite well.

This dealer was energetic and likeable; a picture of innocence, with a round, childlike face on top of which flourished jet-black curly hair reaching out in the form of individually placed coil springs. His looks and countenance earned him the nickname 'Vorsprung'. While laughing and joking, soaking up his daredevil humour, Vorsprung touched on the subject of advertising. He explained how he got the best results when formulating the next sales plan. 'In each case, I use a tester ad in a journal with the most discerning readership, and believe me extracting money from them is like wringing blood out of a stone. Although I do not want to be racist, the issue that comes to mind has to be the *Jewish Telegraph*. You know you're onto a winner if you can get a result from that sheet!'

They all burst into laughter, and you could see that Vorsprung wanted to elaborate further on his success, so they adjourned to the pub to enjoy his story.

'I can't believe it was only a couple of years ago I was returning from a holiday abroad, with the wife driving a little MGB GT sports coupé through West Germany. We stopped the night in the small Roman Catholic town of Limburg, a quaint historic place blessed with an immense church and town centre populated with several bars and restaurants. One of these was a Scots beer cellar with a steak house above. Tartan fabric decorating the walls and tables gave a sense of international harmony. Here was the last place in Europe you would expect to find a group of jovial Yorkshiremen partying away and enjoying an evening drink together. Far from home and taking less care over their words due to a certain amount of intoxicating influence made their conversation audible throughout the room. The group's principal member voiced his opinion of the British Leyland Group in a loud Yorkshire accent. 'British Leyland, a chaotic behemoth currently accounting for forty per cent of its home market, is now in a position of undercutting itself with massive capacity for supply only offset by the actions of its stark raving bonkers unions.' 'The time to join this conversation was now, so I made myself known to him.

'Couldn't help overhearing that you appear to be in the same trade as me, I threw in.

'Import-Export?'

'No, no. I have a tremendous outlet for used cars back in Bury, Big Rock Motors', I exaggerated in true holiday style!

'Without being rude, I couldn't help hearing of your connection with British Leyland and am always in the market for clean part-exers wherever you're based.'

'You'll have a hard job,' he countered. 'I operate from Zeebrugge in Belgium. I don't touch second-hand at all. I am in the business of selling brand-new Leyland cars, all left-hand drive, back into the UK.'

'Never!' I was astounded. 'How could that possibly work?'

'The British public has always been made to pay thirty per cent more than the Europeans for anything ranging from razor blades to cars. Usually, the bureaucrats have managed to keep it that way – until now. Probably bring it on themselves with their anything-for-an-easy-life attitude. The politicians proudly endorsed the Treaty of Rome to render the paperwork for importing and exporting cars less complicated than selling savoy cabbages!'

'At that, he enquired, 'With whom do I have the pleasure?'

'The name is Vorsprung.'

'I could see that his face began to crease with the effort of suppressing a spontaneous smile that might explode into uncontrolled laughter. He was trying to lower his eyes from staring at my hair.

'Well, Vorsprung, here is my card. My name is Julian. You need to have been registered for VAT and have no criminal record. Give me a bell when you get back, and I will fax a price list to you.'

'On my return to the UK, it did not take me long to contact Julian. He promptly replied with the price list. Rejuvenated after a fortnight with the wife, I applied myself to the feasibility task with the renewed vigour of a man who senses an opportunity. With the figures to hand based on the Austin Mini, it became clear that I could make a decent profit after converting from a left-hand drive back to a right-hand drive at an incredible twenty-five per cent discount on the new price! Flushed with the urgency of a gold prospector, I placed my tester into the classifieds of the *Jewish Telegraph*. Some days later, the blarter began to rock! Pennies from heaven, no! More than that, you know the feeling.

'Two days later, I was back in Belgium to stay a night with Julian and his young family. He invited me to sample the delights of a French restaurant in the beautiful city of Bruges and explained the details of the operation. Basically, his company would do all the paperwork up to the point of entry. The main risk would be paying the cash upfront and getting it to him. However, a further bonus was the favourable business exchange rate in Belgium. I just had to try this scheme. There was no incentive for Julian to scupper his business for the sake of one deal. His other customers confirmed his excellent status, and I paid for two Austin Mini 1000s, which he jokingly vowed would beat me back to Hull on the North Sea Ferries, which they did.

'After the long drive up from Manchester on a sunny morning, we arrived at the docks and, blow me down, there the Minis were – two little beauties sitting on the quayside. As usual, we endured the expected delay in completing the necessary paperwork. In those days, it could take hours just to tax a vehicle. Our day had started at two in the morning, so we were thankful to be sorted out by one o'clock and made our way to the hospitality complex at the port for a well-earned nosh up. I pushed against the restaurant door, but it would not budge. Then I pressed my face to the glass and peered inside. The self-service counters were all lit up on the other side of the large dining area, but nobody was around. The aroma of cooked food drifting about the place only boosted our already growing hunger.

'No use trying to go in there at this time of day,' a voice behind us called out. As he approached, a well-built, stocky dockland person with a weather-beaten face seemed to be enjoying a joke. 'The shop stewards and the local committee of the trades union have negotiated a deal with management.'

'Done in the true spirit of the Pentonville Five,' he laughingly continued. 'They held out for the one-and-a-half-hour lunch break for every member working the wharves. This, of course, includes the restaurant workers. So the place is shut between twelve and two!'

'Are you telling us seriously that they shut the restaurant for lunch every day?'

'Yes, that's the size of it. It could only ever happen in this God-forsaken place,' he replied, hooting with glee as he retreated to whence he came.

'Anyhow, the importing got underway. Changing the vehicles over presented no real problems as the intrinsic designs were all made to accommodate both options left and right. I enjoyed travelling to Belgium far better than standing for hours at a motor auction. One morning with a hold-all filled with cash in the boot of my E-Type, I decided to check the tyres' air pressure. The sixth sense of fear shrouded my person when crouching down to remove the rear Shrader valve cap. I turned and looked up in the cold of a total eclipse of the sun. There looking down at me was Harry Longworth, one of the hardest men in Manchester, not two feet away from my money! I always liked Harry. Once, he'd told me that he wished I could have been his son. I'd been on his car pitch many times, and knew of his connections with, let's say, the men who kept the city in order after dark with methods not allowed to the police.

'Hi, Vorsprung. How's it going?'

'Feeling much more relaxed, I thought this was just a coincidence. 'Not so bad, Harry. How goes it with you?'

'Could be better. Have you heard the news that the old Dutch and I have split after forty years – the old firm is no more.'

'Sorry to hear that. I hope the pitch is still in full flow,' 'I tried to continue normally.

'Of course, nothing as terminal as that! Look, the reason I'm here on the motorway was to meet Charlie and get this back.' He reached into his pocket and fetched out a silk cloth in which was a large pure blue-white diamond ring.

'She disappeared into the wild blue yonder with that still on her finger, all three carats of it. I felt obliged to send big Charlie Muffin to retrieve it – without hurting her, of course. You know Charlie, taught by a craftier man in his childhood than Fagin. He easily managed to catch up with her on Pollensa Beach, shook her by the hand, and passed on my best regards with my ring now in his hand.'

'Well, Harry, I'm off down to a closed auction at Farnborough. I'll see you back on the pitch sometime. Best of luck with the other.'

'It'll be fine.'

'I remember well how good it felt looking down the chevroned bonnet of the E-Wagon, relieved as I pulled away.

'Things got a little more challenging after a few months of easy trading. Part of the process of converting from left to right involved the replacement of steering racks. They had to be new, and the only suppliers were the British Leyland dealers, who insisted on supplying on an exchange basis as dictated by the parent company. This was fine but involved a fair amount of travel. Unfortunately, the day came when we started getting our own left-handers back! Parallel importing was occasionally beginning to be reported in the press, and more dealers began to jump on the bandwagon, removing the cream from the deal. The last car from Belgium was a handsome Wolseley straight-six Princess. An extremely impatient customer came for the handover. Still, Roger Wrench was nowhere in sight with the vehicle, so I made an excuse and dashed round to his workshop to find him in the pit fixing the power steering hoses to the new steering rack.

'All done now,' he cooed triumphantly as he jumped out of the inspection pit and into the car. 'It's been easy peasy. This one just had to connect the two PAS hoses.' 'With that, he fired her up and eased her into drive. Hands at a comfortable quarter to three right-hand down, the car turned sharply left, narrowly missing several parked obstacles! Unfortunately, the offside wing suffered minor damage and would require repair. Roger's cherry red hair standing on end had the look of a Turk's head paintbrush and so no use to anybody.

'Sorry, must have put them the wrong way round.'

'The last transaction I did was a couple of transporter loads of right-hand drives. I viewed them in Liverpool, and from there, they were transported to Dublin and then straight to Holyhead in Anglesey without even touching base at the dealership! This was several months ago now. Most of the profit has now gone in tax and a fair bit of self-indulgence. So I'm up for a new venture. I have been in touch with the Japanese outfit Mitsubishi. Is either of you two interested in a partnership?'

'Not for me just now. It sounds like you had a good run with that one, Vorsprung,' replied Miles. Mark nodded and confirmed he was too busy.

'Funnily enough, I've got Eddy the Spanner suffering a spell of selected amnesia. At last, he is about to start work on a Wolseley 1800/2200 auto, the previous model to yours, affectionately known as the old 'Landcrab'. Just over a year ago today, we sold this veteran lump with the vast saloon accommodation to Adrian Spades, a professional bridge player. The purchaser required such a lemon to convey fellow card partners from venue to venue while playing practice hands. Our revered customer was of a corpulent disposition standing five foot six with inset alert eyes. He was quite at ease with being overweight due to a lack of exercise, a healthy appetite and a propensity for beer and good wine.'

'Some weeks later, he returned with the car to complain politely that the gearbox was slipping its gears. In his own words, he informed us, 'I do not need a courtesy vehicle: somebody else can do the driving for a change. But if you could fix it as soon as possible, I would be most obliged. I will phone you in a week or so.' Eddy, our mechanic, took this lack of urgency to heart.

The parts would be hard to find, which necessitated the weekly fobbing off of 'It'll be ready next week.'

'Eventually, the calls stopped coming in. We heard nothing from this intelligent well-mannered person for months. Eddy, of course, with his never-ending queue of desperate aggressive punters that always kept him busy, resulted in the old Landcrab gathering dust in the corner of the workshop.

'Then, out of the blue, three months ago, a smart gentleman arrived with an immaculate Rover 3.5 litre Coupe P5. Tall and thin with a gaunt, worried face, he introduced himself as a close friend of Adrian Spades. He was well dressed in a lounge suit and tie and struck me as likeable, but his request was counter to my business instinct. His asking price for the Rover was £700. The car would readily retail for much more than that. The drawback to this was that he wanted the cash now. All the documents were present in his name; he showed me his licence and passport, which matched. I phoned the police to check it was not stolen and performed all the HPI checks available. I could see that this beautiful car was his pride and joy, but he would not disclose his reason for the sale. Despite this, I decided to go to the bank and cash the cheque. Knowing I had taken a risk, I marked her up nervously at £1,195.00.

'I never needed to put any undue pressure on myself, and most mornings breakfasted at around 10 a.m. My great aunt Gwen frequently made those intrusive calls an hour or two earlier. She was under the impression that everybody lived as her ex-army officer husband. He who had served in India rose every day at 6.30 a.m. promptly.

'Are you still in bed?' the haughty imperial voice asked.

'Yes.' She was probably only trying to help, as my wife was teaching from the early hours. Anyhow, this set the mood for the morning. Slightly irritated on my arrival at the showroom, I could clearly make out the slim figure of yesterday's P5 vendor. I was more than ready to do battle with him in my present mood! Before I could say a word, he gesticulated with a friendly wave and greeted me.

'Good morning. I have come to buy my beautiful 'horseless carriage' back. I see it's up for sale already.'

'Now, wait a minute. I've got to earn a living. I am not a moneylender. You must understand.'

'Quite so. The new price seems reasonable to me for such a distinguished conveyance; my wife and kids are waiting at home, ready for a trip to the seaside. I have the cash with me and would not dream of asking for any discount."'

'If you insist, but I am prepared to . . .'

'I'll hear none of it, as you just remarked you have a living to make.' He then produced a wad of cash and counted out the £1,195 in full. I tried to hide my astonishment, being extremely grateful to share and eager to join him in whatever happy state of affairs had come to pass. Curiosity got the better of me when the final hand back took place.

'Have you inherited suddenly from a great aunt?' I was taking a cue from my great aunt's start to the day.'

'Nothing like that.'

'It's not always the best policy to ask if a customer is well or how the car you sold him is, but again I could not resist.'

'Yesterday, I was on my uppers, as sometimes happens in my business. I was due to play an invitation-only poker game and had no money. My luck held, and the £700 brought winnings of £18,000. A good night's work!'

'Have you seen anything of Adrian Spades recently?' I tentatively enquired.'

'No, but this I do know − he lost his licence on a drink drive about nine months past. He conveniently moved his game over to the south of France.' That all took place a good twelve weeks ago, which brings me to yesterday.'

'Everyone deserves a bit of luck in this world. It's a rare man such as that who brings it to your door,' commented Mark. Vorsprung concurred.

'As I said, Adrian contacted Eddy yesterday to politely ask, 'Is my car ready yet?' He gave the stock reply in his usual way that it should be OK for next week! On my return to the workshop this morning, I duly noted the old Landcrab still covered in dust but with its bonnet ajar and having the battery charged.'

'SPANNERS!!! How long do you think that thing's been lying there?'

'Er, about a year, Boss. Funnily enough, the owner's been on, and I've promised it for next week – again.'

'Very patient man that. Ninety-nine per cent of the population would have bent your ears back eleven months ago. Now listen to me. Have you actually road-tested that machine?'

'It's that long. I can't remember if I'm honest.'

'Which on this occasion I doubt. Get it out, and we'll both give it the once over.' 'As I expected, the gears changed smoothly, and we cruised the motorway for several miles.

'Ever played Monopoly? Probably not. There's a square on the board called 'Free Parking', and you have just been had. That bridge player has just made three no-trumps at the first time of asking! Return the car to Adrian and don't elaborate. Just give it back. At least it's out of our comprehensive warranty, and, on balance, the cards have been kind to us of late.'

They both noticed Mark was quieter than usual. He was pensively just sipping his ale.

'Anything to report from your direction, Mark? It has not gone unnoticed that you appear to have pulled your nightly ad. The one with a handsome portrait of your good self dressed as a man of the cloth, complete with the dog collar and benignly smiling down on the caption 'Would you buy a car from this man?'

'Yes, that's right,' mused Mark, staring into his drink. 'A few months ago, a man answered the advert. He arrived on the pitch dressed in T-shirt, jeans and strapped sandals. You know the type. 'The name is Simon Lawrence,' he graciously announced. 'After several more visits, it became evident that he was not interested in my stock but keen to learn of motor traders' methods and manners of communication. Over the next few weeks, this stranger began to enlighten me with much science and religion. He began to fascinate me, and it occurred to me that he was gaining influence over my mind with his logical theories. In return, I impressed him with our inborn talent for convincing people of what we think they need. Not like politicians: more spiritual than that.'

'Sounds like you're becoming obsessed,' Vorsprung advised.

'I am obsessed,' Mark confessed. 'One night, he asked me for a defining live experience of life that I had personally witnessed. Out of all the so-called important events, all I could think of was that night at Old Trafford many years ago. You were there,' he said as he looked at Miles.

'The FA Cup replay against Preston North End, I remember.'

'That's it; so do I. I'll never forget we walked in step, entrapped in a vast crowd, each person shoulder to shoulder marching to the stadium. For some reason, the combination of thousands of individual minds lived to be part of the event. Soft night air filled with expectation. Long queues snaked towards the Stretford End with turnstiles clicking among the fans. Two stanchions towered above us into the night, each with forty or so floodlights banked on top and shining down past the brilliant white goalposts and onto the hallowed green turf out of sight to us, still in the dark, outside. Remember, young Alan, a slight, agile lad who, yielding to the desperation of being locked out, hoisted himself upon the shoulders of the crowd and ran over them, shinning his way up a drainpipe and climbing into the ground. The turnstiles shut, and panic set in. We were at the back and could see educated, sensible, law-abiding men and boys begin to push each other towards the big red exit gates. The giant doors began to bow and twist. Unbelievably, you and I joined the throng as shouts of "Heave! Heave!" could be heard from the very people who would be crushed to death if the gates held firm, which they did. The crowd at the front was now flesh and blood compressed by the power exerted by those behind them. The prospect of death on the *Titanic* could not have induced such madness. A police sergeant, holding his loud haler high to make himself heard and followed by his constable, rode their horses into the rear of the horde. The sergeant bellowed and frantically repeated over and over, 'The turnstiles for the Old Trafford paddock are still open.'

Bodies began to turn and jog towards this football salvation; others followed until 4,000 dispersed to the far corner of the arena. But all the turnstiles throughout the ground were closed long before his announcement, as he well knew. However, the two unsung police heroes saved hundreds of lives that night.

'Simon found it extremely interesting that such an event should be important to a 'streetwise' person like me but quickly analysed the reason.

'You see, if one thinks about it, that mounted policeman at that particular time and place with his freedom of choice proved that he had been given a purpose in life. This instance is no random event. The more we research, the more it becomes an irresistible fact that a creator would require a sophisticated tool such as *Homo sapiens* for an unknowable future reason. You subconsciously chose an episode to demonstrate its importance,' Simon pointed out.

'That was some weeks ago. Between then and now, we have bought a church overlooking the Staffordshire plain, complete with graveyard and grass parking for fifty cars – just in case – but currently a place of worship, at very handy money, I have to say! We will use this as a base on our return. To continue our research, Simon has arranged for us to stay with some friends in Fuheis, not far from Jordan's capital, Amman. We have contacted and agreed to terms with several publishers to print the results of our endeavours in various issues. They will, in the main, take the form of a sermon. It would be helpful to send either of you two copies for safekeeping in case of any resulting controversy. Nevertheless, I doubt you will see much of me around for a long time.'

'That's no problem to me, Mark, if Vorsprung is OK with that,' Miles offered.

'This appears to be a big step; you've obviously thought long and hard on this one, so best of luck with it,' was all Vorsprung could say.

'And we will aspire to hone our individual reason for being here by buying and selling as many motors as possible,' he cheerfully concluded.

They bade Mark farewell and, true to his word, never saw him or Simon again for years to come. Occasionally, they heard bits of news about him on TV. Miles enjoyed reading the missives, which arrived regularly and, as promised, kept them in safekeeping. The first of which came some weeks later in the following form.

Mark and Simon's First Composition

Intelligent men across the motor trade depended on a small book to assist them in purchasing and selling vehicles. They considered this monthly issue, 'The Glass's Guide to Used Car Values', to be their Bible. The authors of this tome were all dedicated experts in their field. These carefully chosen, honest professionals judged auction results and the details of trades throughout the nation to arrive at their conclusions. However, within its pages, there are many contradictions. Its monthly market appraisals were based on hearsay and were therefore erroneous. Dealers would often refer to it as 'Glass's Rumour'. The book's real value was knowing how to read it and extract the truth when needed. The froth within was what the scribes believed to be fact at the time. On numerous occasions, it included unhelpful information that they assumed should be incorporated to enhance the veracity of their observations.

To the clear-sighted motor trader who comes into contact with all manner of individuals ranging across the full spectrum of classes in society, the Holy Bible appears to share similar attributes to their guide. There are evident contradictions within its pages, and some, but not all, of its historicity is suspect. There are no historical dates within the Old Testament, and no scientific theories are revealed to its many adherents by God or anyone. Many of its early stories appear in a similar form written on ancient cuneiform tablets in Mesopotamia hundreds of years before the Old Testament's existence. These hallowed accounts became sacred to generations. It makes sense that Abraham and his contemporaries migrated from Ur in Mesopotamia to safeguard their content and hand them down by word of mouth.

However, with no dates and scientific enlightenment, further studies reveal that the underlying stories derive from cataclysmic or provident events that actually happened. But to quote the famous English comic Eric Morecambe, 'Not necessarily in the right order!' The patriarchs who eventually transcribed the word to written form took great pains to avoid detail. Nevertheless, their paranoid dread that provable inaccuracies and errors in the scriptures would invalidate the whole thing has turned out to be unfounded. God would never reveal the finer details of Einstein's theory of relativity or, for that matter, enlarge on the complete destruction of two cities as described in Genesis.

The need to know and require a deity or God resides in the human gene pool made up of every variant of the nineteen/twenty thousand genes within our DNA. A process of increasing self-awareness and intelligence appears to accelerate between 30,000 BC and 1845 BC. In this cosmically short period, civilisations independently on the now separated continents take root. *Homo sapiens*, with his inbred genome that demands the superintendence of gods, build the foundations of civic life around religion in every case. The population of the top fifteen countries as per current boundaries of today in 1845 BC was:

(1) India 20,703,067
(2) China 12,703,988
(3) Mexico 4,982,886
(4) Brazil 3,396,441
(5) Turkey 2,942,662
(6) Iran 1,957,777
(7) Egypt 1,869,332
(8) Bangladesh 1,409,776
(9) Peru 1,225,110
(10) Pakistan 1,221,109
(11) Italy 1,200,219
(12) France 1,194,442
(13) Spain 1,188,664

(14) Iraq 986,309
(15) Russia 980,887

In this early world, the scribes' advantage was less distraction, more time, and being there. The understanding of human activities, religion, and science was based on observing and controlling the 57,570,669 people living on the planet.

The written word is 'werry unwyliable', unlike the Volkswagen Golf portrayed in the iconic Japanese vernacular used in the famous seventies car advert. The first-known example of basic writing is on the Kish tablet, inscribed in 3500 BC, starting from pictographs and then realism to abstract forms of letters to formulate words. Although the development and improvements to any species' general condition are still in line with Darwinian theories, scientific observations are now prominently interested in studying DNA and the genetic codes that give instructions to the body parts and the functions of the brain. We must first consider the origin of language to produce the written word later. We have the 'chicken and egg situation with no recorded evidence. The implication that comes to mind is that no other species of birds or primates have evolved to speak, let alone go on to achieve thoughtful words with meaning as Darwin's theories seem to suggest they should. The logical answer must be that language, and other traits singularly accorded to *Homo sapiens* are genetically coded.

Following on from these facts using our present knowledge of DNA, quantum science, and so on, the only logical conclusion is that no scientist can disagree that there can be only one God or no God at all. There are 100 trillion atoms in a blood cell and 37.2 trillion cells in an average human being. The most significant chromosome in your body is chromosome one, with its 10 billion atoms. All these exist with the same orderliness as the universe. The chances of this all originating at random must be less than nil multiplied by infinity. An all-embracing patient creator must have designed the origin of life to evolve using a set of mysterious formulas. The purpose is not currently known to us and is beyond present-day understanding. At this time, no words exist to describe science written directly by God, our given name for the Creator. We have to rely on many different fallible texts in the Bible for human understanding of God's word given to humans and duly recorded without the benefit of modern-day electronic devices. Our first step forwards is a meticulous study. The search for clues within the ancient texts and their relationship must bring forward contemporary scientific thinking to substantiate their veracity.

The nuclear fusion of four hydrogen atoms to form one helium atom at a rate of 500 million tons per second has been taking place on the sun for 5 billion years. This process emits energy in the configuration of electromagnetic radiation. Part of this provides light. Solar radiation transfers heat and other vital properties to sustain the creation of life intended on a planet positioned in orbit 93 million miles away from the sun. Around 4.5 billion years ago, the solar nebula began to form planets from particles comprised of dust and gas. The forces of gravity and motion attracted heavy elements such as rock and similar dense material to the centre. The mighty solar wind swept the lighter hydrogen and helium from the core. In this way, the terrestrial planet earth, now with its magnetic field and gravity in place, was formed. Today's scientists have named this process the 'Core Creation Model'. We can find a simple explanation of these prehistoric events in the Bible:

Genesis 1:2: 'In the beginning of creation, when God made heaven and earth, the earth was without form, and void, with darkness over the face of the abyss, and a mighty wind that swept over the surface of the waters. '

Mark and Simon's Second Composition

Life began to rise relatively quickly on earth. Archaeologists have found evidence of biotic existence formed 4 billion years ago in Western Australia. At this time, messenger RNA began to assist

DNA – the molecule of life – in the miracle of replication. One billion years later, photosynthetic organisms appeared to make it possible for cells to derive energy from the sun. The planet struggled through a further 2.5 billion years, during which it suffered four 10-million-year ice ages, referred to as 'snowball earth'. The brilliant white globe's iridescent light dazzled the solar system, resilient and proud, never giving up on its resident emerging life forms. Four mass extinction events failed to halt the progression intended for the earth's purpose. The fifth and last of these was the Cretaceous Paleogene extinction. This event marks the end of the Mesozoic era, known as 'the age of the reptiles'. The predominant species were gigantic and grotesque, flourishing and multiplying for some 180 million years. Birds were as big as modern-day light aircraft, and aquatic behemoths swam beneath the seas, while dinosaurs taller than double-decker buses roamed Earth's luscious paradise.

Nevertheless, wholly at odds with the stability of Earth's existence in 66 million BC, the Decca Trapps, a volcanic mountain range in north India, began to erupt. The ensuing lava flow covered a million square miles while simultaneously choking the atmosphere with sulphur dioxide. In addition to this planetary disaster, an asteroid measuring between 11 and 15 kilometres screamed through the sky to hit what is now Chicxulub, Mexico, with a force of 100 million times that of the largest ever tested 50 megatons H-bomb, the Russian Tsar Bomba. Seventy-five per cent of all species of plants and animals instantaneously became extinct. No tetrapods over 25 kilograms survived. Crocodilians, small mammals, and sea turtles did well, however. The author of the book of Job in 1700–1600 BC could not have been aware of these cataclysmic facts. God explained to Job that He is all-powerful and can do anything. Even in tremendous adversity, humankind must respect this fact.

He refers to this in Job 40:15–19:

'Behold now behemoth, which I made with thee: he eateth grass as an ox.
Low now, his strength is in his loins, and his force is in the navel of his belly.
He moveth his tail like a cedar tree: the sinews of his stones are wrapped together.
His bones are as strong pieces of brass: his bones are like bars of iron.
He is the chief of the ways of God: He that made him can make his sword to approach unto him.'

Mark and Simon's Third Composition

Over the years, the sculptors depicting the greatest minds of Classical Greece did not patronise their subjects with godlike aesthetic features. Long faces, large beards with bland eyes set over powerful bull necks fashioned out of cold stone or bronze are preserved to this day in museums worldwide.

Pythagoras, the philosopher and mathematician, who lived from 570 to 495 BC, is considered the most superior intellect to emerge at that time. In 530 BC, he founded a commune for like-minded thinkers at Croton, Magnia Graecia ('Great Greece' in southern Italy and part of Sicily, an ancient Greek settlement). His numerous followers are known as the Pythagoreans. They employed mathematics for essentially mystical reasons. Analytical design led them to suppose that all things are numbers and form, not matter with a specifically organised world and universe. Pythagoras believed in metempsychosis (the transmigration of the soul into a new body at death). Both his philosophical and scientific perspectives influenced future intellectuals from Plato to Copernicus. Among the myriad of topics discussed and researched at the commune is that he proposed the hypothesis that the earth might be spherical.

Socrates (479–399 BC), a philosopher from Athens, left no written words for posterity. However, contemporary playwrights and historical accounts from his student Plato give enough comprehension of his work. After being sentenced to death by a court with dubious legitimacy, they forced him to commit suicide.

Plato (428–348 BC) was an Athenian philosopher influenced by the Pythagoreans and his teacher Socrates. An accomplished mathematician, he was famous for his theory of forms and Platonic Realism. He founded the Academy in 387 BC, where his star student Aristotle studied under his wing for twenty years. Academics widely accept him as the principal mind that supported the Pythagorean Western philosophy concept. In line with his mentors, he also believed in metempsychosis. Almost all of his written work has survived to the present in one form or another. Incredibly, 250 notes from his lectures are still extant.

Aristotle (384–322 BC) left the Academy after the death of Plato in 348 BC. At the invitation of Philip of Macedonia, he departed Athens to tutor Alexander the Great in 343 BC. He encouraged the future military Macedonian with his views on Greek supremacy over Persian or, for that matter, most foreign nationals with his 'just war' rationale. Nevertheless, we regard this polymath as one of the most influential people in almost every field of human knowledge who ever lived. Islam named him the first teacher. One of the greatest thinkers in politics, psychology, and science advocated that in traditional religion, the worship of local deities was patently false but politically necessary to maintain the civil order of the masses.

Nonetheless, personally rejecting this, he favoured a supreme abstract creator who was the ultimate cause of movement and change in the universe but is Himself unchanging. Without knowing about DNA and modern science, Aristotle describes the living soul (cells) as being split into three categories. One is plants – the vegetative soul, reproduction and growth. Two is the animal – the sensitive soul, being mobility and sensation. Three is the human –the rational soul, being thought and reflection.

His book on the heavens (350 BC) concludes that the earth is round. A fact (not a hypothesis) based on observations of visible constellations as you travel further away from the equator. The Bible predates all these celebrated Greek masters!

The prophet Isaiah recounts in 700 BC, ISAIAH 40:22:

> 'It is He that sitteth upon the circle of the earth, and the inhabitants thereof are as grasshoppers; that stretcheth out the heavens as a curtain and spreadeth them out as a tent to dwell in.'
> The book of Job, purported to be the oldest Old Testament book, written in Hebrew, the language of Canaan, between 1700 and 1600 BC, incredibly explains that the earth is a planet and its position is in space, the final details of which were confirmed some 3,000 years later by Copernicus.

Job 26:7: 'He spreads out the northern skies over empty space; He suspends the earth on nothing.'

Mark and Simon's Fourth Composition

The last Ice Age accumulated snow and ice to form the polar ice caps, depriving the oceans of enough water to reduce the sea level by 400 feet. Consequently, the coastlines enlarged outwards as much as 100 miles. The dryland between Siberia and Alaska surfaced and became known as the Beringian Land Bridge. By 10,000 BC, enough people had migrated across here to boost the indigenous population of the American continent to 2 million-plus. These immigrants might have followed herds of bison or other game, or just their genetically coded instinct of curiosity. Around 9,800–9,300 BC, the Melt Water Pulse 1B event raised the sea level ninety-two feet over a period of 500 years and submerged the land route. As the ice cap, which covered the north down to present-day New York, steadily melted, the river beds and valleys flooded the great plains and drained the resulting freshwater back to the sea. The formation of inland lakes fed by never-to-be-seen-before relentless gliding, swirling, and furious water leaves the human spirit in no doubt as to the existence of God. By 7,000 BC, the oceans had reclaimed most of the coastline. The population of the Americas stood at 3.8 million.

European glaciers provided the Black Sea with meltwater, which flowed downhill into the Mediterranean on the other side of the world. The Ice Age years had reduced the Med to lakes 400 feet lower than the oceans worldwide. The onset of Melt Water Pulse 1B now induced the European glaciers to flow north, leaving fertile farmland the size of England and Wales on the former east coast of this freshwater sea. After 3,000 years, the Med approached its previous level, with the Black Sea now 300 feet lower and just the strip of land at the Bosphorus separating the two. Melt Water Pulse 1C, a minor geological occurrence from 6,000 to 5,400 BC, was the straw that broke the camel's back. The first sign of water creeping over the land at the bottleneck many might have assumed to be a high tide. Within hours the water cut a deep gulley and transformed that into a cavernous ravine gushing millions of gallons in a vast cascade down to the Black Sea 300 feet below.

The sheer force of impact produced clouds of mist and spray: those in range could hear the noise 100 miles distant. Sunlight shone through the vapour above this raging gorge to form a perfect rainbow arch from the ground up into the sky and back downwards to the ground. To the people scattered about, this was a celestial gateway through which all sacred waters should flow. It was not long before the prosperous farmers of the fertile delta regions in the east realised that the seawater was advancing at a mile a day to reclaim the former sea bed. Their holdings were between 5 to 700 miles away from the source of this cataclysmic phenomenon. They had no idea of the reason for the unfolding catastrophe before their eyes. The husbandmen took what little they could and retreated with their families to higher ground north, east, and west to avoid the oncoming tide. On reaching relative safety, exhausted, the survivors must have fallen to their knees and prayed to the sky above to stop the seas from drowning the whole world. To endure such an occurrence with no end in sight must have been terrifying.

After six weeks, the sun's rays sparkled on a stabilised ocean that lay before them with their places of work 300 feet below the surface. The people's prayers had been answered. No waterfall at the Bosphorus; only a water strait into the Black Sea with currents and tides that now obeyed the laws of nature. So, the former inhabitants dispersed to many parts of the region, taking their experiences with them, relating the happening and their salvation to many others. By 5,500 BC, the population of Asia stood at 7.5 million.

During the deglaciation period, the world sea levels returned to present-day proportions. Flood stories and myths through oral transmission in the early years to the written word abound worldwide. However, no archaeological evidence exists for a significant event other than the related ones. The oldest written tale on the planet is the epic of Gilgamesh, which predates Noah by possibly 1,200 years. Genesis reveals the correct dimensions for a ship of that size, Noah's ark, but these could well have been inserted by a devout scribe years later. The flood myth inscribed on a tablet in 2,100 BC is almost identical to Genesis, apart from the names.

Mark and Simon's Fifth Composition

Basket babies is another recurring story from ancient times. During the years leading up to 3,228 BC, the tyrant king Kasma was subject to a prophecy that his sister Devaki would bear eight children, the last of which would be a son destined to kill him. He imprisoned Devaki and her husband Vasudeva and, just to be on the safe side, ordered each new baby to be murdered on the day of its birth. On the advent of the eighth arrival, their prison cell was filled with coloured light to announce the earthly presence of Lord Krishna. Vasudeva immediately secreted the infant in a waterproof basket to cross the raging Yamuna River. He exchanged his son for the daughter of Yashoda and Nand, also a newborn that day, and Krishna was saved.

The birth date of Sargon the Great is unknown. His mother, a priestess, which may have involved a certain amount of prostitution, bore him secretly. As needs must, she placed him in a reed basket made waterproof with bitumen and clay. She launched the tiny vessel from her home Azupirance on the banks of the river Euphrates. Downstream a man named Akki, a lowly gardener in the royal court of the king of Kish at Ur-Zaraba, salvaged the tiny craft. Akki brought Sargon up in the majestic surroundings to mature into the first emperor of a multinational empire in the history of humankind. His reign lasted from 2,334 BC to his death in 2,279 BC.

Pharaoh Amenhotep was well aware that the enslaved Israelites were using the human tactic of intense breeding to increase their number. The population of a prosperous Egypt, estimated at 2.16 million, shared his unease. The Bible tells us a pharaoh of oppression decreed that his people should throw every newborn Hebrew boy into the Nile. Jochebed, a desperate mother, put her son into a reed basket made waterproof with bitumen and clay. She proceeded to conceal it among the reeds on the banks of the River Nile just as the mother of Sargon the Great had done 900 years before. Pharaoh's daughter rescued the child, conveniently placing a Hebrew infant at the centre of the Egyptian royal court. It also records that he later murdered an Egyptian overseer he caught in the act of beating a Hebrew, further emphasising his Hebrew origin. This suspicious story, possibly copied from the previous two, would prove beneficial propaganda to promote the 'Hebrew Che Guevara', an Egyptian prince born of the royal family. After much research by modern historians, the most likely candidate is the enigmatic eldest son of Amenhotep III, Thutmosis, Moses, the saviour of the Israelite nation and the world's three monotheist religions.

In 1,368 BC, the fertile lands of the Nile Delta, known then as Goshen and the homeland of the enslaved Israelites, began to undulate ominously. Israelite feet rode the motion of the ground beneath them but took fright. They stared anxiously up into the night, searching for their God among the falling stars of the universe above. Far away across the sea, static electricity sent bolts from the sky to arc down behind the horizon. Wondrously coloured spectral lines appeared as a divine light made its way from behind the distant rim. The elders of the tribes took no convincing that these events were the work of their God. They did not hesitate to let God's appointed disciple Moses lead them to freedom back in Canaan, their homeland, 400 years after they had entered Egypt, for, brought up and educated in the royal palace, Moses had access to the pharaoh.

Steam-driven discharges behind the faraway horizon announced their presence daily, culminating in the detonation of the volcano Thera. The unimaginable explosion was 800 times more powerful than the 50-megaton Tsar Bomba, blowing the top off and producing a caldera eighteen miles wide. The cacophony would reach Egypt in forty-five minutes and later reach places across the planet over 6,000 miles distant. The vast fallout cloud began to darken the skies as it travelled westward of Goshen to middle and southern Egypt, leaving Israel's land relatively unscathed. Comparisons with more minor eruptions at Mount St Helens, USA, and Krakatoa, East of Java, confirm that not just one but all of the biblical plagues may be geological after-effects of a blast.

Exodus 7:21: 'And the fish that were in the river died; the river stank and the Egyptians could not drink of the water in the river, and there was blood throughout all the land of Egypt.'

Heavy with its ignoble consignment bound for the heartlands of civilisation, the boundless grey-brown cloud took the opportunity to deposit tons of red iron oxide, a corrosive toxin, into the rivers and reservoirs below. Combined with foul-smelling pumice, it turned all the water blood red, undrinkable, and killed all the fish.

Evolution requires frogs to produce multitudes of frog spawn to guarantee the survival of the few. Their predators, the fish, were dead and unable to control their number, so the land became infested with frogs.

Exodus 8:5: 'The LORD said unto Moses, tell Aaron: stretch out your hand with your staff over the rivers, canals and ponds and cause the frogs to come up unto the land of Egypt.'

Thankfully, their numbers could not be sustained after some time and began to die off. However, so many carcasses became a nursery for lice, and then swarms of flies came to harass the people once more.

Exodus 8:16: 'And the LORD said unto Moses, say unto Aaron, stretch out thy rod and smite the dust of the land, that it may become ridden with lice throughout the land of Egypt.'

Exodus 8:21: 'Or else, if you will not let my people go, behold I will send swarms of flies upon thee and your servants, and upon thy people, into thy houses: and the houses of the Egyptians shall be full of flies and also the ground whereon they are.'

An avalanche of volcanic bombs followed by the release of magma clasts, formed by the interaction of magma and water, remorselessly progressed. The air was filled with fiery minute grain-sized rock particles, chemicals, and glass that resembled a cosmic hail storm. In the years to come, the dreadful consequence of this volcanic eruption was to devastate the countries in its path. Birds and livestock perished while humans suffered thermal injuries ranging from boils to skin-cell death by charring. Ironically enough, in this case, and some others, these conditions can be conducive to growing cash crops, wheat and spelt. The abundance of these attracted the interest of ever-increasing numbers of seething locusts who proceeded to devour everything edible in their path. The gigantic cloud above cooled and condensed, releasing its fire on the land below and obliterating the sunlight, turning day into night. Anyone who has woken up in a strange room in total darkness knows the absolute powerlessness and disorientation felt by the blinded Egyptians below.

Exodus 9:10: 'And they took ashes from the furnace and stood before the Pharaoh, and Moses scattered them toward heaven. And they caused boils that break out in sores on man and beast.'

Exodus 9:18: 'Behold, tomorrow about this time I will cause it to rain a very grievous hail such as not been in Egypt since its founding until now.'

Exodus 10:4: 'Else if you refuse to let my people go, then tomorrow I will bring the locusts into thy country.'

Exodus 10:21: 'And the LORD said unto Moses, stretch out thy hand toward heaven, that there may be darkness over the land of Egypt, even darkness that may be felt.'

Moses is now in high regard at the court, and amidst all the confusion, he leads the Israelites using the sight of Thera's towering plume of fire in the north to guide them. On reaching the coast, Moses turned east with the column now behind them to cross a tidal land bridge across the Sea of Reeds (a saltwater lagoon connected to the Mediterranean called Manzala). The fate of the pursuing Egyptian army can be explained by the water withdrawal (due to tsunami activity) on the seaward side, leaving the lagoon side above sea level. An incoming tsunami wave would crash head-on with the overflowing lagoon side engulfing anyone or anything in between under countless tons of water.

Exodus 13:21: 'And the LORD went before them by day in a pillar of cloud, to lead them the way; and by night in a pillar of fire, to give them to go by day and night.'

Exodus 14:22: 'And the children of Israel went into the midst of the sea on the dry ground, and the waters were a wall to them on their right hand and on the left.'

There is indeed no trace or evidence of the events surrounding Exodus itself apart from the Bible. Perhaps sceptics could accuse the scribes of back-testing the geological evidence into the story. They could not have been aware of the scientific details and had to rely on observation alone. Nevertheless, no one can deny the Egyptian reactions, which are manifested and documented. In light of all these bitter occurrences, Amenhotep III lost no time in ordering the erection of an unprecedented number of statues to appease Sekmet, the goddess of war and destruction, the lady of terror and protector of pharaohs. Many of these are still in existence today. Examples reside in museums worldwide and those still in situ across Egypt.

Mark and Simon's Sixth Composition

Matthew Fontaine Maury, a descendant of Huguenot ancestry, was born in 1806 to a sizeable Virginian family. In keeping with his parentage, his father imposed strict religious training for him to observe. Maury joined the navy and, when out at sea, furthered his interest in navigating the oceans. At thirty-three years of age, he broke his leg in a stagecoach accident that ended his maritime days.

Nevertheless, the 'Pathfinder of the Seas' pursued a scientific career, studying meteorology, navigation, winds, and currents. He produced many books. In 1855 his *The Geography of the Seas* was published, which remains the standard today. Matthew had many religious friends worldwide who admired his ambition to seek the paths of the seas. He was inspired from the beginning by his knowledge of the ancient texts of the Bible.

Psalm 8:8: 'The fowl of the air, and the fish of the sea, and whatsoever passeth through the paths of the seas.'

Job 38:16: 'Hast thou entered into the springs of the sea, or hast thou walked in search of the ocean depth?'

Ignaz Semmelweis, a Hungarian, was born in 1818. When posted to Vienna General Hospital, he was alarmed to discover that thirty per cent of women died at childbirth in a hospital as opposed to ten per cent by a midwife at home. He deduced by trial and error that doctors should wash their hands with running water before each examination, unaware that microorganisms were a cause of hospital deaths. He correctly surmised that still water would not be effective. Contemporary doctors were offended by his supposition but could not deny that medical staff, by using his methods caused the mortality rate in hospitals to drop to two per cent.

Frustrated by the usual lack of recognition by the establishment, he suffered a nervous breakdown and was committed to an asylum. Known to his patients and front-line nursing staff as the 'Saviour of Mothers', the institution guards beat this outstanding doctor, who died of his wounds at the age of forty-two. Just a few years later, Louis Pasteur confirmed the germ theory. Had Semmelweis's pompous contemporaries consulted the Bible, they would have found the answer written there 3,000 years earlier.

Leviticus 15:13: 'And when he that hath an issue is cleansed of his issue; he shall then number to himself seven days for his cleansing, wash his clothes, and bathe his flesh in running water, and shall be clean.'

Plasma is the fluid that carries all blood cells and components. It is fifty-five per cent of total blood volume. The 700 proteins it carries contain the information and data for blood's purpose. The origin of the non-chemical or physical constituents is unknown to present-day science. The role played by Quantum Entanglement in the delivery of an intelligent signal system into the bloodstream from the universe by its designer is the current subject of investigation. Integral within these are constituents of water, salts, enzymes, antibodies, and proteins. Blood's purpose is transportation, protection, and regulation to sustain our bodies. Today doctors rely on blood tests to discover many ailments. There are 100 trillion atoms in a blood cell and 37.2 trillion cells in the average human body. Modern-day scientists, the best brains in the world, have not yet solved the unimaginable complexity of blood's make-up and cannot manufacture a single drop. In 1,650 BC, its creator explained to an ancient scribe all they needed to know:

Leviticus 17:11: 'For the life of the flesh is in the blood: and I have given it to you upon the altar to make an atonement for your souls: for it is the blood that maketh an atonement for the soul.'

Leviticus 17:14: 'For it is the life of all flesh. Its blood sustains its life. Therefore, I said to the children of Israel, you shall not eat the blood of any flesh, for the life of all flesh is its blood. Whoever eats it shall be cut off.'

Society isolates those diagnosed with an infectious disease from the unaffected. Human fear is born of stories from ancient times when leprosy people were confined to nightmare conditions in leper colonies and later in leper houses. 'Out of sight is out of mind' leads to the consideration throughout history to the present that such a condition is not a topic of primary medical importance and comes low on the list of expensive research. Medical isolation severely tests an individual's rights against the general public. There are many references to this practice in the Old Testament.

Leviticus 13:46: 'All the days wherein the plague shall be in him he shall be defiled; he is unclean; he shall dwell alone; without the camp shall his habitation be.'

Conversely, quarantine is the control of the healthy majority, which flies in the face of the rights and freedom of the general public. Quarantine is challenging to sustain for long periods. The gathering unrest due to prolonged confinement becomes intolerable for many. It has been employed with varying degrees of success and enthusiasm throughout history but is enormously expensive. There are also many references to this practice in the Old Testament.

Isaiah 26:20: 'Go, my people, enter your rooms and shut the door behind you; hide yourselves for a little while until his wrath has passed by.'

The general opinion of present-day academics regards James Clerk Maxwell 1831–79 as the nineteenth-century scientist who ushered in the era of modern physics. In the Millennium Poll of the one hundred all-time most outstanding scientists, he achieved third place behind Isaac Newton and the winner Albert Einstein. Einstein quoted, 'I stood on the shoulders of Maxwell.'

Maxwell formulated his 'Classical Theory of Electromagnetic radiation' over the years and consolidated his theories in 1873 with the publication of *A Treatise on Electricity and Magnetism*, which explains that electricity, magnetism, and light are different manifestations of the same phenomenon: the interrelated 'electromagnetic force'. This radiant energy travels through space in waves at the speed of light. It consists of radio waves, microwaves, visible light, infrared light (the closest wavelength to visible light), ultraviolet light, X-rays, and gamma rays. There are four fundamental physical forces of nature. The most powerful is strong nuclear force (subatomic), the second is electromagnetic force (long-range), the third is weak nuclear force (subatomic) and finally, gravity (long-range). Today's understanding is that all four are not able to be reduced to a more basic interaction. One of the constituents of electromagnetic force is radio waves. These consist of a spectrum measured by both their frequency and wavelength. All can travel at a speed very close to the speed of light. The better-known examples of communication are long waves, which can diffract around mountains and generally sustain long-distance ground waves. Then medium and short waves that can reflect off the ionosphere to return to earth beyond the horizon, known as sky waves, make instant worldwide communication possible. And frequency modulated wave bands improve overall sound quality. Present-day microwaves can only transmit in straight lines, so they must be relayed via multiple antennas.

The mutation of cancer cells, resulting in abdominal cancer, struck down Maxwell's mother at the age of forty-eight. In 1879 he had difficulty swallowing and was diagnosed with the same assassin as his mum at the same age. As death approached, he confided to a colleague, 'The only desire I can have is like David to serve my generation by the will of God and then fall asleep.' Surely this gentleman and a respectful person did not need atonement and would be reconciled with God.

Maxwell could not have conceived humankind's scientific progress into the twenty-first century. It is now possible for one man to be listened to and viewed by billions of people across the planet. Discoveries and mass communication are unfolding at an unimagined rate. Conversely, does it now seem impossible that an infinitely old creator could listen to every prayer and thought of the watching billions of living individuals? It might have disappointed him that the world's increased knowledge and education regarding temporal and physical facts have eroded man's expected faith and respect. Human confidence appears to have overtaken religion and driven it into decline. Maybe his brilliant mind would have concluded that if humankind could harness design such as this and yet not create the means, his belief in God is still justified.

Astronomical objects and lightning emit the only two natural examples of radio waves. Yet, converting electrical pulses into the spoken word was revealed to Job 3,500 years earlier in the Bible:

Job 38:33: 'Knowest thou the ordinance of the heavens? Canst thou set their dominion over the earth?'

Job 38:34: 'Canst thou lift up thy voice to the clouds that the abundance of waters may cover thee?'

Job 38:35: 'Canst thou send lightnings, that they may go, and say to you, "Here we are"?'

Ron Palmerston

Jim's hearse, a Rolls, with him in it, bore him on his last dignified journey. The arranged meeting point was outside his old semi-detached home of many years. A group of people, there to pay their last respects, positioned their motors to form an orderly procession behind the old polished meat wagon. By this time, the professional chief mourner Cecil was standing to attention. His black feathered top hat was formally tucked under his left arm to lead the funeral procession on foot. Curiously enough, anyone within reasonable proximity could not help but notice Cecil's distinguished set of brilliant white teeth, which many of the motor traders present might have deemed to be a perk of his job.

Nevertheless, the sight of the man's visage appeared to lighten the moment. Like a colour sergeant major, he marched slowly forward, leading the cavalcade down the suburban street lined with fifty red-brick semis on each side. As the funeral procession approached the houses, front doors began to open, and the neighbours tumbled out to wave and applaud the line as it passed by. Jim had been at Dunkirk and had stormed Gold Beach on D-Day. He'd never had any ambition to be any more than a private in the army but was an extremely useful and practical man who could see the funny side of things. Jim loved to recall that on day three of the allied invasion, a captain confident of his newly established bridgehead position summoned him in a somewhat military fashion.

'Private Perrin! I hear you're a wheelwright's son and dwell in rural parts.'

'Exactly so, Sir.'

'That's a cow over there, is it not?' He continued.

'I believe it is, Sir.'

'Then please go at the double and milk her as we are all desperate for a cup of tea.'

Jim obliged, as the neighbours knew he would have.

On our return to the house for light refreshments, we noted that Dot had not appeared on her doorstep as expected. Ron volunteered to pop across and check her out and duly reported a definite presence within due to a constant whirring sound from inside. He was always one with the words. He announced there would have to be another occasion such as this. The police forced entry to discover that poor Dorothy had been dead as a dodo for at least two days. Rigour Mortis had set in, and she was still sitting bolt upright on her stairlift, travelling up and down until the sergeant considered it appropriate to switch the damn thing off.

Some of the guests politely made small talk, and the wives and girlfriends socialised. They reverently touched on Dot's untimely demise but, more importantly, foraged for the latest gossip. Meanwhile, the menfolk discussed the general state of the motor trade.

'How's the upper echelon of the profession going, Ron? It's got to be a better bet than the bread and butter models that are hard to find and difficult to sell.'

Too much a master to show unease to his select companions, Ron would never elaborate on his work details. The acquisition of retail stock at 'the top end' would remain a mystery to the envious human satellites desperately searching for the key to gain access to the world of celebrities and their wealth.

'Personality, charm, and wit are my stock in trade. I always try to be kind and befriend my clients.'

'Victims more like,' joked the enquirer.

'We are all victims just trying to finish as near to the top end of the stairlift, so to speak,' countered Ron.

After a few drinks and reminiscences that involved our late mutual soul mate, the wake began to break up. With her hat and coat already on, Ron knew his time was up as his wife, Barbara, approached. She thrust his mac towards his hands, not yet ready for the burden offered.

'Time to make tracks, my dear,' she rejoined. 'Long day tomorrow. Busy-busy.' The most respected man concurred and left arm imperially in arm with his better half. Safely back home, the couple began to make plans and check the proceedings for the next day.

Lord Prescott enjoyed life at the Nixe Palace Hotel in Palma and, as was his usual custom, booked a tennis court for 4 p.m. British time. Ron, impersonating his trusted chauffeur cum butler Maitland, had contacted his Lordship to confirm that Ron would collect his car from the main agent two days earlier than planned, as he was due his annual week in Scotland. His Lordship apologised for this lapse and faxed the main agent accordingly. This part of the operation was complete. Barbara applied herself to perfecting Ron's attire for the assignment. She had acquired a unique talent under her mother's and several aunts' supervision for sewing and embroidery art forms. She attended to every detail, including the Prescott coat of arms stitched to the chauffeur's hat and discreetly to his jacket breast pocket. Her man about the house could be relied upon to perfect the necessary documentation. Ron duly obliged at a champagne party to celebrate the concrete-pouring ceremony at Johnny Offisrocherty's new pad. The assembled guests from the pop-music world, all high on drugs and booze, were having a great laugh as they pushed Johnny's Silver Shadow into the oozing grey mire. They adapted words of the famous number one hit for the occasion: 'The taxman's taken all my dough, this car has got to go,' were cheerfully sung by one and all. His motor settled under the more than adequate solid floors of his mansion to be, forever in its concrete tomb. Tactfully Ron bided his time to suggest that Johnny would no longer have much use for the logbook and documents pertaining to the dormant beast.

'Hey man, you're right,' he said and laughingly exchanged them for a few lines of coke before promptly letting the trappings of this materialistic world carelessly slip from his addled mind.

On the morning of the collection, Barbara saw to it that Ron was in tip-top condition for his work later that day. She drilled him night and day like a ballet dancer to achieve a flowing, balanced movement and a gentlemanly upstanding gait. They purchased a pair of 'Dave Clark Five' four-inch Cuban heel boots to boost his height to the desired six foot six. He now sported a pair of well-groomed pork-chop sideburns to accompany his elegant but restrained moustache. Barbara put on the finishing touches of makeup and stood back, glowing with pride.

'You'll do! You look more like Maitland than Maitland does!'

On arrival at the main agents, our chauffeur removed his hat and tucked it under his left arm as Cecil would do. He took care not to conceal the coat of arms as he strode through the showrooms to the reception desk. With his heartbeat under control, he coolly checked that the service book had been stamped (for appearance's sake) and followed the service manager to the forecourt.

'Nice to have the door opened for me. Makes a change that does.'

'We've valeted the vehicle top to bottom, and the complimentary paper seat and floor covers will see you home.'

With a grateful smile, Ron thanked him for that and took the rather splendid Rolls Royce Silver Shadow with him.

Barbara welcomed the homecoming breadwinner and his spoils. The meticulous preparations had worked yet again, and her inner joy was hard to conceal. Daddy had brought home one of his children. This best-selling Rolls in LeMans Blue with a champagne leather interior complemented by a sumptuous walnut dashboard and fittings is motoring perfection. The newly fashioned number plates were now on the car. The proud father was busy with his acid and punch to align the engine and chassis numbers to conform with their recently procured log book counterparts.

'Pack your bags, Babs. I'll have her ready before the night's out.'

'Oooh, are we off on a jaunt, Bun-Bun?'

'Early start tomorrow, my love. The car is sold and needs to be out of the country in forty-eight hours. Our first port of call will be The Tartar Frigate in Broadstairs to give 'Hans the German' plenty of time to cross the Channel. We'll then bash on to the Hotel Du Vin at Tonbridge Wells for a well-earned five-star stay.'

Cruising the Shadow down to Broadstairs was a privilege. Sitting behind The Spirit of Ecstasy evokes a British grace and movement with a benign imperial intention different from the Mercedes Bonnet Star, which tends to arouse a feeling of forward motion to invade a neighbouring country. Better not to inform Hans of that! However, the freshly serviced supercar effortlessly purred along at eighty miles per hour. Beautiful day to ride with Barbara by my side to reach our destination at the appointed hour.

The Tartar Frigate is an enchanting English harbour inn. The attractive little bar stocked with various coloured bottles adorned with a photo of our most revered yachtsman and prime minister Edward Heath was a welcome sight. At the end was Hans, clearly visible despite the comfortable, discreet, but subdued light. He was six feet tall, had short blonde hair, was very powerfully built, and had blazing blue eyes. His youthful good looks were still intact at the age of twenty-nine. He was leaning on the bar dressed in his trademark attire, a white polo neck with navy blue slacks that rendered the impression to anyone present that he might be a heroic U-boat commander of yesteryear.

The deal took no time to conduct. Both parties knew each other well; without the need for unnecessary pleasantries, Hans handed over the agreed price in the full knowledge of the car's doubtful pedigree. He appeared delighted with its condition and rapidly departed for Germany. Ron and Barbara felt the same and took the next train to Tonbridge.

***

A year or so later, Ron unexpectedly found himself in the company of Detective Sergeant Harry Nuell and his partner DC

Benn while visiting his old friend Malcolm at his car pitch. Good police work often finds itself most productive when confronted with the coincidental good fortune to find that tenuous lead. Malcolm Thoms, the Red Star Garage's proprietor, laughed with the detective as they stared at the crude hole battered through the brickwork of the office. The inconvenience of repairing such a chasm did not trouble Harry, as his attention switched to the solid iron safe in the corner.

'The three visible burns around the lock indicate the use of the old "jelly" to me. Better get this fingerprinted, Benn. A determined attempt to get at your bundles of illicit cash, Mr Thoms?' fished the DC.

'Lost the keys years ago,' replied Malcolm, testing the detectives' powers of deduction.

'DC Benn, call for the police cracksman* immediately,' Harry urged.

'That really will not be necessary.'

'Why so? What are you concealing?' nosed Harry.

'You are making the same mistake as those idiot thieves last night,' advised Malcolm.

DS Nuell and DC Benn surveyed the cleft in the wall and observed the damaged safe again with funnelled brows.

'It's not locked. Never has been for years,' quipped Malcolm as he carefully opened its door.

'See, it's empty save for this old *Telegraph* lining its floor. Look at the headline, 'Ron "Another Rolls Rollover"'. I always wondered where you acquired your stock. I'm only joking!' A slightly irritated Ron thought the joke in very poor taste but successfully concealed his nerves standing beside the detectives.

'Operation Mr Jeeves is a serious ongoing investigation,' the embarrassed detective sergeant retorted, now taking notice of Ron's presence. Inadvertently betrayed by one of his own, the time clock to Ron's arrest was now ticking.

The Queen's Counsel for the prosecution paced back and forth in a stately fashion to address the twelve good persons before him.

* A cracksman is a safe breaker

'Ladies and gentlemen of the Jury, I would like to thank and emphasise the police's honest endeavours, and our witnesses in this not-so-tragic case. I find it hard to believe that this series of robberies could be the work of one man. After hearing all the evidence, there is no doubt that the man before us is an extremely intelligent person motivated to premeditate elaborate schemes to commit theft for his personal gain. By the illusionary nature of some of the evidence put before us, hard and fast facts are hard to come by. You must not doubt the reality that he willingly deprives honest, hardworking people of their property. It would be best to find a verdict of guilty of all charges. I rest my case!'

'Members of the Jury, the Counsel for the Defence will not bandy about with pleasantries to gain your favour. We have heard the defendant's testimony. He believed then, as he does now, that he is sanctified from above to be the chosen person responsible for the future and current existence of Rolls Royce motors. He has explained to the court that alternative forms of economics and distribution have been experimented on and thoroughly tested. These range from Communism to National Socialism. He correctly points out that the former is disintegrating, and the latter suffered total destruction. Capitalism is now without competitors. My client believes that a certain amount of deception is unavoidable in this prosperous new world. Today's government is printing currency to pay for excessive wage demands, causing monetary inflation and robbing everyone. He prophesies that they will use quantitative easing to counter the opposite, deflation, again at the general population's expense in the not-too-distant future. His mind pictures that Members of Parliament will authorise helicopters to drop vast amounts of paper money for the needy public to pick up and spend in a few years. What can possibly be the difference between the methods granted to him and these future financial instruments? The voice through Palmerston's third eye, the pineal gland, repeatedly reassures him that relieving one owner of his Rolls to pass on to another for a small handling charge is the most efficient and ethical way of operating. Using his insurance payout to replace his missing Rolls, the original owner fulfils Aristotle's theory of cause and effect. My client's consequence of obeying his mystical instructions to his inner being is that two Rolls Royce cars now exist. A similar result was achieved in his mind's eye by the DNA molecule to replicate as ordained by God, our creator. We have heard the testimony from the forensic health professionals that his belief is constant and genuine. He advocates the love of humankind but not their inflexible temporal rules. Directives that take no account of his otherworldly personal contact messages. I put it to you, ladies and gentlemen of the Jury that Ron Palmerston's actions were a product of a mental condition possibly not understood to us at this time. It is your duty to recognise this and find him not guilty by reason of insanity.'

Before uttering his summary, my Lord Judge Hastings took serious stock of the matter before him in his court, which some say consists of theatre and tradition. At the back of his mind was the thought that his fellow Judge Prescott was now parading around in a Rolls Royce Corniche convertible – probably (though not proven) due to the acts of the defendant. His insurance company's over-generous settlement to such a high-standing person as his good self was also a consideration. His direction to the jury needed no legal explanations in this instance. He regaled that opinion outside the court should play no part in their decision-making process. His Lordship pointed out that the whole civilisation's rules of law and order have been bonkers all along or, if not, Mr Palmerston in the dock was! His closing words had been proclaimed many times by many judges to reassure juries they were supposed to be confused: 'If you find my views on the evidence helpful, you may adopt them, but otherwise, you should ignore them unless, of course, you agree with them.'

The jury's deliberations did not take long. The foreman arose to announce the verdict of not guilty by reason of insanity. Judge Hastings now had the psychiatric reports in front of him. They contained all the information required to make his legal order. Palmerston must be confined in a high-security institution indefinitely to receive corrective treatment. Accordingly, he committed the defendant, now referred to as 'the patient', into the Northern Mental Institution's care, formerly known as the Albert and Victoria pauper lunatic asylum.

After not such a comfortable ride accompanied by too many male nurses for his safety, the silhouette of a large manor house against a starry summer night sky became discernible. The hospital omnibus made its way up the winding drive to stop beneath the imposing clock tower central to an aristocratic façade. The Victorian establishment erected such institutions to further the cause of psychiatric medicine in line with their other multiple achievements. The explosion of progress ushered in by the British Industrial Revolution always seems to outpace practical medicine. This became transparent to Ron as it was getting on for midnight when they conducted him through poorly lit corridors to his allotted dormitory with a bit of impatience and a trace of force. Once in bed, he could concentrate on his current surroundings. Echoes of sound, some distant ripples of disquiet, lapped up to him from the stone walls. A twinge of pain accompanied the mournful background noise. A half-mile distant, the village church bells rang out every quarter to comfort Ron that his present whereabouts were only temporary and far preferable incarceration to the inescapable prisons over the land such as Strangeways or Dartmoor.

Curiously, Ron slept well and awoke early. The room was still in darkness, but the pull-down blackout blinds perforated with tiny holes were pinpricked with morning sunlight shining through. They were numerous as Abraham's promised descendants, some of whom were unfortunate enough to have satisfied the others regarding their suitability for tenure in this wretched foundation.

At 6.30 a.m., the attendants determined to establish control from the day's outset advanced with handbells swinging into the wards. In this profession, the 'old ways' are best. So, with varying degrees of kindness and brutality, the patients are readied in the same fashion each morning as they had been for nearly a century. The ideal of self-sufficiency, an admirable aim prescribed for the disturbed men and women, was accomplished with duties ranging from artisan crafts to farming on the 300-acre estate. Nonetheless, the gulf between inmate and carer continually widened as the day wore on. With everyone beginning to tire by early evening, the environment was fraught with tension. Attendants vying with patients was the perfect catalyst for cruelty, abuse and oppression. As the darkness of night approached, the hallucinatory chaos became real. The natural order did not coexist in this world of black shapes and straitjackets. Injuries were commonplace, and the terrifying screams of misplaced thought permeated the dark passages and cellars below.

Ron, of course still in possession of his ordained vocation, sought out the company of the institution's longest-standing resident, Lady Violet Venetia Trowbridge. After supper, the meeting took place in her private rooms during the early evening anarchy.

Sixty years before, Lord Trowbridge took the sensible decision to keep his wife Violet as distant as possible from his acquired American mistress Miss Scarlet Fox. His Lordship had her committed, saving political embarrassment all around. Many years later, his trust fund continued to keep this long-forgotten lady in her private and supposedly privileged situation. She explained to Ron that she had always been aware that her everyday life had been stolen. With the help of the Establishment, his Lordship left her future firmly in the control of others. However, she had managed to fill her days with some kind of purpose. For some reason, while strolling in the gardens or anywhere for that matter after tea, she would burst into tears and cry for precisely one hour. For so many years, this daily event tended to stoke irritation among the attendants. Pity would be the last reason to desist from their mindless abuse and taunting.

'Lady Violet, the reason for your tears is you have no one or nothing to love. Some people survive because they love themselves, but this is just conceit, and I cannot allow myself to consider it. My maker consigns me to deliver you from your torment. The trust fund has paid your 30 per cent deposit and requires you to make monthly instalments of peace and love to your friends and oppressors alike. Please graciously gain entrée to your Rolls Royce Silver Cloud and gently grasp the wheel with both hands: it's automatic. There's no need to let go. Let The Spirit of Ecstasy lead the way at all times!' Even Ron was amazed as Lady Violet stood up, hands on the wheel with her eyes alert to everything before her as she joyfully glided out of the room.

Ron's fellow residents in the Trentham Ward took no time noticing the silence after tea as the noble lady swept by dry-eyed in a state of serene euphoria. Conditions were ideal for the application of his profession. It was not long before he made tentative enquiries for a similar opportunity to acquire an example of the world's ultimate form of transportation for themselves. Ron clarified the terms and conditions of the hire-purchase agreement to everyone as before with Lady Violet. The 30 per cent deposit would be found for them but emphasised that any contract breach would terminate the deal. The only thing out of their control would be his dealer's offer and warranty to the bankers. As long as the powers that be assured his presence within the institution, there could be no trouble in that direction.

Ron supplied many different illusionary models: Phantoms, Spirits, Shadows, Ghosts, and Clouds. The outcome of so many satisfied customers cruising around the wards, hands unflinchingly on the wheel, was happiness and peaceful coexistence – a state of affairs previously unknown inside this troubled sanatorium. Within a few weeks, tea and supper passed by with no incidents, and the attendants had a much easier time of it. In the splendid earlier sunny days of the empire, the Victorians built these substantial piles far from the public gaze, hidden at the end of a long winding drive. Those receiving treatment therein were referred to as 'round the bend'. But they foresaw, now, a perfect habitat for an evening jaunt in one's Rolls!

Abraham Lincoln's quip 'You can't please all the people all of the time' certainly applied to the governors and medical staff who were becoming uneasy as the improved situation continued. The present harmonious accord under their wing might make redundancies and reductions to financial grants unavoidable. The current benefits to their charges might even result in a sharp cut to their very own considerable stipends. Retrieving them at a later date would be difficult. It was acknowledged that something had to be done about the root cause of these benign circumstances.

This committee of seniors had an army of lawyers and psychological experts at their disposal to solve any inconvenient complications that might come their way. After a short while, they summoned Ron to placate his mentors with a solution.

'By whose authority have you managed to sedate our invalid community?'

'The same being that bestowed freedom of choice to us all,' Ron politely affirmed.

'Be that as it may, we have concluded that you are as sane as we are. You have pulled the wool over the court's eyes.' Ron thanked them for their deliberations and turned to exit the room with only one thing on his mind: Operation Repo! 'In light of our considered opinion born on 100 years of experience, Judge Hastings will be asked to reconsider your case. You will be remanded in custody when he is obliged to agree.'

One by one, the trustworthy buyers of Trentham Ward and all of Ron's clientele were informed of the disaster to come. The hire purchase agreements were unenforceable due to his dealer's offer and warranty failure. The hire purchase 'snatch back brigade' remorselessly repossessed every illusion of pride and hope. The evil black shapes of the all-powerful bringers of misery were on their way. The heartfelt sound of Lady Violet's tears ushered in the return to chaos and the nightmare hours of darkness.

Ron could only bless his innocents as he walked across the open fields to the village church in the early evening dusk. He passed through the small gate and crossed the graveyard to the locked shed; the one Barbara had switched the padlock of to safeguard the velocipede placed within. He quickly found the keys hidden in John Lovelady's final resting place and accessed his predetermined transport mode. His loyal spouse, with her meticulous planning, had come up trumps once again. The Dawes Super Galaxy tourer equipped with Reynolds 631 tubing, front and back panniers packed with provisions, money, and a new passport (did he have to be German?) would be more than adequate for the long journey ahead. Hans had acquainted him with a basic knowledge of German, which he intended to polish up during the lonely journey.

So Karl Weber undertook to tread the pedals across northwest England, boarding a ferry to Ireland and sailing to France. The Spanish sunshine lifted his spirits to carry him to the port of Denia and over the sea to his final destination, the beautiful town of Arta. His small handling charge allowed him to purchase a four-bedroom terraced house fashioned of local stone, very comfortable, on the town square. It was the perfect situation where the world could do its best to forget Ron and Barbara Palmerston.

6
1975 Cadillac Eldorado

(Lido Green Convertible with Cotillion Pinstripes)

It was a Grade II listed chapel on the corner of Shelverton High St and Hill Lane. The large grey façade was quite imposing because of its sheer size but otherwise architecturally rather plain. The early twentieth-century construction was mainly in red brick with two concrete pillars running up the sides of the grand oak double doors of Norman-arched design to overcome the dreary Edwardian effect. The estate agent ceremoniously inserted the heavy brass key and pulled the doors open to reveal the substantial eighty-foot body of the church. Our two prospective purchasers dutifully followed Anna, paying some little attention to her sales pitch, and noticed the handcrafted polished wood gallery above, surrounding three sides of the auditorium. They estimated this split-level place to accommodate over 1,500 seated paying guests, which would suit their future requirements. After several diplomatic visits to the planning office, they persuaded the bureaucrats to make it clear to the vendor's professional agents that they would never be in the mood to allow a change of use from a place of worship.

Consequently, the dream of converting it into yet more two-bedroom flats for the benefit of the townspeople was dashed, rendering it almost unsaleable. Simultaneously, the local planners were more than amenable to the frontispiece's tasteful embellishment with neon lighting. Anna and her colleagues, all skilled operators in the property business, were now well aware of the situation. Giving due consideration, she advised their clients to accept Simon and Mark's rock-bottom price.

The respective solicitors exchanged contracts and completed the purchase shortly with no unwelcome issues to resolve. After forty years of roaming the Middle East and studying at many European universities, both men were ready to accept a fresh challenge from the newly established headquarters at Shelverton. Friends and followers volunteered to renovate the church, and tradesmen from Eastern Europe transformed the premises into a high-tech auditorium. A 292-inch micro-LED high-definition wall TV adorned the altar. The joiners replaced the pews with individual power seats, each with mini keyboards for questions and voting on topics covered in the minister's address. The computer programmers and engineers connected the church's website and YouTube for worldwide distribution. As in all things temporal, revenue streams to finance growth ambition are necessary. The two men sat down to assess the mission's progress and were satisfied that all the financial arrangements were in place. Advertisers had not been hard to come by, and the 1,500 seats for the first premiere service sold out at £100 each. Simon turned to face the now-ageing Mark to say, 'I know that in the main, I've been responsible for most of the research and development, but was the purchase of that space-waster Yankee motor of yours necessary?'

Mark paused to think. He knew that Simon dressed the same as the day they had met and had no taste for the flamboyant. He was eternally grateful for the religious and scientific enlightenment given to him by his friend but felt he had to remind him of the role Simon had selected for him in the first place.

'Our Lord Jesus travelled from Bethany to Jerusalem, riding a donkey to be with his people on Palm Sunday. Let no one be confused as to who we are. I am just a modern-day man once of the motor trade in the wonder of the universe who has scientific facts unavailable to the public from those days long ago, until now!

'Consequently, on our opening night, I shall arrive in the Metallic Lido Green Eldorado Convertible, complete with Cotillion pinstripes. A thing of beauty: the interior decked out in white Sierra leather, an original eight-track and powered by its five-litre V-eight engine.'

'Fair enough. I suppose we have to market the product in keeping with the current need for instant fulfilment of their theological instruction,' Simon conceded with a faint sigh. 'I'm sure your natural instinct can be relied upon to augment the proceedings with due reverence for such an event as expected by me.'

By 7.45 p.m., the audience was comfortably in their seats. The lighting above them slowly dimmed. The arrival of their host in his Cadillac was screened on the giant TV before them. A nervous energetic excitement permeated the room. Vidor's *Toccata in F* boomed out through the Wave Micro Super Hi-Fi system to announce Mark's imminent presence. He appeared through the double doors smartly dressed in a cream polo-neck shirt emblazoned with the logo C21 (after the Dave Clark style) with air force blue slacks. A dark-blue gown that loosely resembled university graduation attire draped from his shoulders as he imperiously swept up the aisle.

Exuding academic confidence, he stood before the lectern and activated the electronic devices to raise the platform to pulpit height. Automatically the lights dimmed, leaving the audience in darkness while spontaneously illuminating his form in a soft purple glow. 'You see displayed before you on the screen in front an image much magnified of an atom. The science of quantum mechanics developed over the previous century demands that human imagination – that's your imagination, or faith, Ladies and Gentlemen – must accompany the most sophisticated technology constructed for scientific advancement. With this in mind, together here in the room, we will look closely at the history and then the structure and functionality of its system.

'The atom and the universe can be as small or as large as you want them to be, so we will begin our journey back in November 1967 at the Anfield Football Stadium in Liverpool. Roger Hunt scored to put Liverpool ahead and looked comfortable when big Tommy Lawrence, their goalkeeper, hoofed the ball skyward out of defence to some tune. As the ball reaches its apex on the screen, I'll freeze the frame and replace it with an image of our single atom back in its place.' The assembly gasped as the image reappeared, expanding faster as the simulator zoomed in at the speed of light.

Mark then continued: 'Imagine two traffic cones placed on a table before me, with the open ends facing away from each other, one trying to resist collapse primarily consisting of antimatter behind the other, which has an infinitely dense small portion of matter. The two opposite charges, as theorised, are intent on mutual annihilation. They produce a cataclysmic explosion of energy to send most antimatter and time within the first into retreat to suffer a deflationary collapse.

'Conversely, the latter's open-end taking a tiny proportion of antimatter in its stride is free to expand and occupy the infinite space and time available in front of it. A millionth of a second after the Big Bang, the forces of nature become apparent. First is gravity, the strong nuclear force, followed by the weak nuclear force, and then the electromagnetic force. The nascent universe delivered through an astronomically 2 trillion degrees hot thermal fireball now has all the future composite energy and matter it will ever need. The arrow of time points forwards into the future. Immediately, the nuclei of hydrogen, helium, and lithium and their quantum properties of protons, neutrons, quarks, and antiquarks set out on a journey to perform their future role in creating the stars. Later, electrons joined to complete and harmonise the charge within the atoms in the system. The resulting rapidly expanding universe began to cool from the initial extreme temperatures. Uncountable trillions of hydrogen, helium and, to a lesser extent, lithium and beryllium atoms joined in occupying the stellar nurseries in the sky, or molecular clouds. Under the relentless force of gravity, they compress to heat up and ignite. Atomic fusion could now mature them into dazzling stars to take their destined place in our cosmos' galaxies. These billions of years old primordial fusion reactors produced a range of atoms to form the lighter elements from helium to iron. Iron will just not fuse at this point! However, these elements account for ninety-six per cent of a planet, such as Earth's mass. The star progresses through its Red Giant phase to emit some heavier elements into its planetary nebula to scatter into the interstellar medium. The doomed Red Giant continues onward to become a White Dwarf.' The wall screen was filled with wonderful colours as the heavenly events unfolded.

'These supermassive fusion reactors in the sky do not exist as long as the average star. They morph into super red giants that swell to a size big enough to encompass the Solar System. The iron core of this gargantuan entity has contracted to reach the end of the line. Neutrons begin to saturate the core. Neutron caption reactions of the slow process and the rapid process create further heavier elements. Despite the turbulent chaos of protons, neutrons, and electrons tearing themselves apart, they miraculously find a way back to dance together again. Quantum mechanics is now the master of classical physics as electron degeneration struggles against the whirlwind maelstrom to obey Wolfgang Pauli's exclusion principle. Somehow, during the titanic explosion, the old reactor survived just long enough to complete the assembly of the natural elements of the Periodical Table. The supreme engineer observes his cosmic event, a supernova so big it illuminates the entire galaxy hundreds of light-years distant to announce that he has met the conditions for intelligent life on a small planet among the stars.' The screen now settled on the approaching image of the atom. Mark triumphantly peered into the darkness of the auditorium and sensed that his congregation were silently in thought. With this in mind, he raised his voice a tone or two.

'No atoms mutate! They do not evolve or change in any way ever! They do not age and do not relate to the concept of time in the future or the past! An atom of gold is precisely the same as it formed billions of years ago. There is no day and night in this stable system other than through chemical and nuclear reactions, with different elements partaking in the same atomic world to provide the universe with reality. The enlarging form on the screen begins to demonstrate duality and mystical simplicity. It is the building block of and still occupies the same location as the football stadium and its 54,000 clamorous fans. It and they might as well be as far below as the universe is above now in this perspective, invisible to the human eye from here. Neither of the two versions of reality is visible to the other. It is a mechanical tool to implement the working of the universe. No living entity in this domain has a hand in its function. As you can see, our approach displayed on the screen to the outer circumference reveals that the structure is nothing like the imagined planetary system perceived by most people. On our last glimpse of the whole in its proportional size – to the football – through its translucent negatively charged environment known as the electron cloud, the nucleus is still not visible some two miles distant.'

Still transfixed in silence, the audience looked fixedly and wide-eyed as the quantum microscopic simulator slowed its advance to portray its entry into the cloud. A panorama of a seemingly infinite backdrop of nothing came into view. 'You will notice a small sheet of violet lightning emanate as an electron jumps to a lower energy state. It is in the business of converting mechanical energy into electromagnetic energy. The colour represents the wavelength of the photon it has just emitted. Various theories postulate the reasons for its disappearance and return on its journey to shed more energy to stabilise the atom's structure. We can follow its course by observing the divine colours blue, blue-green, and red. However, there is no way of predicting its future whereabouts, only estimating where it may probably be. As it travels around the nucleus, it appears to be moving in the fashion of a standing wave, adding further protection from a collision with the positively charged protons in the core. Ladies and Gentlemen, we cannot dismiss the suggestion that this tiny cosmic body is predetermined. We are now just 100 feet from the nucleus. It is visible, and, on closer inspection, we will examine its properties and try to resolve its functionality.'

The nucleus drew nearer on the screen. The first impression was of an embryonic transparent but dense body with a kind of thin pinkish icing around the perimeter. A subtle shape change accompanied by a small amount of oscillation was discernible on the surface. Everyone in the room sensed a maelstrom of activity within its form. There was no tangible sign of this, just a telepathic impression that nobody present could interpret.

'Each one of you consists of 7 octillion atoms. That's seven, followed by twenty-seven noughts. Your hydrogen atoms are over 13.5 billion years old, and the rest, billions. I suggest we wish them and ourselves a happy birthday! I can feel your nervousness and admit that it is pretty shocking. So firstly, I will outline the features of their nucleus as understood by today's scientists. – the details of which are in your order of service.'

'The interior of the manifestation before us is one of perpetual infinite creativity. The two main constituents of the nucleus are positively charged protons alongside neutral neutrons. The only exception is the lightest and most common atom, hydrogen, with only one proton and no neutrons. As we recall, the hydrogen nucleus and its isotope, along with helium, were instantly created in their countless trillions at the **Big Bang**. They must be considered the blueprint for the future production of everything. The electron's addition with its negative charge to complete the atom's structure is a mechanical event involving no life form. Everyone must accept that there is no Darwinian evolution involved here. These minuscule high-tech mechanisms are designed. They could not be the result of random origin. They cannot replicate anytime in the billions of years ahead of them. They do not die.

'In the subatomic world, protons are made up of three quarks; two up quarks with a +2/3 charge each and one down quark with a −1/3 – a net positive charge of one. These bind together and dynamically interact with at least eight gluons that mediate the strong force, creating three strongly colour-charged forces. On the other hand, the neutrons have one up quark with a +2/3 charge and two down quarks with a −1/3 charge each. These interact with at least eight gluons resulting in a net-zero charge. Virtual pions that consist of a quark-antiquark pair – which the rules of classical physics insist should annihilate each other – materialise from nothing to complete the strong nuclear force enabling multiple protons to combine with neutrons in the nucleus. This binding action allows the atomic system to harness numerous electrons. The flexible number of electrons in harmony with the protons balances the system, currently in standing waves with their wave-particle duality and probable position orbiting the nucleus in cloud formation.

'They now can allow covalent and ionic bonds to empower practically all chemical combinations to perform the miracle of building complex molecules that include carbohydrates, proteins and the molecule of life, DNA. There's more! As every motor dealer knows, any mechanism that touches moving parts has a very limited life span. It would be prudent to avoid a guarantee as to its future performance.

'Unstable atoms obtain a more stable ratio of protons and neutrons due to the weak nuclear force. The W bosons, both charged negative or positive, carry this force less, so the Z boson is neutral. By emitting a W boson, the weak nuclear force changes a quark's status, which turns a proton into a neutron or vice versa with no contact despite its microscopic range. The resulting atom now represents a different element, isobar or isotope. Science refers to this process as beta decay. It can be considered a small part of its defence system. Beta−, the conversion of a neutron to a proton emits an electron with an antineutrino.

'Beta+ is a proton to neutron emitting a positron – an electron with a positive charge – with a neutrino to stabilise the atom described above.

'Electron capture, the third mode of beta decay, is when a proton-rich nucleus in an electrically neutral atom absorbs an inner electron to change a proton into a neutron and simultaneously emits an electron neutrino.

'The atom can adapt and answer any physical functions asked of it. It obeys the guidelines imposed by great men and women of science. It can readily operate with the imposition of intrinsic properties such as quantum spin, charge, and mass. Quantum superposition states that its composite particles can exist in multiple states of motion in concert. The Pauli exclusion principle states that no two identical fermions, or particles, can simultaneously occupy the same quantum state. The Schrodinger wave function rules whereby particles can become waves. It still follows the conservation rules of classical physics while maintaining energy and charge in which quantum quantities such as the barium and lepton numbers are conserved.

'The origins of the natural universe consist of constituent subatomic particles. The simple activity of these creates all electricity and magnetism. Humankind's representation of this is the Standard Model of Particle Physics. This diagram portrays leptons and quarks' matter particles, all of which have an electrical charge except the neutrinos on the left. The force-carrying particles are on the right; the photon transmits the electromagnetic force; the W and Z bosons convey the weak force, and the gluons carry the strong force. The electron absorbs energy and proceeds to a lower energy orbit to emit electromagnetic radiation to transmit radio waves and light up the skies. The proton and neutron structures with complex composite subatomic particles allow nuclear fusion and fission reactions. Nuclear fusion facilitates the configuration of our sun and all the stars of the cosmos. The numerous protons bound together in the nucleus by the strong nuclear force allow multiple electrons to empower the chemical bonding of the elements.

'Be assured the atom has more secrets not yet made known to us mere mortals. We are no nearer to understanding the fundamental reasons despite our recent scientific discoveries about why things behave as they do. The established media berates us with the idea that the twentieth century was the age of technology. No such thing! It was the era of perfecting the inventions and discoveries of the nineteenth and indulging in worldwide warfare. Most of the Standard Model of Elementary Particles is derived from observing the outcome. Back-testing results from construing its theory may well be accurate but is a country mile from the understanding of the cause. Some of the unanswered questions for this planet's inhabitants to address are:

(1)   'What exactly is energy, and where does it come from?

(2)   Why is the colour charge not on the Standard Model of Particles? Gravity and its force carrier are also missing, as no one has figured these out yet.

(3)   Where did charge and spin originate from orchestrating all electricity, magnetism, and electromagnetism?

(4)   Why is the nuclear weak force the only force concerned with spin?

(5)   Quarks interact with each other. They emit and absorb different gluons to assemble the colour force. No scientists today can explain their origin.

(6)   Why can no one understand the cause of the complex, paradoxical juggling act involved in controlling perfect order in the nucleus? The forces of nature are each allotted individual tasks to perform.

'The weak nuclear force controls the fuel consumption rate in our sun and the stars. Without this force, with its minuscule range, the universe would not function. On the other hand, the strong nuclear force maintains order in the nucleus guaranteeing an unfathomably complex system. We must remind ourselves that the atom has never malfunctioned since its inception. Should it ever do so, the universe would collapse!

'The deeper we go, the more we realise our lack of knowledge and the many more mysteries to be discovered in the quantum world.

'Undoubtedly, this purposeful infinitesimal entity that enables the universe's functioning and the smallest living cells has been designed. The originator must be all-knowing and can learn nothing more. Therefore, we can deduce that we have been given life for a purpose accompanied by a divine omnipresence watching over us. Three thousand years ago, King David came to a similar conclusion inspired by what he knew God to be. He wrote Psalm 139. I will read verses 1–6 while the simulator prepares for its return journey:

> 'LORD, thou hast examined me and knowest me.
> Thou knowest all, whether I sit down or rise up;
> thou hast discerned my thoughts from afar.
> Thou hast traced my journey and resting-places,
> and art familiar with all my paths.
> For there is not a word on my tongue
> but thou, LORD knowest them all.
> Thou has kept close guard before me and behind
> and has spread thy hand over me.
> Such knowledge is beyond my understanding,
> so high that I cannot reach it.'

The pulpit lights now dimmed to leave the room in complete darkness. A deafening silence prevailed to accentuate the blindness one feels when one can't see anything, which removes all sense of spatial awareness. Not knowing the whereabouts of the simplest objects one takes for granted in life induces a slight sense of panic. The hint of panic melted into a kind of dread bordering on fear. Tiny specs of light appeared on the screen of receding atoms compressed into an unrecognisable picture of shapes in shadow. The illustrious company present, held in suspense, willed the simulator to evacuate them from this intermediate commonwealth of an unassembled compound of matter. The essence of near-death experience prevailed.

To everybody's intense gratitude and relief, the football reappeared. Bobby Charlton gracefully trapped it, calmly wheeled a three-sixty, and, as was his style, put in a sixty-yard perfect pass without looking up and out to the left wing. The sound waves issued forth from the home supporters in the Kopp Stand loud and clear.

'Where's 'ure 'andbag? Where's 'ure 'andbag? Where's 'ure 'andbag? Georgie Best? Where's 'ure 'andbag? Where's 'ure 'andbag? Where's 'ure 'andbag? Georgie Best!!!'

The 15,000 standing fans from Manchester behind the far goal replied (to the tune of Jim Reeves's number one hit, 'Distant Drums'), 'We hear the sound of distant bums over there! Over there!'

In the meantime, George easily collected Bobby's pass and was on his way toward the Liverpool defence. All seven octillion of his borrowed atoms on this earth combined with his world-class coordinating balance and fascinating motion as this spritely figure alone with the ball began to weave his spell. Instinctively pushing down his left thigh and swivelling his hip, he stopped. One of the hardest men in the league, Tommy Smith, was now in his wake as George accelerated into newfound space. With one thing on his mind, Chris Lawler, their experienced left-back, advanced to cut George off or scythe him down – either would suffice. Jinking first left and then to the right, George put the ball into flight. Every fan or player treasures this magical moment for what seems like minutes, but it is only seconds – time stops. Big Tommy Lawrence was not on his own now, and players from both teams appeared to be in still-life form, paralysed as the ball passed them by on its way into the net.

The screen turned to a sympathetic saver mode as Mark, again illuminated behind the pulpit's lectern, continued to preach.

'Yes, dear guests, we are back in the living world. The atom bonded into elements will not shape our destiny. It is merely the building block in the construction of everything. We remain a fallible – as the lads playing for Liverpool will attest – evolving and perplexing entity. The twenty-first century has ushered in a new optimism. Maybe the long-awaited technical revolution is here. History tells us that humanity has been allowed to satiate itself with the cruelty of war, destruction, envy, and hatred to accompany the natural goodwill of humankind. Perhaps the media, scientists, and politicians will listen to our message. We must find a way forward with the help of new resources such as quantum computers and artificial intelligence. Dare we think our self-inflicted horrors have been allowed as a safeguard against a wrong turn in our evolutionary process? As in present circumstances, our development of high-powered, multitasking electronic brains must have a failsafe mechanism to avoid being overrun by our creation. The human brain is unmatched on this planet but now calls for an upgrade of human intelligence due to the inevitable scientific advances about to take place.'

'Our God has constructed an undeniable physical atomic system to accommodate the planet and the universe with infinitely diverse forms of beauty to accompany us on our sometimes painful journey to the destination of His choice. Please look into your soul to find His presence. We must find the strength to liberate the force granted to us while adhering to Jesus' message of peace and love. Retain your given unique originality armed with our "Theory of Certainty" to understand the task before us!' Mark paused before continuing.

'Demographic trends across the world's advanced nations show that an incredible 125,000 abortions occur daily. That's 50–70 million a year. The organisation, 'The Women of the World', grows month by month, and its message subconsciously permeates the adult female mind. The interests, achievable ambitions, education, and financial security of modern-day life are beginning to contest the words in

Genesis 3:16: 'I will make your childbearing pains very severe; you will give birth to children with painful labour. Your desire will be for your husband, and he will rule over you.'

Mark then leaned over his rostrum to demonstrate his point with arm gestures.

'The birth rate is plummeting. One hundred and eighty-three countries out of 195 will soon have a fertility rate below the replacement level. The most optimistic estimates are that by the end of this century, with things as they are, there will be 401 million under-fives instead of the current 700 million. The population of the over-eighties will rocket from 141 million today to a staggering 900 million. The twenty-first century's supposedly educated and dynamic generations are sleepwalking into catastrophe.

'Let us imagine a virus could wipe out the elderly to provide an answer. Inevitably it would lead to a small, declining population of inexperienced, largely uneducated youngsters fighting for survival and men labouring in the fields as countless generations before them to provide basic sustenance. Not long after the fall of the Roman Empire, the people of mainland Europe lived among the giant aqueducts, roads, and imperial ruins, not knowing what they were or who had built them. These mainly rural inhabitants had absolutely no idea they were man-made. This nightmare scenario, to welcome back the Dark Ages once again and restart the process of scientific advancement from scratch, is an actual probability.

'God must require us to survive to carry out his purpose. Most people across the planet only need to create a comfortable existence for themselves and their families. While doing so, their dreams and needs are catered for by improving their lot. This slow form of evolution requires centuries. The possible threat of extinction within the next 150 years means we can no longer afford to squander the aforesaid time.

'The forecast for the end of this century means that every twenty-four-year-old male is not only asked to support his family financially but will have to maintain an average of seven eighty-year-olds. The automation of industry and recreation has been evolving for 100 years to provide non-essential commodities with built-in obsolescence. Fewer manual workers will construct the necessities for the quality of life and advancement in a new world. The competition for unskilled operatives from the very few countries with growing birth rates in Africa will intensify. In the new environment, it will become clear that the cycle of educating a human being for twenty years to achieve just forty years of work and research generation after generation is entirely untenable.

'If medical knowledge had made it possible for Isaac Newton, James Clerk Maxwell, Albert Einstein, and their contemporaries to realize a lifespan afforded to the patriarchs in the Bible, humankind would be much closer to fulfilling God's purpose. The long-lived patriarchs, purported by religious scribes for thousands of years, had missions to fulfil. I put it to you that history tells us that they never accomplished these moral and cultural assignments. We believe the time has come to reverse this process due to the possible decline in population, contagious diseases carried by ever-increasing human contact, and the technological possibilities ahead.

'Unfortunately, the days of personal risk and heroics are over. We must peacefully revolutionise the planet's nations into one state for the common good. With the Manhattan Project's success in mind, initially, we intend to persuade the world's governing bodies to create seven cities dedicated to worldwide medical and scientific research – space-age metropolises with all the facilities for dedicated research and development. It would be a multinational effort to provide unlimited finance to equip laboratories to attract top scientists from every nation on the planet to live and breathe together, researching their chosen field and sharing their acquired knowledge in an intimate environment purposed. A combination of a worldwide internet vote and the agreement of politicians will decide their location. They will become advanced state-of-the-art international territories to lead the people to peace and cooperation.

'The first and most urgent of these is age reversal. Imagine the benefits after seventy years of life experience you could take with you to university for further enlightenment to enhance further progress toward our desired goal. Space exploration and travel would become feasible. The future universities would be attended on starships transporting settlers to distant planets. These pioneers will colonize the nearest habitable cosmic bodies with instant communication to Earth. The remote settlements will make an immediate return to unfettered human population expansion indispensable.

'Doctors, oncologists, and scientists will be rewarded handsomely to work in harmony at our glittering second city to rid the world of one of its most lucrative industries, the people-killer – cancer! It is hard to conceptualise that establishing an all-encompassing environment in a single location with every means of apparatus and provision at their disposal could be any more expensive than the fragmented well-meaning worldwide attempts to find a cure today.

'The third city's construction is no less urgent – the study of quantum, molecular, and classic biology. To conquer the world of sub-microscopic, parasitic living particles is paramount. In tandem with the city of Silvanus, they will examine the solvable mysteries of DNA, the biological blueprint for the human condition. Comprehension of the chromosome and the orchestration of gene activity will be the highest priority, with any results instantly being available to the other two cities.

'The fourth city will be spectacular. Its buildings will be like gold with windows sparkling like diamonds. While being scrupulously regulated, the privileged computer engineers will build and operate their mind-blowing quantum computers, not linked in any way to the worldwide internet.

'The fifth city will augment the fourth and appear just as brilliant. Contained within a larger area, it will be responsible for space travel and astronomy. They will build future space stations to orbit around the solar system's planets on this enormous facility.

'Our sixth city will be born with the long-awaited nuclear fusion reactor to supply the planet's energy needs. Subterranean pencil trains capable of moving thousands of miles per hour will replace air travel. The engineers worldwide will surpass the Victorians in laying the tubes in which these trains will travel. Our environment will sigh with relief as hydrogen and electricity finally put paid to the primitive fossil fuels of the past.

'The world's religious leaders must congregate in our seventh city to iron out their not-so-intangible differences. As I have done tonight, the people will grant them the splendour to debate their case that there can only be one creator, the atom designer. Whether individual or national, the violence must stop for us to have any reason or purpose. This city has to host and listen to all to achieve peace and unity as we advance to answer for our earthly activities. John describes his vision of the cities to come:

Revelation 21:19: 'The foundations of the city's walls were adorned with every kind of jewel. The first was jasper, the second sapphire, the third agate, the fourth emerald.'

Revelation 21:22: 'I did not see a temple in the city because the Lord God Almighty and the Lamb are its temple.'

Revelation 21:24: 'The nations of the Earth will walk by its light, and the kings of the Earth will bring their splendour to it.'

Revelation 21:25: 'Gates shall not be shut at all by day (there shall be no night there).'

'Until next time, my friends, when we shall explore the role of DNA and the origin of life for further guidance as to our purpose! I would like to thank everybody for their valued attention. Please confirm on the keyboard to the right of your seat if you wish to attend the next meeting. Also, I would like many of you to consider our invitation to join our movement seriously.'

Mark paused for a moment, still shrouded in the subtle light. An image of the slowly rising morning sun on the wall screen cast soft red light across the room, becoming brighter as Mark straightened his gown and raised his hands to quieten the anticipated applause. Now with majestic grace, he alighted the pulpit to a standing ovation. The screen radiating bright sunlight behind him and the Wave Micro Super Hi-Fi system playing Purcell's *Trumpet Voluntary* was a sure catalyst for louder cheering and applause from the congregation seated both at ground level and above in the galleries. Enjoying the adulation, Mark took his time to vacate the building and depart in his mint-condition Lido Green Cadillac Eldorado with the Cotillion Pin Stripes.

Some weeks later, on an overcast Wednesday morning, Mark began to consider the unqualified success of his inaugural endeavour while musing over the completed final touches to his sermon. Worldwide interest and the unprecedented number of website hits exceeded his highest expectations. The burgeoning revenue streams assured his partner that their movement had the potential they had envisaged years before. He hoped to build on this initial success with his second attempt.

It was understandable that Simon, born and bred in the different world of academia and study, might have some reservations about some of the dynamic recruits making themselves available to further the cause. Before making such commitments, he insisted that his agreement was to be sought by fully disclosing the applicant's history and pedigree.

One such person was William Cardwell, otherwise known as Puffing Billy in yesteryear's motor trade due to his addiction to smoking tobacco using a calabash pipe. Bill started to make his real money by bluffing his way into signing a lucrative contract to fill disused mine shafts up in the Mendip Hills. A dangerous undertaking at the best of times. He borrowed the money to buy a truck and trailer to transport the colossal bulldozer from Measham Motor Auctions in the Midlands. He was resourceful enough to accommodate the wishes of the captains of industry and the establishment's leaders at the time to dispose of any awkward artefacts that might attract unwanted public attention. A brave man of honour and total discretion as far as Mark was concerned, Simon demanded that he accompany him to Bill's

Tudor farm in the rolling countryside north of Brighton. Mark swivelled his chair to peer down from his first-floor office above the church through the Regency sash window onto the high street below and reflected on the deals he had done with Bill back in the day. It didn't seem that long ago, in harsher winters, when, driving down the A5 from Cannock, they could see lines of lorries parked with small fires under their engines to prevent diesel freeze. Black shapes against the morning snow were waiting their turn to rejoin the busy link to the relatively new M1. Passing the Brownhills junction gave one a sense of freedom from the ice-bound foggy North.

Nevertheless, it seemed more fun back then. Warren St, the thriving centre of the second-hand car trade, was in its last phase of life, but it was still common knowledge that a private man could not walk its length without being sold the car of his dreams! Simon arrived in his sports utility vehicle, so Mark collected his case and made his way down to join him (wishing he was going alone in the Caddy despite its fourteen to the gallon!).

'Morning, Simon.'

'Morning, Mark,' he cheerfully replied. 'I've put the postcode in, and we should arrive early afternoon as planned.'

With all the functional benefits such as satnav, speed limiters, and so forth, a modern car possesses, there was not much else to do but chat. They ran over the text for the next ministry and several new applications they had received and agreed everything was going well. The broad strategy for the domestic operation would be a network of churches across the country, each with the technology and design enjoyed by the original at Shelverton. To run each establishment, the movement would require persons acquainted with diverse business experience and dealing with the public, backed by a team of enthusiastic, energetic university graduates.

'The very reason for our meeting with Billy. Please do not judge him on first impression. He may well light that infernal pipe and disappear in a cloud of smoke. He used to think it gave him an edge to weigh you up, but when his protective nebula clears, an oddly deformed Sherlock Holmes stands before you. Puffing Billy is not his only nickname.'

Mark leaned toward Simon to clarify his point. 'It's a long time since I last met up with him. Be prepared for his unusual appearance. He is a quick-witted man with sharp, intelligent eyes that, unfortunately, are squinted to convey the impression that neither is looking at you. The nose that separates them is petite, hooked and has a slight but off-putting buckle to it. On top of all this, he stands at five foot eight, slightly overweight, with rounded shoulders to compliment him with a somewhat comical demeanour. I am sure he was aware that the trade laughingly knew him as "The Male Model for The Local Gargoyle Company". He may be a bit eccentric, but he does not let any of this bother him. He has succeeded in becoming extremely wealthy. It's not far now – about two miles past Amberley.'

Simon's jaw dropped as they drove through the picturesque village.

'Don't even think about it,' Mark admonished. 'The church is not for sale!'

A few miles on, the lady in the satnav gave them their instructions in the usual school ma'am voice, 'Your destination is 200 yards on the right,' and, sure enough, they arrived at the magnificent pillared gateway entrance to Motorhead Farm. Simon obediently announced their presence to the grill, conveniently placed at window height in the red brick pillar. Silently the majestic gates opened. The long driveway wound its way through beautiful landscaped grounds and gardens on the approach to the house. The traditional and informal setting tastefully lent itself to the interconnected water features with bridges to pleached paths bringing the natural world close to the home. Well-ordered topiary adjoined and surrounded the reception area in front of the imposing façade. There was no one around as they approached the door and pulled the antique bell-pull. The old clapper did its best to resonate the sound of the toll throughout the house. Billy's wife of fifty years answered the door, still blond and very smart, with a look of amusement about her.

'You must be the distinguished visitors' Mark and Simon; my husband has arranged to meet. Please follow me to the main lounge, and I will inform him of your arrival.'

She turned her head and politely asked if they wanted anything to drink.

'Tea, coffee or something a little stronger, perhaps?'

Simon deferentially declined, and she gracefully departed into the house. Not knowing what to expect, they took stock of their surroundings. The large drawing room was quite dark as the windows did not admit much light. The furniture had quality and comfort but was visible only as silhouette outlines in the fading luminosity. Above all, it was quiet, and Mark noticed that Simon was a little edgy as they looked at each other.

Still slightly ill at ease, the muffled sound of music emanated from beneath the floorboards. Somewhat perplexed, they recognised J.S. Bach's *Toccata and Fugue*'s opening bars in D Minor. The volume increased with every note, and the whole place began to shake when the 'Mighty Wurlitzer Pipe Organ' appeared through the floor, hitting the throbbing base notes at full blast! Lights and mirrors accompanied the instrument's ascension into the room as the pianist with brilliantine well-groomed black hair pounded out the piece's main body. Without a moment's hesitation, he expertly concluded his rendition with a very solid performance of 'Kitten on the Keys'.

A formal bow completed Billy's grand entrance back into Mark's life, and he advanced to greet them with a broad smile. The annals of time had matured Bill's presence with a Mediterranean complexion that did not entirely conceal his prevailing imperious imperfections but improved his overall appearance.

'If you would be kind enough to follow me, I will show you my evolutionary collection, and perhaps we can have afternoon tea while discussing your project.'

After a short walk through the leafed pathways, they came upon the first of several former agricultural outbuildings behind the main house. Bill, complete with deerstalker hat, but thankfully no calabash pipe, led them in and switched on a bank of floodlights.

'On our left is an 1886 Daimler – we have the first petrol-engine four-seat vehicle ever produced. Once Gottlieb Daimler and Will Maybach established the basic design, it did not take the rest of the world long to improve and adapt. The Model T Ford introduced in 1908, 'The Tin Lizzie' mass-produced on assembly lines, eventually sold 15 million by 1927! In the pre-war years' style and performance began to be dictated to by the increasingly demanding public.'

As they passed from one barn to another, Billy, in his element, described the objects of his passion. Stutz, Hotchkiss, Bugatti, Packard, Pierce-Arrow, and Rolls-Royce from the Roaring Twenties. The glamorous Talbot-Lago T26 Grand Sport, MG TC, Bristol 400, Riley RMC Roadster, and the Jaguar XK120 followed the Second World War. Buick Riviera, Cadillac 62 Club Coupe, Jaguar XK140-150, Austin Healey 3000, and the MGA were born in the 1950s. Elvis Presley joined the queue to own this Rolls-Royce Silver Cloud to befit his 'King of Rock' image. The swinging sixties introduced a revolutionary art form style with the Austin Mini, the Mini Cooper, Jaguar XJ6, Ford Thunderbird, Ford Mustang, Aston Martin DB5–DB6, and the sexiest car ever made, the Jaguar E-Type.

'As you can see, there are a few more cars from the seventies until the present day, but I am sorry to say functionality overwhelmingly replaced art to the detriment of pleasure. Coincidently pop music and fashion, for whatever reason, seemed to abandon originality for common-sense boredom at approximately the same time.'

Having finished his tour in grand style, Bill led the way back to the drawing room with his guests suitably impressed. Afternoon tea – sandwiches, cakes, coffee, and tea – had been laid out. They both declined the more substantial liquid refreshment on offer and settled down to listen to him.

'I've been following your letters and YouTube submissions for a long time. My team of researchers, including an Oxford Don, one professor Lovall and a team of graduates, are here in our Brighton laboratory, working out the mysteries of genetics and DNA to pursue age reversal and understand God's purpose for us. You won't believe it, Mark. Remember all those years ago? I made my first fortune filling disused mine shafts. Well, my team got wind of the fact that the core of the landfill was beginning to heat up, so we checked it out, and, sure enough, at 100 feet below, the temperature had reached fifty degrees Celsius and was rising. After fifty years, I was the only person who knew their precise location. So, I made it my business to purchase all the plots with mineral and exploration rights! The prospect of a cheap renewable source of green nonpolluting energy has earned me further vast wealth. More importantly, your – our – foundation afforded me access to the corridors leading to the very top of political power. I would like to impress my honourable intentions regarding your movement upon your good selves. I will not be viewing this as a profit-making enterprise but will require some assurances that no one can take financial advantage of us. Charities across the planet are merely a vehicle for executives to collect massive salaries. I have an army of lawyers who can draw up the necessary framework for domestic and international operations for you both to consider. I have taken the liberty of putting an offer in for a Methodist church. I think its location is perfect, close to the centre of Brighton. Here are the particulars.'

Billy passed the brochure to Simon. The latter thoughtfully browsed their contents. At the same time, Bill continued, 'If you could get your guys to bring it up to the Shelverton standard and connect it to the network, I will arrange at no charge a peppercorn lease. Then duly engage quality staff to assist me in managing this local mission.'

'Mark and I will need a little time to discuss your generous proposals. At this stage,' Simon nodded to Mark, 'we can see no difficulty at all in your joining us and look forward to welcoming you aboard to help change the world.'

A few days later, after much deliberation and a great deal of work ironing out the small but significant details, not least of which was Puffing Billy's eccentricity, Simon and Mark welcomed him as an equal member of the board of governors. The Eastern European tradesmen worked night and day to ready the church at Brighton in time for Mark's second major address. Billy would be allowed to 'compere' the televised rendering at Brighton. Mark would announce the result of the internet election for the seven cities' locations at the end of his address. Again, both churches were a sell-out.

Throughout the weeks to Mark's long-awaited second address, the 'Twenty-First-Century Movement' membership increased beyond possible expectations. Revenue streams from the burgeoning worldwide community and the internet afforded the establishment of many more churches up and down the UK. Creating an international network began to formulate in the governors' minds. Each mission was to be run by an experienced man or woman of commercial business backed up by a team of devoted university graduate followers. By now, numbering twelve, most of the governors earned just a living wage plus expenses and maintained rigid discipline throughout the group. They, of course, were answerable to the trinity of the original undertaking.

The Lido Green Cadillac swept through the high street in majestic style as before. The wall screen displayed Mark's arrival, making his way through the immense crowd outside, cheering in adulation. Speakers and screens were in position along the length of the street for the unfortunate individuals without tickets. Mark advanced to the pulpit with a trailing dark-blue gown, enjoying every moment of the vibrant atmosphere spiced with a dash of fanaticism. Arms aloft, he quieted the assembly as the overhead lights slowly dimmed to welcome the brotherhood near and far. The image of the hydrogen atom appeared on the screen.

'If we can start on a lighter note, Ladies and Gentlemen, the hydrogen atom displayed on the wall screen has been replaced with a stylish Ferrari 250GT Berlinetta. I remember

Champagne Charlie was quite pleased with himself when he availed himself of my company to boastfully reveal the fact that he had just paid a small fortune for the privilege of owning one. I hastened to remind him that a good friend of mine a long time ago experienced a mysterious vision whilst driving his beloved Lancia 3B coupe, a car that its designer incidentally chose for his personnel use.'

An image of a deep-dark-blue Lancia 3B coupé appeared, almost immediately replaced by a moving film of a humble Austin A40 scrambling past two A35s approaching a race-track bend. The sound of its A-series 945cc engine struggled out of the hi-fi system! A still shot of all three cars graced the considerable wall screen for the bemused audience to consider.

'To the uninitiated, the motors before you are just three diverse examples of automobiles. However, anybody with the slightest knowledge of vehicle design would recognise the compact A40 with the curved front wings sweeping aerodynamically along the straight practical flanks aside the bonnet leading up to the grill, the work of only one man, the unique Pinin Farina.' Mark began to emphasise his point as the atom briefly returned, succeeded by a single living cell's magnified picture.

'I would like to thank the hundreds of thousands of members who took the trouble to vote on the last meeting's oratory and have great pleasure in confirming that ninety-eight per cent – almost unanimous – voted that the atom is predesigned, rendering the certain existence of a designer. My point for this session is to determine the designer of a relatively simple product – car, art, or music – by merely listening and observing. But seem to have great trouble determining the origin of everything now alive on this planet. I suppose the scientists, all doing their best, will not bring themselves to admit, as with the atom, that the first living cells cannot have just appeared given as much infinite time at their disposal by random chemical reaction. On close examination, it is clear that the living cell, although different, bears many similar characteristics to the intrinsic design of the atom. A Rembrandt is a Rembrandt, a Farina, whether Ferrari or the humble A40 is a Farina. Albeit with hindsight, their development is precisely predetermined, and I hope to show you why.

'The planet Earth spent the first 700,000 years of its existence preparing to introduce life – a very different place than it is today. Another poorly understood event by scientists, the faint young sun paradox, should have rendered the environment a lifeless snowball. However, as if by divine order, our star burning at eighty per cent capacity and much cooler than it is today became subject to magnetic storms that released cosmic rays to penetrate Earth's atmosphere. These reacted to produce ultra-insulating greenhouse gases to keep the watery haven below a warm and suitable laboratory for the intended purpose.'

Behind Mark, the wall screen displayed the drab brown lifeless landscape below. Pale yellow sunlight filtered down as the camera raced across the sky. As night's darkness approached the horizon, a flicker of colour flashed in the twilight. The ancient nocturnal region gave rise to the many shades of a trillion-electron spectrum to form a perfect aurora over the barren land.

After straightening up his notes, Mark continued: 'The atom is the basic unit of matter. The cell is the basic unit of life. Both are fundamentals for certain things. Organisms can't exist without cells, and cells can't live without atoms. The two forms are inextricably linked.

'The cell is the smallest living unit in every organism. One or more make up all living things. Every cell replicates and proliferates from pre-existing cells – except the first! Any mistakes in the process, which began 3.5 billion years ago, would terminate any future life form. They fall into three categories called domains, divided into kingdoms further down the tree of life devised by biologists.

'The unicellular *Prokaryote archaea* occupies the first domain. It has a membrane with modified lipids with different stereochemistry from its successors. They contain one circular plasmid for DNA and have a range of 491,000 to 5.7 million base pairs. They use Transfer RNA to decode the message of DNA to build proteins. They can have an outer cell wall and flagella but contain no nucleus. It takes an estimated 300 million atoms to make up this fledgling cell meticulously drafted to withstand the most extreme environments to come its way.

'In the second domain, "bacteria", we have the prokaryotic cell more abundant than the archaea from the same stable devoid of a nucleus, which is unicellular but with different characteristics. Its nucleoid region stores only one circular chromosome with its DNA genetic information. It has no nuclear envelope. It is at one loosely in the cytoplasm held in shape by a cytoskeleton. Their resilient plasma membrane encloses the cytosol, a secure area to allow all the biochemical reactions to take place there. DNA and ribosomes combine to produce proteins to gather nutrients and reproduce. Their size, however, is small. The surface-area-to-volume-ratio-limit restricts the growth limit because they have less DNA for protein. Some have flagella to enable movement, while others have pili to help bacteria adhere to surfaces. The prokaryotic cell reproduces asexually with binary fusion – with no membrane-bound organelles or complex chromosomes to consider, it merely splits duplicated DNA into two separate cells. The one circular double-stranded supercoiled DNA chromosome can have between 160,000 to 12.2 million base pairs in bacteria. The simplicity of the structure makes it possible to proliferate almost everywhere on Earth, including in our own bodies. The prokaryotic cell is programmed to undertake uncountable diverse tasks to protect and generate life, with the old archaea still operating at a base level when needed.

Mark strained forward to captivate the audience's attention: 'There are no evolutionary steps from the bacteria to the third "domain" Eukaryote. No intermediate stages; just a giant step to a sophisticated solution based on the primary chassis of the two existing cells, all based on the exact intrinsic design. The primary data they had to offer was to assemble a product designed to operate for billions of years to come, the eukaryotic cell!

'One thousand times larger but still microscopic to accommodate the necessary machinery to furnish the planet with plants, animals, fungi, protists, and, not to forget *Homo sapiens*. The eukaryote is the prime mover but is still accompanied by bacteria and archaea performing their basic tasks.'

Fritz Lang's silent movie Metropolis brought to mind the busy production and transportation in the industrialised Roaring Twenties. The wall screen began to pulsate with chemical and electrical movement, and the people were mesmerised as before with a sense of abstract mystery. Before them, the magnified image portrayed a much more sophisticated engine of nature – no silver escalators between black-and-white skyscrapers and factories with busy people transporting goods with the urgent need for progress.

The screen's beautiful representation showed the plasma cell membrane with various forms consisting of protein and a phospholipid layer.

Mark continued: 'This selective barrier keeps the unwanted outside, and all that is necessary inside. The nucleus is protected by its outer shell at the heart of the cell, unlike the prokaryotic cell that stores DNA in double-helix linear strands tightly wrapped around protein histone spools to form chromosomes. Between the nucleus and the plasma membrane are the membrane-bound organelles. The mitochondria are the powerhouse to supply the adenosine triphosphate – ATP – molecule to fuel the cell. The endoplasmic reticulum – ER – is the principal regulator of cell function interacting with other organelles. The Golgi complex moves molecules from the ER to their target destination. It packages, folds and is responsible for the end products. The ribosomes are the micro-machines for making proteins: translating information to link amino acids is central to the process. The lysosomes are responsible for conducting a unique mosaic of crucial assignments. They break down worn-out cell parts and are mandatory for defending against invading viruses and bacteria. All these are stabilised and supported by the cytoskeleton, which sends signals throughout the cell. It consists of three filaments.

'Microtubules are microscopic cylindrical tubes involved in mitosis, intercellular transport, and cell shape. Microfilaments are tiny protein polymers of actin that react to produce muscle movement, cell division, and order. Intermediate filaments provide support for the plasma membrane, do not use energy, and desist from motion. Centrioles assist in cell division. A watery substance called cytosol surrounds all the organelles. A thick solution called cytoplasm fills the inner space to host enzymatic reactions and metabolic activity. A cell is now ready to advance to the twenty-first century multiplying by mitosis starting approximately 1.5 billion years ago to produce infinite numbers of genetically identical daughter cells to their mothers with not a single chromosome, more or less. On the other hand, a little later, they were enjoined by meiosis, which divides twice to produce four daughter cells containing half the genetic information gametes, sex cells: sperm is male, while eggs are female.

'The naked world had waited long enough with its skies of assorted colours in the morning and sundown. Gravitation helped to push back the shallow waters into oceans. The night aurora's spectrum is glorious in blue-green, yellow, orange, and shades of red, performing their art to nothingness and no one below.

'Genesis 1:9: "Let the waters under the heaven be gathered into one place so that dry land may appear."

'The now-dry land and seas wrestled with the anarchy of the primordial weather conditions to gain a foothold for its first solitary living cell. The archaea were engineered to multiply in the asexual process of binary fusion by duplicating exact copies of its unfathomable molecule DNA into two new cells. These similarly divide within hours to four and then deliver in a matter of weeks two billion, one hundred and forty-seven million, four hundred and eighty-three thousand, six hundred and forty-eight identical cells. In their wake, the eukaryote quickly follows each one pre-programmed to produce specialised cellular organisms for life on the planet.

'The first evolutionary need was to acquire energy to sustain this rapid proliferation. Our ancestor cells achieved diversification under the instruction encoded in the DNA's base pairs sequenced to produce long chains of amino acids collectively known as protein. This information determines their three-dimensional shape and formulates what they do.

'We cannot consider at this stage a cell to have free will or in any way be conscious, and it, therefore, must act under its ordered instructions for its progress,' interjected Mark to remind the audience of his presence.

'The dynamic organelle chloroplast with its own small proportion of DNA added to the eukaryote introduced the giant step of photosynthesis. The two diverged, one to form multicellular plant life and the other to kickstart multicellular animal life. These basic building blocks, over immense time, behave similarly to the atom. As atoms bond to form the Periodic Table of Elements, cells behave as instructed to create multicellular organisms. Common sense tells the modern man that a 3.5 billion-year process for life can proceed only if you have an error correction system, another structure in the chromosome: DNA polymerase.'

Mark stood back to make his final address of the night.

'It now becomes clear that the most complex molecule in the universe, DNA, with its infinite command configuration and abstract orders, cannot have originated on Earth within the first living cell at random. Who has primarily compartmentalised the operating system for its safety as with the atom? Most bacteria have one or two circular chromosomes comfortable in their primitive environment. The mitochondria contain a small amount of DNA. Subsequently, after following the arrow of time, the matured coordinator of animal, plant, and human life, the chromosome functions in the security of the eukaryotic cell's nucleus. From here, the DNA must issue its instructions for growth and replication.

'There are twenty-two pairs of chromosomes – autosomes – and one pair of sex chromosomes – allosome – located in the human cell's nucleus. These are long strings of DNA shaped like a double-helix spiral ladder. At the end of each rung is a base pair made from two of the following: A-Adenine with T-Thymine, G-Guanine with C-Cystine, and one at each end. A selected stretch of this is a gene. There are 6 billion base pairs of DNA in the human cell. The average number of atoms per human cell is roughly 100 trillion. The number of cells in the human body is 37.2 trillion. The length of an unwound strand of DNA in each diploid cell is two metres, which is 100 trillion metres per human. Placed end to end, this would reach the Sun and back three hundred times! Chromosome one, the largest, consists of 247 million base pairs: 3,000 genes. All twenty-three pairs add up to 34,000 genes. Once encoded by the chromosome, the gene regulates the protein's size and shape, determining its function. Proteins make up cells, which make tissues and tissues make organs.'

Mark paused for effect and continued.

'The two hundred or so different cells in our bodies thankfully can be regarded as reasonably stable entities. The DNA molecule empowered by its ability to sustain these diverse forms using simple encoding is mostly beyond present-day understanding to decipher a sequence to perform a realistic treatment. It has been doing so all of history. Residing in its protective layer – the nucleus – the mind-boggling process of transcription and translation occurs all the time in your body. The information in a strand of DNA is copied into a new molecule of Messenger RNA – known as mRNA – by the enzyme RNA polymerase at transcription. DNA also encodes mRNA to exit the nucleus, enter the cytoplasm, and travel onto the ribosome with its newly acquired template. Steady motion takes it through to its appointed sites in the ribosome. To a lesser extent, the ER patiently waits for Transfer RNA – tRNA – to decode the approaching mRNA to match its complementary anticodon sequences to produce an amino acid chain – polypeptide – which later folds into protein to perform its cell functions. After translation, the mRNAs degrade at a defined rate when the cell's protein requirements are met.

The whole process is called gene expression and is the stage in a cell's working-life interphase: the time spent building up health fitness while making and replicating more DNA in preparation for the never-ending bouts of cell division mitosis and meiosis. The goal of mitosis is to produce genetically identical daughter cells with not a single chromosome, more or less. Their primary purpose is to grow through multiplication, not size, orchestrated by the chromosome to produce all the composite parts of living organisms like us.

'On the other hand, the purpose of meiosis is to produce gametes, the sex cells sperm and egg. In human reproduction, crossing and transferring genetic information results in DNA variety and new gene combinations to make us unique.'

Mark crossed his arms on his chest and intensified his speech with an invigorated passion for inciting his followers' zeal. Images of ecstatic supporters worldwide appeared on the wall screen, captivated by every word.

'Yes, mitosis is now in the business of cloning cells to produce trillions of plant and body parts. Lungs, kidneys, livers, hearts, and so forth, forever!

'Yes, meiosis is now in the business of mixing coded genes for individuality: living plants, animals, frogs, birds, and humans; humans with different eye colours, skin colours and personalities are the only species coded for consciousness and exchange of information through speech!

'If time means anything, it did not take much of it in the grand scale of things for the chromosome to engineer these living forms' existence to occupy every square inch of the planet.'

Mark raised his eyes and began to tremble with emotion.

'There are uncountable trillions of treacherous hurdles for the building blocks of life to pass over, any one of which would be insurmountable for random events to succeed. This is not the survival of the fittest − it is a design for future purpose!

'As with the atom, the design for purpose is fundamentally at hand from the beginning. Everybody now understands that no living cell in all of time has existed without DNA. The information stored within this molecule has been expressed through coding so that *Homo sapiens* should benefit from chromosome 7 Fox P2, the power of speech and the activation of a gene somewhere in the ninety-eight per cent of non-coded DNA for consciousness. The gift of humankind's dominion over all living things is in these genes.

Genesis 1:28: Then God blessed them, and God said to them "Be fruitful and multiply and replenish the earth and subdue it, rule over the fish in the sea, the birds of heaven and every living thing that moves on the earth."

'Buried in the undeciphered strands is the instruction that humankind must have faith in God and his intended purpose. Do not cast aside your holy books and scriptures yet! It is too early to say that our designer did not inspire the meaning of some of the words written by *Homo sapiens* to guide us through difficult times to the present day. Science today can easily deal with inaccuracies if it wants to. Nevertheless, the immaculate conception, miracles performed, and the resurrection of Jesus do not stretch our imagination today as science cooperates with our ingrained faith and renders our quest more certain.'

Beads of sweat were now running down Mark's face due to his oration's increasing tempo.

'The acquisition and distribution of information during all the living cell's stages to the present day is key to understanding that evolution is a pre-programmed system. Charles Darwin believed that God existed as a first cause without the knowledge of genetics. Albert Einstein was much the same. Our movement closely examines the existence of intellect in the first stages of the human embryo.

'People are continually deliberating with their God across the globe in preparation for the end of the beginning. Billions of minds seek telepathic contact to establish the next stage of development. The time has now come to harness this power of thought. Our movement is ready to lead the world with discipline and peace into a new age!'

Mark concluded his second address with arms now raised and reminded the listening multitudes to vote for the locations of seven cities. Once again, he descended from his rostrum to tumultuous acclamation.

7
Jaguar V-12 E-Type Roadster

(Finished in Heather with Purple Leather trim)

They say that success breeds success in many a quarter of the motor trade, a maxim certainly truer of the old days than now. (What the saying has not changed is that money usually follows money.) Mark and Billy had recognised the odd familiar name crop up on applications to join the movement. However, on Mark's triumphant exit, it came as some surprise to notice two such characters among the adoring crowd: Johnny One Leg and his old partner Hans the German. Later he touched on this with Simon, who, as we know, believed in God and certainly not in coincidence. He possessed a sceptical persona that bordered on paranoia that matured into full-grown apprehension when confronted with characters from Mark's long and illustrious past. Shouldering a busy mind, he spent a restless night pondering over the emergence of a strong-willed, necessary High Order to govern their movement.

The church at Shelverton, many moons and sermons later, now had a different attendance. Stylishly clothed, fanatical senior members now occupied every seat in the auditorium. Flags and banners flew high in the streets outside – this was a rally for all intents and purposes. The would-be idealistic converts of the early days were still very welcome but were duty-bound to attend at any one of the now fifty churches situated across the realm. The growing European and worldwide following could witness the events at Shelverton on the internet.

A table spanned the church in front of the altar. The twelve top administrators suitably attired in dazzling uniforms as befitted their high rank sat imperiously, proud of their loyal subjects present in the hall. The wall screen showed panoramic views across all the continents. After much debate over the past weeks, each fully subscribed and paid-up member used their votes to decide the location for the seven cities. The digital clock counted down to zero at the top right-hand corner adjacent to the CC21 logo and ended the election.

In today's centre chair, Billy sitting with Hans the German to his left and Miles Beaumaris on his right, stood up at the appointed second. All three men adorned in regalia as befitted their status looked fit and healthy for their years.

'Ladies, gentlemen, followers, and all of humanity, I have the honour to announce the results today. The world leaders will be waiting with you in anticipation of our decision on this historic day. We hope God above will look down on us and appreciate our willingness to serve his divine purpose.'

Miles Beaumaris drove down to Brighton in Hans's esteemed company some months before this momentous event. The V-12 E-Type, finished in heather with a dark purple leather interior and a classic solid dashboard in matt black, sped through the driving rain that streamed up the chevroned bonnet towards its windscreen. The polished chrome wire wheels spun the water away. Despite the weather, it was a very pleasurable trip. Both men had met many times before and discussed the burgeoning movement and ways to keep control from the top. Loyalty to Mark and Simon was undisputed, but the immediate reason for their visit to Billy was top secret. The two of them knew to avoid this hallowed subject without the presence of Billy.

Miles eased the Jag through the grounds. Looking younger than ever, Louisa answered the door, conducted the pair into the discreetly lit lounge, and retired. In familiar fashion, The Mighty Wurlitzer Pipe Organ heralded them with a hearty rendition of Beethoven's *Ode to Joy* (presumably for Hans's benefit). Billy hurdled over his stool and greeted them warmly.

'Afternoon, Bill,' Miles acknowledged him with a raised hand with a sardonic look on his face and further remarked, 'You and your good wife, Louisa, look three years younger than when we last met!'

Hans reflected that all three of them knew why. However, the healthy new lifestyle could not improve Billy's keen, angular Quasimodo form!

'How do, Hans? Did you have a good trip over?'

'Ja. Sehr gut.'

'Excellent. We all appreciate why we are here. So let's get down to business. We will prepare the way for Mark's forthcoming announcement. I'll go first. As you both realise, my scientific Oxford team here in Brighton has made a limited but staggering breakthrough. We now have enough to proceed in conjunction with Hans's operation. My English team has now joined the Germans at a location unknown to either party to continue their research. Most scientists involved are only aware of their part of the total programme. We acquired a remote monastery situated in a ravine close to the pinnacle of one of the planet's highest mountain ranges. Of course, you are aware of this as governors of the movement; you all approved the colossal expense of converting the buildings into one of the world's largest and most advanced medical centres. Nevertheless, no one knows its exact location. At every stage, we constructed the facility in total secrecy. All past and present employees are transported there by windowless aircraft on automatic pilot. Aircrew and experienced aviators are always on board in case of emergency. I must impress on you that we must take extreme measures for the safety of the operation and ourselves, owing to the usual human political rationale. Only the inner circle possesses the wherewithal to conduct the next stage. High-powered disciples – best not to refer to them as salesmen – will spread the word across the globe to convince nations' leaders. We can't have an airliner full of politicians, and car dealers trusted with the universe's future, can we? Wouldn't seem right, would it?' Billy laughed.

'Anyhow, it is now time for our first visit to our facility to undergo genetic modification. We will join the 150 hand-picked operators selected for our mission tomorrow morning. Some of these we already know. Put plainly, it will be an induction to prepare you to persuade your allotted politicians to back our cause. We will explain the necessary details of Hans's and my team's research on our arrival. There's no need for that now. Louisa and I volunteered for the trials at Brighton, and we can confirm we've never looked back!

'We both know the nature of the process, Bill, and can't wait to start. I had an idea you had gone with the trials and, with the two of us working together, who knows? You're both looking good,' commented Hans.

'I'll park up the Jag, then, and maybe we can go for a few beers down at that local pub in the village,' Miles suggested.

'Good idea,' replied Billy. A terrific evening out and a good steak meal contrived to make for a decent night's sleep.

The assembled party went across the tarmac to the unmarked silver airliner the following day. These experienced men exchanged banter catalysed by slight nerves and humour. Once aboard, Miles recognised familiar faces among the group. Hans and Billy were out of sight at the rear of the cabin. The aircrew seated the rest of them comfortably four at a table facing each other. The breakfast menu was fruit juice, full English or American. It felt strange as the plane with no window view accelerated to its take-off speed and lifted, driving its way up into the sky.

Sitting opposite Miles was a dealer nicknamed 'Cheque-less in Cardiff'. Miles's mind travelled years back, smiling to himself as he remembered. Information technology was in its earliest days. The Labour government had relaxed the credit controls that squeezed the potless* working man out of the car market in its zeal for modernity. The established franchise dealers, happy in their coexistence with their upper- and middle-class clients, preferred things as they were! Not so on the second-hand pitches across the land. One of whose was Cheque-less.

Some well-meaning Derbyshire doorstep money lenders hatched up a scheme to revolutionise vehicle finance. They took it upon themselves to target their familiar areas (with 'no deposit finance'). The directors, therefore, stuck with their old doorstep favourites: Liverpool, Leeds, Cardiff, and Manchester. Marlon Brazil (Cheque-less) pleaded with them not to appoint specific dealers with short-term strategies (greed) and that The Workingman's Car Bank (TWCB) would be well advised to steer clear of these areas of dubious creditworthiness. However, after a few months, rumours abounded that these punters were not paying off their loans. To make things worse, the agreements might even be unenforceable in law. Marlon looked at Miles and knew what he was thinking.

Laughing, Marlon reminded him. 'There was I signing the punters up like there was no tomorrow. The cheques came a few days later. It was like pennies off a plate! Until, of course, after some time, they didn't. Convinced these happy times were over, paying a visit to these double-breasted suits became necessary. A lady receptionist met me on the ground floor of their multi-storey office block and provided a cup of coffee. She politely asked me to wait for Mr Ormerod, head of vehicle finance. I was ready to go in heavy to get what I could, but instinct held me back.

***

'Ah, Mr Brazil, I've been looking forward to meeting you in person at last. One gets so little chance to meet real people outside this ivory tower.'

---

* Potless means a working person who is slightly better off than being penniless

Marlon thought, 'If you got to meet some of the people you've been lending money to recently, your first wish would be to remain safely within!'

Marlon duly followed Ormerod down to the basement. Down the well-lit marble stairway, the two of them trooped and then along a corridor illuminated with wall lamps to a double door resembling a bank vault entrance.

'If you don't mind, Mr Brazil, would you please step well back as I put in the combination?' He then theatrically entered a series of numbers and led the way into a room that should belong to the world of James Bond and *The Man from U.N.C.L.E.*

'This room is the centre of our operation,' Ormerod proudly announced. 'In here, we have the latest twentieth-century banking technology.'

On the surrounding walls were large spools of what looked like tape-recording gear sporadically moving around an inch at a time. Housed below these were long black chests fitted with instrument panels of all kinds. All very impressive. Still, Marlon wondered, 'Does it record all the payments clients from the over-spill towns are not making?'

Sitting opposite, Marlon could not help laughing after all this time while Ormerod continued to enthuse as he danced around the room and cheerfully asked if he could borrow Marlon's pen. Beginning to enjoy the moment, he duly obliged.

'Oh, ye of little faith, Marlon. I'm surprised at you! What do you think that machine in the middle of the room is?'

In those days, Marlon thought a computer was something the kids played with, so he demurely hazarded a guess: 'A computer?'

'No! No! No!' Ormerod replied, gesturing in a superior way at all the surrounding electronics. 'The computer is what surrounds us. No, that's the cheque-printing machine, and it's broken down.'

Immediately, Ormerod pulled a chequebook from his jacket pocket and wrote a cheque for the amount they owed Marlon. However, they lost millions and ceased trading a short time later.

***

'All part of life's rich experience, Marlon. Our movement consists of men of the world with guile and accomplishment. The scientists know the value of being in good hands,' said Miles as he and Marlon chatted over a wholesome breakfast and briefly joined the two strangers at the table in casual conversation. After a few hours, the aircraft assumed its position, ready for descent and smoothly coasted down through the snow peaks to the valley below.

Above the sheer ice cliffs on either side, wall-to-wall blue skies trapped the plain beneath in splendid isolation. The low temperature sustained the newly fallen snow but was not cold enough to restrict the river's meandering flow. A flat escalator transferred the travellers and their luggage to their appointed accommodation. Their destination, Franklin Town, consisted of modernised single-storey cottages tastefully arranged around the medical facility and a town square with every possible comfort: bars, restaurants, sports, and function rooms. At 5 p.m., after a decent time to settle in, our company of about 150 persons met as requested to listen to Professor Lovall detail his plans for our forthcoming treatment.

'Good evening to you all. I hope the trip here was pleasant enough. I am sure you will find it worthwhile. The course will take ten days to complete, and other than attending the various procedures, everyone is free to sample the local attractions available. Nevertheless, please adhere to the guidance for suitable clothing for the outdoors and follow the guide to social distancing in your welcome pack. The genetic engineers and doctors from England and Germany have perfected their procedures for a limited time of age reversal: fifteen years. After which, you will begin to age again to give an average of thirty years of extra life – adequate time for our cities of the future to develop further solutions.

'Secrecy at this stage is paramount until our "disciples here" have completed their mission. Judas Iscariot, a disciple of Jesus's closest followers, betrayed him for a paltry sum. An outcome we cannot contemplate concerning our objective. Therefore, we must put certain safeguards in place. I think we can all agree on that. In the unlikely event of one of you risking your long future years, we have the means to cancel out any work done. In the years to come, the world will maintain law and order by cancelling extra years of life as befits the crime. The days of sacrificing human life are over.

'Without going into too much detail, I will outline the course of action for the week.' The professor had keen blue eyes and had clearly gained his patients' trust with his mannerism. Exuding a knowledgeable presence, he continued, 'Our protein engineers, after lengthy research, can now control codon usage to custom design "mutant libraries". We can employ advanced DNA sequencing to make new proteins. Our computers design DNA templates that can code for specific amino acid sequences. In your case, these DNA mutations will transfer to your chromosomes. They will translate into proteins for the elongation of your telomeres and the rejuvenation of their protective caps. Your stem-cell therapy will reduce your senescent cell presence and require a general anaesthetic. We propose conducting vasectomy for men and total tubal sterilisation for women during this process – a condition of receiving this operation, as previously agreed. On no account can your new genes be inheritable at this stage. The portable hyperbaric pressurised oxygen chambers supplied to your rooms should be used for one hour a day during your stay. We are all on this fantastic adventure together, and I look forward to meeting you throughout the days ahead.'

The regime for their treatment was necessarily subject to discipline. However, it still left plenty of time to discuss the approach to the difficult days of their stay ahead. As hard-headed business people, it was not difficult to agree on methods that might seem undemocratic to achieve their objectives. There was no other way. Simon and Mark, both willingly there to undergo the treatment, agreed that the end justified the means for them to fulfil God's purpose.

Not long after their return, the hierarchy and influential sales executives armed with their new life expectancy awaited

Billy's momentous announcement. Behind him, the wall screen revealed a lush green volcanic atoll set in the blue ocean. 'With a substantial majority, the city's location for age reversal and associated genetic engineering is a tropical island off the coast of Brazil. It shall be named Geras!'

The wall screen changed as the drone camera flashed east across the Atlantic Ocean. The chosen location for the city selected to find the answers that lie in our genetic code was Boa Vista, a volcanic island off the west coast of Africa within easy reach of Geras. Top scientists from every nation-state could congregate on this beautiful island in the city of Silvanus to specialise in genetic research.

'Another popular choice to triumph over the immortal, immature dividing cancer cell will be named Hera Hera, a few miles north of Rabat, Morocco. I will hand you over to Hans for the next results.'

Hans began, 'Our membership has decided that the southern hemisphere is the safest place to develop quantum computers. Therefore, I can confirm that the almost unanimous choice is New Zealand. This city will be known as Quantum Springs and, hopefully, will provide all the help our other cities will need as information becomes available.

'The city that requires the most space and cooperation with the world's most advanced nations will be in Australia. The planet's terrestrial space station is accessible to every future astronaut from whatever race or creed. As with all our cities, it will comprise every facility for research and a high standard of living extracted from the most modern means.'

Hans began to highlight the excitement of the future while not forgetting the quest for our granted purpose. Transfixed by his presence, the audience listened to his final words: 'The glistening and brilliant stepping stone in Australia to the eternal universe will be named Cosmos!' With that, he introduced Miles Beaumaris.

'We all thank Hans for his announcement. I am pleased to inform you of the membership's final two decisions. The next city is to develop a fusion reactor, bringing clean, cheap energy to the world. Due to our chancy record concerning nuclear power – remember Vice Admiral Vasily Arkhipov – it is evident that such a blueprint must be a joint effort in a singular metropolis. The unequivocal location has to be Switzerland, in the brand-new city of Cratos.

'We must now update *Homo sapiens*' different approaches to serve God, the knower of all things. Understanding universal love and trust will become more apparent when we begin to achieve our goals. The importance of this is fundamental. The ability to exchange information freely with one another is a gift we possess but have not always taken advantage of to the full. Tribal and international competition has yielded some results regarding our dominance and survival as a species. Now it is time to work toward our maker. We urge doctors of faith to come together from every corner of the planet to reconcile their differences. The way forward has to be a combination of science and spiritual love given to us by the Lord. The 104 billion souls who have lived or are still alive today depend on our faith to take brave steps forward! Egypt is the city of splendour's location to accommodate the world's spiritual leaders for this divine purpose. The chosen name for this seat of learning is Armana.'

Miles accepted the arena's deafening applause as a Roman emperor would at the games. After some considerable time, he raised his arms to quell the veneration. With style suited to the gods at Delphi, confidently plotting humanity's future, he handed the chair back to Billy.

'Brothers and sisters, we will go out from here to convince the leaders of the great and wealthy powers of the urgency for our cause. Although none of the locations is within their boundaries, they will profit from the vast investment opportunities and international cooperation results as never before. Our trained advocates know what to do to spread the word across the planet's continents. We will update as soon as possible when we make significant progress.'

At this moment, the occupants of the top table filed down the central aisle in a dramatic but disciplined fashion. The now-expected commendation of the frenzied crowd accompanied their exit.

Within a few years, the new twenty-first-century church continued to inspire a large and growing proportion of the world's population. The running of the now substantial operation was no longer possible from offices at Shelverton. They established the new headquarters in London at a prestigious brand-new glass-fronted block, 'Lambeth Cross', furnished with every modern contrivance to assist the cause's hierarchy. The updated churches of learning and worship appealed greatly to information technology's younger generations.

As time passed, the belief that God connected to daily scientific discovery prompted followers to link in and satisfy their genetic curiosity, creating another self-fulfilling body of research. The steady growth of respect and trust of the older generation to get things done without bloodshed increased the movement's somewhat unorthodox leaders' support. It was no surprise to the panel of dignitaries assembled in the control room in Lambeth Cross's depths to witness the small delegation's safe arrival in Washington DC on the wall screens.

It was a beautiful sunny springtime morning over there. The lead car, a V-12 E-Type in heather with a deep purple leather interior, looked resplendent – hood down while keeping to the speed limit and making its way down Pennsylvania Avenue. The rest of the representatives followed in a luxuriously appointed Winnebago generously supplied by the Americans. The unannounced visit attracted no crowds or onlookers. The hosts had organised permission to pass by 1,600 Pennsylvania Avenue – the White House – and a suitably clad group of troopers genially waved them through.

Among the twenty or so observers in the control room, Miles sat between Simon and Mark, rapidly beginning to take a keen interest in the proceedings in Washington DC displayed on the wall screen.

'That Jaguar wouldn't be the one I sold to Billy for his collection, would it?'

'Good observation, my son! And quite correct. Billy and his civil service colleagues agree that the Jag would be the most suitable classic sports car to befit an honorary RAF chaplain. He persuaded Air Vice-Marshal Ron Wallington and his good lady wife, Barbara, to come out of their early retirement to head our delegation and conduct our diplomatic affairs at Camp David. We hope your exquisite example of sports motoring will go down in history.'

'Can we zoom in on the vice-marshal? I seem to recognise him.'

'If we must,' replied Mark. Simon looked uncomfortable and restless during this turn of conversation. On the magnified screen, the driver in command of the vehicle, with the gait of a professional chauffeur, revealed a familiar face from Miles's illustrious past!

'No relation to the revered right honourable third Viscount Palmerston, prime minister at the height of British power in the reign of Queen Victoria Empress of India, I presume?' quipped Simon.

'A very searching question, that is,' acknowledged Mark. 'There may be some hereditary genetic resemblance. I must say that the highest authority advising the elected British government vouches for his pedigree. A very private man, though. His history is a bit hard to get hold of, but Billy assures us he is the best man for the job. He has established a great relationship with his backup team, and everyone is confident of his exceeding expectations.'

Ron's wife, Barbara, relaxed back into the purple leather as he smoothly gained speed, leaving Washington's suburbs behind. At a comfortable distance, the Winnebago was visible in the rear-view mirror. The road ahead was typical of the many that English and Scottish engineers had designed worldwide. The terrain that frequently called for no overtaking was mainly a single carriageway with double yellow lines in the centre. Nevertheless, the smooth curves fashioned with perfect camber to cope with the gentle ascent into the forested ramparts of the Catoctin Mountains made for a paramount driving experience.

Barbara had always loved Ron. As the wood-scented slipstream whistled past the side of the drophead roadster*, she sensed with pride that together, they faced their most challenging but exciting task ever. With Billy's help, she procured all the accoutrements to assemble a complete wardrobe for their mission. The road trailed its way upwards through Frederick County, Maryland, to the small town of Thurmont. Further on, Ron surmised, 'This must be the Hog Rock Vista pull-in, Babs. We're in the Catoctin National Park, the Blue Ridge Mountains foothills that form the Appalachian system.'

'There's no mountain high enough, as the song goes. Let's stop here for a coffee and take stock,' Babs replied.

Ron joined his team aboard the Winnebago for the last briefing to remind everybody of their mission's importance.

'It's going to be a relaxed and informal meeting, but on no account, drop your guard.' With that, he alighted the motor home with a cheerful wave. In Ron's short absence, Barbara put the final touches to her already immaculate presence. She had decided to combine her two-carat Burmese ruby and diamond ring with her simple 24-carat gold necklace to display her marriage's longevity to Ron. Babs pulled on a plain white silk Queen Elizabeth II headscarf to counter any suggestion of opulence. She looked her Air Vice-Marshal over. No jewellery or fine medals, dressed in Royal Navy-blue casual slacks and top to make the best first impression.

Behind the wheel and at one with the Jag, Ron motored down Park Central Road and turned right past a wishing-well sign inscribed 'Camp David'. Both vehicles passed through the gatehouse to the central car park, where a small reception awaited them. Two rows of junior naval officers immaculately dressed in blue and white sailor suits stood to attention on either side of the path to Aspen Lodge, the President's private quarters. The President's chief of staff and two aides conducted Ron

*   Drophead roadster is a convertible sports car

and Barbara through the naval ensemble to be welcomed by America's First Family on the sun terrace. A reception committee politely escorted Ron's small supporting group to their allotted cabins and invited them to make free use of all the leisure facilities to hand.

The President, six foot three with broad shoulders, was cordial and friendly and soon understood that Ron was of the same caste. He immediately dispensed with official titles in favour of first names. Dwight (the President) introduced his wife, Kelly, and their two sons, Bobby and Vincent. Ron responded and introduced Barbara and himself. After a few minutes of small talk, Dwight suggested they could stroll around the facility, to which everyone agreed. They passed by Laurel Lodge, the venue for the first meeting at 6 p.m. The fresh air and scenery were exhilarating. Of course, the Americans knew of the movement's goals and privately concurred with their objectives. Their respective civil servants stressed the importance of the relevant members of the President's cabinet being present. Everybody spent the early afternoon ambling among the nature trails and tall evergreen trees. However, the time arrived to prepare for the evening's conference, and Barbara, true to form, fussed over the vestments.

A long refectory table to accommodate ten persons per side, more if necessary, with a chair at each end, furnished the stateroom for the forthcoming talks. The American emissaries consisted of the chief of staff, the secretary of transportation, the secretary of energy, the presidential science adviser, the director of homeland security, the secretary of commerce, the attorney general, the secretary of state, the secretary of defence, the secretary of the treasury and, of course, in the chair the President of the United States. The envoy of the Twenty-First Century Church sat facing these honourable men. They consisted of the first clerk for age reversal, the professor of cancer research, Professor Lovall, the head of genetic engineering, the first clerk for quantum computer research, the professor of astronomy and quantum mechanics, the chief coordinator of interplanetary space travel, the professor of classical, quantum and nuclear physics, the director of transport, and the chief administrator of religious integration with Air Vice-Marshal Ron Wallington in the chair.

As the President, accompanied by Air Vice-Marshal Wallington, entered the room, everyone stood to their feet and subsequently took to their seats. The President opened the proceedings with a hearty welcome and invited the Honorary Chaplain Air Vice-Marshal Wallington to take the chair. Ronald arose to speak, now dressed in formal RAF attire adorned with the appropriate chrome badges of office.

'Your kind hospitality is much appreciated to make it possible for me to enlighten you and your cabinet on recent developments that will undoubtedly affect the current world order. I am sure everybody in the room has been briefed and is well aware of our movement's progress and published objectives. We have now reached a difficult time. The next steps into the future require the cooperation of the world's most powerful nation-states. The odds that the atom, which consists of 99.9 per cent of electromagnetic space, could create itself by random events over infinite time are incalculable. In fact, impossible! The primary building block of the universe is also the fundamental constituent of the first microscopic living cell. We must replace faith in God's existence with certainty.' Ronald glanced compassionately down the rank of hardened American politicians. His representatives maintained a serene presence opposite their hosts.

'My team and I are here to persuade you to begin to abandon the old civilisation of nation-states in favour of world cooperation. Economies are converging towards a social capitalist order where the best systems will prevail under the auspices of decentralised local government. That, however, is for the future. With this in mind, we must focus on constructing the seven cities. The world must undertake the seven programmes in unison, any one of which could result in a nation-state gaining world domination under the old system. I am sure you are all aware that the ever-competing countries are becoming restless about the predominance of space in and out of the world's atmosphere. The media spreads suspicion to foster human fear, the most significant driver of the paranoid stampede to mass insanity. No one suggests that you should drop your guard – far from it. Let us consider the words of Isaiah.

Isaiah 2:4: "He will be the judge between nations. Arbiter among many peoples. They shall hammer their swords into ploughshares and their spears into pruning hooks. Nation will not lift sword against nation and never again will they learn war."

Isaiah 14:26: "This is the plan prepared for the whole Earth; this is the hand stretched out over all nations."

'Nevertheless, the world's leaders now have to work closely together, bonding over many years into beneficial executive power. Control and practical use of the new resources provided by scientific advancement in our cities will be universal. We will demand today's leaders form a civil service executive to oversee the cities' growth and integration to benefit humanity. They must remain within this domain to nurse the nation-states out of their childhood when out of political office. With information exchange at your fingertips and what we are about to propose, it must be feasible to form a senior senate on Earth comprised of experienced world politicians. It will be your responsibility to oversee the independence and that the research results are shared among the citizens of the planet. Scientists and members of the medical profession from all corners of the world are flocking to join our cause. They all appreciate that their nations have educated them and will continue to do so. However, the enthusiasm for a combined effort such as this has overwhelming support.'

Ronald sensed that the Americans were becoming restless due to no concrete news to get their interest. You could tell they wondered why they were here listening to somebody else's dreams. They assumed the USA held the technological lead in most things over the rest of the world. But they were wrong!

Smiling, Ronald raised his voice a little: 'Mr President, Ladies and Gentlemen present, what I am about to tell you must be subject to the utmost discretion, at least in the short term. Shall we say secrecy? Our movement elects to conceal the location of the research facility in Franklin Town from the world's surveillance, including yours. Our teams of genetic engineers, doctors and scientists have perfected this establishment's age-reversal procedure. We can offer everybody in this room thirty years of extra life with more to come. Almost certainly, with the worldwide effort, we seek much more. The opportunity on the table for you and yours here and now is to live at least one hundred and twenty years!'

Ronald now had the room's undivided attention as the host's presence of mind began to swim. 'Men must undergo vasectomy, and the women total tubal sterilisation to avoid any possibility of their newly activated genes becoming inheritable. The suggested age we have put forward for participation is sixty. Your wife will be eligible, and when the time comes, the immediate family also. Each participant's age will eventually reverse to forty-five and resume ageing back to sixty and returning to natural life expectations. We have all undergone Professor Lovall's ten-day therapy and can confirm the benefits of getting younger by the minute! The Professor will explain the treatment programme to you as it was to us on arrival at Franklin. You will find the location very hospitable, with all the amenities for social mixing. There will be many nationalities with you, and we strongly advise everyone to steer clear of any political discussion. Plenty of time for that in your long future together. I will now ask my colleague, Professor Lovall, to give you a brief outline of what lies ahead.'

The professor rose from his chair directly opposite the now incredulous Americans. 'Thanks, Air Vice-Marshal. I regard it as my duty to brief you on events so far. I am sure that you have acquainted yourselves with the undeniable conclusion that the atom and the origin of life, the living cell, is the work of an intelligent designer. Mark – who is now looking forward or backwards to his fifty-fifth birthday once more – has broadcast his irrefutable evidence worldwide.

'Of course, some die-hard evolutionists challenge our conclusions. For some reason, they don't seem to understand the role DNA and its junior partner Messenger RNA played in the four billion years of God's evolutionary plan. If evolution is just a series of random events to achieve the survival of the fittest, the world would be full of species with the ability to talk and exchange information by now. We do not argue with all life evolving from a common ancestor, just as humans grow from a totipotent zygote stem cell. On the contrary, we applaud the fact. The scribes of old interpret this with the limited discovery of scientific reality contemporary with their time. They had no idea of DNA and had to rely on philosophical thought, transcendent experience, intense meditation, inspired visions, and mental contact with God to satisfy the genetic instruction to seek spiritual reality. We can extract many examples from ancient Scripture. Let us examine, for example,

'Ezekiel 1:1–28. Ezekiel, a Jewish prophet exiled in Babylon 597 BC, had two fantastic visions of the future but wrongly interpreted them as predictions of the eventual salvation of his nation.

'Contrary to evolution, these were messages intended to show present-day generations, not his, that quantum physics and my field of genetic engineering were pre-ordained for us. In the first, he describes the arrival of supernatural light. He cannot know what he is witnessing but writes in simple indisputable words his observations. His vision is a manifestation of Einstein's discovery – E equals MC squared – that matter is light consisting of vibrating energy, ninety-nine per cent of which is ordinarily undetectable by human senses. Matter, energy, and light are interchangeable.

'In the second vision,

Ezekiel 37:1–10, only his words will do here:

> "The hand of the Lord came upon me, and He carried me out by His spirit and put me down in a plain full of bones. He made me go to and fro across them until I had been around them all; they covered the plain, countless numbers of them, and they were very dry." He said to me, 'Man, can these bones live again?' I answered, 'Only Thou knowest that, Lord God.' He said to me, 'Prophesy over these bones and say to them, O dry bones, hear the word of the LORD. This is the word of the Lord God to these bones: I will put breath into you, and you shall live. I will fasten sinews on you, bring flesh upon you, overlay you with skin, and put breath in you, and you shall live; and you shall know that I am the LORD.' I had begun to prophesy as He had bidden me, and as I prophesied, there was a rustling sound, and the bones fitted themselves together. As I looked, sinews appeared upon them, flesh covered them, and they were overlaid with skin, but there was no breath in them. Then He said to me, 'Prophesy to the wind, prophesy, man and say to it, these are the words of the Lord God: Come, O wind, come from every quarter and breathe into these slain, that they might come to life.' I began to prophesy as He had bidden me: breath came into them; they came to life and rose to their feet, a mighty host."

'These prophetic words point to the possible and allowable; they emanate from the divine. Our research into nuclear reprogramming is advancing at a daily rate. We now have all the DNA necessary in an adult nucleus to develop an induced totipotent embryonic stem cell. The need for embryonic stem cells has long caused ethical concern and is, therefore, now not an issue. Our human embryogenesis and stem-cell biology can reprogramme adult cells to embryonic ones, taking the adult cell and fusing it into a recipient egg cell. We all know the potential of this rarely discussed research.

'Today, a consequence of the Human Genome Project is that genetic diversity has been hugely underestimated. Before this, ninety-eight per cent of human coding DNA used to be regarded as junk. The key is to comprehend the non-coding DNA. Each new gene must arrive from a pre-existing one that re-emerges from the genome's vast barren portions. It is not a mutation but a suppressed gene no longer required in the evolutionary process that lies in the predetermined blueprint of DNA . . . Regulatory genes control the act of suppression, of which the Hox gene is one that, simply put, distributes your body parts to the right place. We are now sure that at least eighty per cent, if not more, of human genomic DNA, is biochemically active and has a biological function. An excellent example is a humble chicken, a distant evolutionary relation of the theropod dinosaurs. I am sure the humour of Johnny-One-Leg will remind us of the maxim "scarce as hen's teeth" while in his pursuit of clean pre-owned stock!

'Approximately 80 million years ago, birds evolved with no teeth and acquired beaks in their descent from the theropod dinosaur. Random mutation would have taken much longer. Dr John F. Fallon, busy with his research into chicken embryos in his laboratory, was utterly overwhelmed to discover that some of his specimens were growing razor-sharp reptilian teeth. Evolution supposedly had dispensed of these 80 million years before. After a great deal of research into regulatory genes and transcription factors, it emerges that working alone or with other proteins is almost undetectable as a promotor, an activator, or blocking, repressing, to recruit RNA polymerase. This means that a recent event triggered their Taploid2 gene to turn the ancient repressed gene for dinosaur teeth back on! The implications of this are staggering. Get your heads around this, boys and girls. The sequencing of activated genes is nearly complete; they are who we are, after all, and are relatively easy to understand with the help of modern computers. However, consider this: ninety-eight per cent of the human genome is still waiting for the discovery of the mysteriously concealed genes within.

'As Ronald advises, we have cracked the initial stage of age reversal. Nevertheless, this is just the start; by the time the worldwide effort gets underway, my team's study of cryptomnesia, from the Greek *kryptos,* meaning hidden or secret plus amnesia, is confident it will be possible to code for memory stored and temporarily forgotten. Awesome! Think of this as if memory is a reconstruction process, not recollection. We can activate a gene we consider present in Chromosome 10 LG11 for total recall to advance with the body's age and parts. Chromosome 18 KATNAL 2 offers the same incredible promise. There is a strong possibility that the gene or genes coding for consciousness lies here. Are we to be blessed with the ability to reprogramme adult cells with genes for memory and consciousness that turn on during the ageing process from the initial embryonic state?

'The search to find and switch on the suppressed genes for memory and consciousness is definitely afoot! At this point, science knows that parts of the *Homo sapiens'* DNA genome are unique to each person. Therefore, discovering the mechanics to activate or suppress genes unknown to us will relegate cloning in favour of resurrecting a personality from a previous life. Is immaculate conception now conceivable? Could it be that Jesus' DNA gifted by his Father was divinely different from our own and programmed for His resurrection? If you had the chance to have a loved one reborn, would you take it? If offered extended life to pursue our intended purpose across the universe, dare we refuse it? We have been bestowed with the intellect and tools to find our designer's answers to these questions. Our ancestors had some advantages. They did not have the diversions enjoyed by present-day man. Many follow a life of religious-philosophical contemplation, and witnesses of all creeds have had to rely on God's inspiration through neural pathways and visions. Let us not ignore ancient scriptures' words while accepting the God-given responsibility to search for the truth:

'Quran 20:55: "Thereof the Earth we created you, and into it, we shall return you, and from it, we shall bring you out once again."

'Ephesians 2:10: "For we are God's handiwork, created in Christ Jesus to do good works, which God prepared in advance for us to do."

'John 13:20: "Very truly I tell you, whoever accepts anyone I send accepts me and whoever accepts me accepts the one who sent me."

'Thessalonians 4:14: "For we believe that Jesus died and rose again, so we believe that God will bring with Jesus those who have fallen asleep in him."

'The implications of our research are apparent, and the infrastructure required will be immense. The preservation of our planet is paramount and becoming more urgent every day. As we have said many times, we must abandon fossil fuels at all costs; with our extended life span, we must apply all our energy to transforming the environment back to its natural beauty. With this in mind, I will hand the chair to our director of transport, Mr Jack Diamond.'

Jack, a thin, fit, good-looking man with flashing blue eyes, rose to speak.

'The pioneering spirit for which your country has been famed is fast becoming a worldwide phenomenon. Thriving economies are achieving comfort and sustenance across the globe. Continents and cities must soon devolve themselves from relying on air travel and other forms of transportation using fossil fuels. It's a tall order, but with cooperation and unprecedented investment, our first step to ensuring global connectivity is building an infrastructure of immersed prefabricated tunnel sections. Today's significant nation-states will build many factories to assemble these to the exact same specification for use below ground level and under the seas and deploy them worldwide. Many steel mills will reopen to a capacity never seen before to provide the various forms of stainless steel compressed hyperloop tubes to the same exact worldwide specifications. These will house the super maglev trains in their low-vacuum intercontinental and domestic tunnels. The repulsive force and the attractive force induced between the superconducting onboard magnets and propulsion coils on the frictionless guideways' sidewalls will generate top speeds of up to 4,000 miles an hour. The emission-free frictionless system will eventually render millions of acres on the surface back to mother nature with its underground location. Imagine for a moment from New York to Los Angeles in one hour! Los Angeles to Bogota in one and a half and on to one of our seven cities, Geras, in just three-quarters of an hour! If it would please you to bash on under the southern Atlantic to Boa Vista, home of our second city, another three-quarter of an hour or, as the mood takes one, London–New York in under two hours. The list is endless: Paris–Moscow, forty-five minutes; Moscow–Beijing, ninety minutes; Beijing–Sydney, just over two hours.

'With our lives getting longer, more time to understand our neighbours and hopefully, as most religions advocate, our new domain will fill with love for one another. No one needs to remain idle as we integrate and bond as one across the Earth to achieve our intended purpose. Future capillary tunnels will replace most road and rail networks to integrate the global system. Nobody will miss the bumper-to-bumper individual motoring chaos of today. We will confine our beautiful art form to motor museums across the world for recreational amusement only. We will shortly replace the experience of free and individual vehicle control with the excitement of interplanetary space travel. Planet Earth once again must be understood as the centre of the universe populated by one united species: us.'

At that, the Air Vice-Marshal stood up and thanked Jack for his brief outline of the aims to save the planet from the past's pollution-based human activities. Deliberately looking over the esteemed company present with his head held high, Ron resumed speaking.

'People forget how fast science and invention are providing solutions. Only ninety years ago, my old granny with one assistant used to log in single-digit arrivals in a small hut at the end of the runway at Ringway, now the vast Manchester Airport. Just imagine that! As we all know, development speed is gaining momentum, not slowing down. The achievements of the peoples of Russia, China, the British Commonwealth, Europe and many more must give us confidence that our global plans will one day be fulfilled. Hopefully, the planet's surface will become one vast international park and host to super-productive farms – on which the arts and friendly international sports, large and small scale, will prevail and become the stepping stone into the universe for all humankind. We are declining to take your welcome questions now but will be available tonight and tomorrow. It will be more appropriate to seek out your opposite number to discuss the possibilities of your personal sphere of interest. So, with no more ado, I hand the chair to our revered host Dwight, the President of the USA.'

'Thanks for your concise and informative introduction, Ron. There is much to dwell upon, and I believe I hear the most welcome sound from the not-too-distant corridors here at Laurel Lodge of a small flotilla of drinks trolleys to help us with our cause! Our good ladies await our company for pre-dinner drinks if everybody could make their way to the lounge bar.'

Good manners dictated a quiet start to the party. The group politely began to mingle and gain an introduction to one another. The men wore semi-formal dress, while the ladies were up to scratch and beyond in the latest fashions. The bar stewards filtered among them to serve drinks, accelerating and producing a comfortable ambience. By the time dinner was announced, the exchange of information was almost at a fever pitch. Everybody present observed the best etiquette to accompany the enjoyment of the finest food and wine fit for the gods. Nevertheless, it was not long before the exhausted dignitaries sought an excellent night's sleep in their allotted cabins.

The following day, Camp David was blessed with a sunny morning. The honorary chaplain, Air Vice-Marshal Ron

Wallington, dressed in summer battle dress casuals, could make out Bobby and Vincent's excited chatter as they approached the camp commander's quarters.

'Hi there, boys. Just call me Ron. I have been in touch with the camp commandant, who has cleared us for this morning's sortie. Your dad will join us later. If we can make our way to the heliport, I've got some things to show you. Follow me.'

'Wow, look at these, Vincent – a USAF bomber and a single-engine fighter,' Bobby enthused. The boys crowded around the model aircraft sitting adjacent to each other on the helipad. The Boeing B29 Superfortress Bomber, finished in polished silver with a 4.5-foot wingspan, glistened in the morning light. As was the American custom, her nose cone art adorned her given name, 'Straight Flush', and on her wings were four mighty propellers. Right next to her was the R.J. Mitchell-designed RAF Super Marine Spitfire MK 1V, slightly smaller and not to scale.

'Which goes first? The bomber may need protection on its mission. But on the other hand, she carries more fuel!' Both lads' excitement was infectious as Ron joined in with exhilaration.

'Our bomber! Our bomber!' they cheered.

'So be it, roger and out.' Ron fired up the four engines, and the B29 began to move forward. Her speakers replicated the sound of Wright Duplex-Cyclone engines as she gained speed and took off. Eyes transfixed and with their breath taken away, the two boys marvelled at the majestic silver bird, now under the guidance and control of its Dynon autopilot, flying past their mum and dad. They were taking breakfast on the sun terrace of Aspen Lodge!

Next, the Spitfire raced down the tarmac, urgently seeking its charge to stand guard around her airspace. The unmistakable spine-tingling sound of its Rolls Royce Merlin V-12 engine reverberating loudly and clearly through its speakers made watchers want to stand and salute as she soared past.

Below, the delegates began to emerge from their cabins, refreshed by sleep and a wholesome American breakfast. They dispersed to stroll through the picturesque grounds to make themselves busy and discuss possibilities within their spheres of interest with their opposite numbers. The models of two old brothers in arms flew overhead to remind everyone of the common objectives over many years.

After some time, the air display had run its course. The B29, still on autopilot with its GPS, now switched to return to launch mode. Ron, expertly using radio control, followed the Spitfire to land successfully behind her. Both aircraft returned together to their original slots.

'Good afternoon, Mr President. I hope you enjoyed our little demonstration. Not too intrusive on your privacy at breakfast, we hope?'

'It's Dwight, Ron. Not at all. The wife and I were both impressed. How was it with you boys?'

'Really good, Dad. We would love to learn to fly them.'

'If it's OK with your people, Dwight, I would like to leave these two models for the boys plus two trainer planes with a flight-simulator tutorial pack for use on any PC.'

'Thanks a million, Ron; that would be great. Can we meet later, say 5 p.m., to assess the progress everyone has made through the afternoon?'

'No problem. See you in the Laurel Cabin, then.'

Ron now retired to the Evergreen Chapel to pause for thought. Surprisingly, he found companionship and a certain amount of comfort in prayer. The burden of responsibility, funnily enough, tended to yield a weakness evidenced by a small tear coursing down his cheek. His mission's immensity soon quelled this as his will to succeed mastered any obstacle that might come his way.

The President and the Air Vice-Marshal duly met in the Aspen Lodge, comfortably seated in traditional leather armchairs. They both agreed that the casual approach of the previous twenty-four hours had been the right formula. However, it was immediately apparent that all the eligible American delegates were of one mind to make the trip to Franklin Town and avail themselves of Professor Lovall's treatment at the earliest opportunity. Isolating the world's quantum computer and fusion reactor would require a League of Nations level of immunity and universal trust. However, working alongside the same age-reversed delegates across the planet gave cause for cautious optimism. The feedback from China was positive: Johnny's team had made a great impression. Whether or not the title given him was an honorary rank or merely a nickname was unclear, but Chairman One Leg suited him, if only as a term of endearment! Mark and Simon reported that Russia was keen to end its colonial ambitions, favouring a united global effort. India, Pakistan, Australia, Japan and many more endorsed the programme.

'In view of the cabinet's and, I hope, your opinion, Mr President, can I report a positive response towards our ideas back to the teams across the world?'

'Broadly speaking, you can confirm a positive response from us. We can set nothing in stone, but yes, a positive response would be in order at this stage.'

Back in London, the Lambeth Cross offices rang with the sound of cheering voices at the news.

8
1985 Sinclair C5

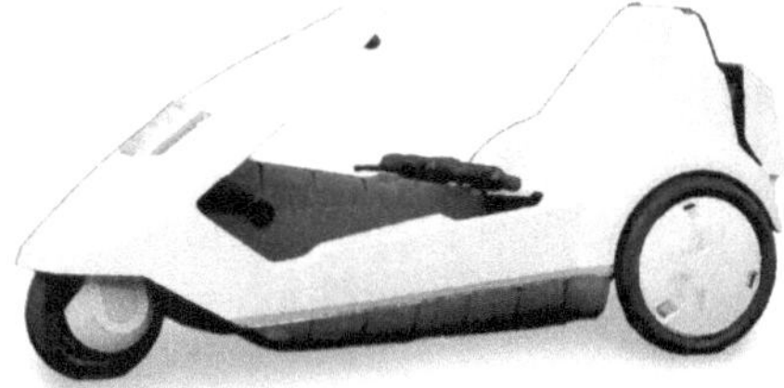

(With Polypropylene Shell in White)

To quote, 'The Sinclair C5 has the distinction of being named "the worst gadget of all time ahead of Beta Max video and Pizza scissors". Intolerably slow, totally unreliable and with an unquenchable hunger for danger, most right-minded traders would direct potential customers to their local toy shop, and even bike-shop men baulked at the idea of stocking such an article. At Lambeth Cross, Benny, Billy, Ron, Barbara, Johnny, and Hans celebrated Miles's one hundred and fourteenth birthday. They marvelled that it had taken seventy-seven years to travel the road into the future for the C5 bodywork to become the prototype for the 2062 personalised maglev Roadtrain.

The Covid-19 world pandemic of 2020 revealed how damaging confined air travel could be to humankind's health. The resulting constraint of its use demonstrated an instant improvement of the planet's atmosphere to further such travel's demise. The progress in exchanging information coupled with the ability to socialise across computerised media rendered the importance of face-to-face contact almost obsolete. Global corporations are perfectly capable of exploiting a golden opportunity for change, and the switch to manufacturing standardised prefabricated immersed tunnel sections took off. The watchful politicians, with their increased life span, attained wisdom. They ironed out their differences and worked together for the planet's good.

The scramble to supply and design a worldwide network of space-age tunnels throughout Earth was something to behold. Joint ventures of train technologies between giants such as China's CRRC, Deutsche Bahn, Russia Rail, India Rail, Union Pacific, BNSF Santa Fe, East and West Japan, Canadian National, and so on transformed travel from air to the subterranean. Equally, the seven cities began to thrive, connected via high-speed vacuum tunnels. European prefabricated tunnel constructors led the way in the early days. Still, it was not long before the world's engineers applied themselves to the job, and the major international and domestic systems were completed by 2049. Fabrication of the domestic subsidiary networks was already underway to complement the primary complex to exact worldwide specifications. At first glance, a personalised small maglev tractor unit with the option to tow similar-sized carriages for family and luggage resembled the good old Sinclair C5.

Capillary tunnels replaced suburban roads. You could now hop into your mini Maglev Mk V and, with minimum fuss, board it onto an ongoing main train to almost anywhere, replete with its own air supply to control the spread of disease and virtual vision of the passing terrain above to avoid any suggestion of claustrophobia. Apart from medical emergencies and the call of nature, all this without getting out.

Realising the remarkable transition of returning the environment to its intended beauty, it took little time for the world's population to adapt to this new transport mode. It was not long before the world's motorways were enthusiastically torn up. In their place, the tunnels proliferated to better cope with freight and passenger traffic. The world's scientists, enjoying a great life in the brand-new city of Cratos, worked together and produced the first fusion reactor. Within fifty years, these reactors were situated strategically across the world and, from their ultra-safe locations, provided unlimited carbon-free clean energy.

The world's people began to find they could no longer return to the old time-consuming way of life. In this new age, the inclination to acquire possessions declined. The requirement of a smaller living space equipped with multi-functional entertainment and educational and career-enhancing computerised facilities at their fingertips did not encourage physical presence. It made sense that wasting time traipsing to and from airports, queuing in traffic jams and travelling to work were dispensed with to accumulate many lost hours. A trip to West Africa or Tenerife for a beach holiday could take less time from anywhere in the world. Cycle paths, and walkways threaded through the farmland, tended by automatic machinery powered by the silence of electricity to enhance the pastoral beauty of the rural countryside. Wildflower varieties not seen for a hundred years began to proliferate into abundance. The night sky here, not troubled by light pollution, held the observer in awe once again. Its reality begged many questions of better-informed men and women still searching the cosmos for purpose.

In the vast cities, electric light vanquished the darkness. Escalators, moving pavements, and, of course, one's mini Maglev Mk V provided all the necessary conveyance. People moved about underneath the coloured neon lights, but, just as in the countryside, urgency and bustle seemed to be missing. Everybody was there to enjoy life but with no inconvenience. The new maids and house servants rendered every service, and personal computers, electric drones, orbiting satellites, and robots tended to every need.

Travelling to follow and support front-runners in any sporting competition, be it professional or amateur, had never been easier. The leisure industry blossomed every year. New worldwide leagues morphed out of the old national tables. Ticket sales and television revenue mushroomed to provide worldwide audiences with the best infrastructure for sporting action. Stadia, with capacities of 250,000, the descendants of Roman amphitheatres, housed the more passionate of our species! Yet, the world's surface still played host to all the traditional sporting events, and the opportunity to attend and participate was still prevalent.

Weather patterns changed to assist the transition from the excesses of the previous 300 years. The traditional seasons began to reimpose themselves. Winter sanctioned the snowlines to subside back down towards the valleys. Springtime returned to stem the tide, and summer yielded the annual harvest. Finally, autumn softly made way for the new life to come after winter.

Mother Nature, however, is not to be tamed by the good behaviour of humankind and resumed charge of the planet. The merchant ships and big holiday cruise liners powered by sail with auxiliary electric engines ploughing across the oceans had to regard her carefully. Despite this, activity in the main was exciting and pleasurable. Industries making use of seventy per cent of Earth's surface continued to flourish.

The morning birdsongs beckoned dawn. The blackbird, regimental as a royalist, keeping post atop the highest tree, sang into the summer twilight, offering the owl his cue to bring forth the night. The occasional thunderclap resonated from the skies to accompany the various sounds of nature. The whistle of the breeze, the howling wind, and the falling rain only managed to interrupt the burgeoning silence. After our first antenatal cry, do we crave the soundwave? Alone without the infernal machines of the past two and a half centuries grinding away on land, sea and air, were they all left castaways on a remote island? One's first instinct was to resort to headphones and tune in to become an individual in the virtual civilisation of a new reality.

The silence on the rural surface appeared to be a catalyst in preparing this intelligent species for survival in the cosmos. However, it became apparent that humankind did not comprehend just how much noise their carbon-based inventions made. Forests and tropical vegetation were busy restoring themselves to house the wild and sometimes dangerous species previously almost overrun by *Homo sapiens* remote in comparative quiet. A subtle evolutionary process occurred while remaining dominant with the species' ability to communicate and kill.

As predicted, the world birth rate plummeted as the younger generations took flight into electronic comfort zones. From childhood to adolescence, with very little guidance instinctively became at one with the computerised world. Youthful exuberance showed little desire to venture further out from the attractions of city life. Apart from the occasional holiday via the maglev, one could explore the world from within the 'Chambre de Reverie'. The live congregations at the worldwide network of Mark and Simon's Twenty-First Century Churches started to diminish in favour of online virtual attendance.

Nevertheless, Professor Lovall's announcement from the cathedral at Geras that his age-reversal programme for thirty years of extra life expectancy could now be rolled out across the globe without delay. The public received the news with ecstatic acclaim. However, by 2061 the professor and his colleagues had gone far beyond that. The church's founding members, the original senators, and leading scientists are now revelling at the rumours of 200 years of life. Privately the professor was working to offer astronauts selected for missions outside the solar system even longer.

'It will not be long before we need microchips, not candles, on our birthday cakes, Miles,' laughed Johnny.

'Don't bother with the song, but a little more champagne may well be in order before our forthcoming review of the seven cities and their phenomenal progress,' Miles replied.

So, our distinguished leaders of the movement sensibly partied into the night. The arrangements were that Billy and Miles should travel in the morning to meet Simon at Amarna near Luxor and then rendezvous with the others at Hera-Hera just south of Rabat, Morocco. The following morning, comfortably strapped in their Maglev Mk Vs, they agreed to set the camera altitude to 400 feet to view the passing terrain on the surface. The interior instrument panel displayed all the information required.

As the vehicle gained speed through the capillary tunnels, it was not long before the compact Maglevs automatically boarded the high-speed intercontinental express to Cairo. The transparent bubble cockpit began to project the English countryside below. It was no different from sitting in a helicopter with broad vision. The frictionless train accelerated into the vacuum tunnel to reach its cruising speed of 3,000 miles per hour. In the blink of an eye, it passed under the English Channel and then the Alps and silently sped below the Mediterranean before relaxing back its momentum on approaching Cairo. It was amazing how these small chariots could glide onto the next train. In a matter of minutes, one was battened down onto a domestic train to move quietly at 450 miles per hour to Luxor. The panoramic scene displayed a tranquil agricultural countryside adjacent to the river Nile. With the transport system all underground, it was akin to travelling back into a biblical era in a time machine.

The two travellers arrived in Luxor in plenty of time to partake of a very civilised lunch at the Sofitel Winter Palace. – a majestic hotel, a favourite winter retreat for Agatha Christie that overlooks stunning gardens by the river Nile. A leisurely amble around the ruins of Thebes on the east bank was an unmissable exercise. Both men were mindful of the mystical interest shown by Professor Lovall in the necropolis (city of the dead) on the west bank.

The men back in their maglev units progressed through a small two-way capillary tunnel seventeen miles long to Armana. They stored their vehicles and moved up the escalator to the surface. In the bright sunlight, a small welcoming party was there to greet and conduct them to an ornamental wooden longboat with some reverence. Over the bows straight ahead, the canal stretched between the rolling desert, and linear dunes drifted onto the rugged rocky terrain. The rowers dressed in brilliant white cotton shirts made smooth progress through the lapping water under the sun. The passengers aboard marvelled at the tall concrete obelisks twenty-five feet apart, numbering fifty on each side. The first on the left adorned the Christian symbol of the cross in deep purple, opposite the green star and crescent of Islam on the right-hand side. The symbols of the subsequent eight world religions had an impressive obelisk with signs ranging from the Jewish menorah to Bahai's interlocking triangles. The colourful sequence is repeated twelve times along each side of the canal banks.

As the boat emerged from the last of the monuments, a sense of comprehension transformed into awe at first sight of Armana, the pyramid city. Across a three-acre tiled plaza, the central pyramid towered before them. Gloss-black solar panels covered the four triangular sides from the apex down to the colonnade below to support the structure above. Other similar attractively designed pyramids but on a smaller scale to complement the appearance of the futurist metropolis. People busily going about their business populated the cafés and restaurants scattered around the ground floor.

Billy spotted Simon at the agreed meeting place.

'Welcome to Armana. Nice to see you in person for a change. Did you have a good trip down?' Simon politely greeted them.

'I still can't get over how convenient these trains are. We are pleased with the progress you have all made here,' Miles exclaimed.

'Yes, the success of our united missionary campaign to de-radicalise the extreme fundamental religious networks is very satisfying. Mark's address at the opening ceremony in 2051 was a wonderful start. His emphasis on there being only one God and the deep exploration of all scriptures to reveal the science of reality has brought a new urgency to find a common way forward. The simple comparison is that *Homo sapiens* took merely 50,000 years to develop consciousness and intelligence. In the past 200 years, this has accelerated to sublime levels. The dinosaurs, the temporary rulers of Earth, did not manage to evolve past the ability to survive in 150 million years of existence. I don't mean to lecture you on your arrival, but when we replace faith with certainty backed by scientific discoveries, we owe our existence to God. People are starting to awaken from their modern delusion that we randomly evolved from nothing. Therefore, the truth coded in our DNA is God's individual blueprint for each newborn person. The sacred scripture of Islam tells us:"

> Quran (2:256) "Let there be no compulsion in religion, for the truth stands out clearly from falsehood. So whoever renounces false Gods and believes in Allah has certainly grasped the firmest, unfailing handhold. And Allah is All-Hearing, All-Knowing."

At this point, Simon beckoned them to follow him into the main pyramid; he reminded them that the living quarters were all below ground and that they should check in at reception. The debating halls were all situated above. You could see the leaders of the various faiths in their colourful traditional dress earnestly making their way about on the escalators and moving paths to attend the day's lectures. The total population of the city amounted to around 60,000. The facilities for enlightenment and research included computers, a vast library, laboratories, wall screens and countless communication devices. Absolute freedom of speech, opinion, and tolerance guaranteed that the world's most talented practitioners and divinity guardians could operate successfully within the city walls. Over the years, the teams within had galvanised a significant and peaceful unity across the planet. They played their part in the partnership to fulfil the plans for the future of the Twenty-First Century Church.

Nevertheless, the meeting with Simon had a serious purpose. Unfounded rumours were doing the rounds in Armana. The three arranged to meet at Simon's residence in the Orange Grove Pyramid, a small distance over the central plaza. On their arrival, after the usual pleasantries, Simon opened the conversation. 'Everyone here is excited at the prospect of burgeoning life expectancy. Our studies will always make use of extra time. It is incredible how much more compliant the world population is becoming with the prospect of a much longer life. The young are fast becoming a minority. Politicians find it increasingly hard to persuade them to sacrifice their many years to come for an abstract ideal. However, the reports or lack of them emanating from the Brazilian city Geras and the West African Silvanus are causing some consternation. There is a rumour that Professor Lovall and his academic friends are enrolling the best teachers and dons for a specialist mission at an unknown destination. I have to ask you, and old friends, are you aware of these developments?

Billy looked at Miles with raised eyebrows to make ready his reply. 'We are constantly in touch as we are with you, regularly using video conferencing to keep up to date with his revolutionary research. He has our complete trust and has only twice asked for financial investment outside regular city expenditure. His requests were approved years ago.

'The first was purchasing an old English public school in West Yorkshire to educate 2,000-plus pupils and provide scholarships for students who passed a common-entrance exam set by himself and his associates. The age range would ultimately be from eight to eighteen.

'The second was a modest investment to convert the disused Franklin Town after transferring its operations to Geras into a fully-fledged university for further education and provide a suitable maglev branch line. It is prudent that the location remains private to undertake their specialist learning undisturbed. His main targets remain to assist the great work at Hera Hera while continuing his undoubted progress at Geras and Silvanus. You can inform your leaders to expect further good news. We intend to announce the details formally during our proposed meeting with his team in a few days. I hope this will be enough to calm any fears our cherished brothers working so hard here may have.'

'Yes, of course, I will ensure the elders are aware of these developments and look forward to the upcoming broadcast. Meanwhile, we can stroll to the Ramesses restaurant for a few drinks and sample Egyptian cuisine.'

The setting sun cast a mystical orange light across the city as our group admired the contrasting architecture. The call to prayer sounded out from the state-of-the-art minaret, part of the imperious mosque of ultra-modern design. Shinto Torii, gateways to nature, stand in unison with the eight-spoke Buddhist wheel alongside brightly lit blue neon Hindu symbols. The upright hand of Jainism in denial of violence at one with the Jewish menorah decorated the small squares between the pyramids. Artistic representations of Sikhism, Taoism, and Bahai were also present as they walked through the city. A purple cross of Jesus adorned the Christian cathedral with a modern design, making Coventry Cathedral look outdated. The construction as a whole poured scorn on the species' historically violent approach to seeking its answers. Instead, the place inspired multicultural open-mindedness with no hint of a 'your God' attitude.

Billy and Miles spent a few days with Simon, touring the city and meeting people. They confirmed that the clear, practical path to the movement's objectives was in line with expectations. On the last morning, they wished Simon well and retraced their steps back to Cairo and then to Hera Hera in Morocco.

Hera Hera, situated a few miles north of Kenitra, was designed from scratch to accommodate the world's finest professors, oncologists, geneticists, and medical practitioners in the comfort they deserved. Its location on the coast of the Atlantic westward and a river forming the east boundary allowed the architects to establish a paradise to rid the world of killer cancer. The maglev international high-speed connection from nearby Rabat made commuting to Silvanus and Geras from Hera Hera extremely convenient. First-class laboratories and research facilities were available here – the exchange of ideas was made easy with the unparalleled leisure infrastructure for discussion before and after work.

The tastefully equipped restaurants, bars, hotels, and even the plazas along the promenade with wall-screen TV for that night's worldwide address to be broadcast by Mark, set the scene. The local governors of this seaside municipality embellished the seafront and many public places with vibrant tropical flowers to mark the special occasion. Distinguished guests from all corners far and wide arrived to attend the celebrations of scientific achievement at this beautiful location.

At 7.15 p.m., the silver sun touched the horizon to emblazon the sky with a deep orange radiance behind the incoming waves of the Atlantic. Shortly Mark, accompanied by his usual entourage, theatrically made his way up onto the magnificent podium. Despite his 114 years, he stood confidently and looked terrific, ready to enlighten his subjects about the progress made at Hera Hera.

Mark looked forward, head held high, authoritatively seeking the soul of humanity to connect on this warm night. With his right hand outstretched, he beckoned his loyal followers across the planet to listen more closely. 'Let me introduce you to the Martialis ant from the Amazon rainforests. This species sensed the presence of the non-bird dinosaurs that lived 245 through to 66 million years ago. A percentage of these vast creatures are known to have suffered from cancer. The disease is not new! However, in contrast, our Martialis ant is now the world's oldest surviving resident still alive. Significantly, its DNA remained unchanged over 120 million years. It does not need eyes, happily living below ground in total darkness with no evidence of contracting cancer. This knowledge alerted the scientists here in this stunning little city that the immortal cancer cell might be born of latent pre-designed DNA coding to control the evolution of individual species. If the random expression and suppression of coding genes were all left to chance, *Homo sapiens* would have become extinct long ago. Logic dictates that, as with computer programmes, complex codes for life can only advance through the ages if a failure-rectification structure is in place. When the programmer suspects his systems may gain an element of self-control, he inserts a small hidden line of code as a safeguard. Was man so scheduled and banished from the Garden of Eden to spend centuries of good and evil to justify obtaining the knowledge he seeks?

'The Egyptians' first documented evidence of cancer was in 3,000 BC. It was discovered in an ancient Egyptian textbook on traumatic surgery and consequently given the name The Edwin Smith Papyrus. The following 5,000 years reveal a general human disinterest in the disease, with people preferring to occupy themselves with politics, war and religion. The twentieth century ushered in three main treatments – surgery, radiation, and toxic chemotherapy – which remained the only underachieving hope. Nevertheless, some groundwork brought here by oncologists and scientists has proved useful.

'The team effort at Hera soon focused on the fact that the information within coding is not a chemical event, and the source driving the structure is unknowable. What is knowable is that information is transported from the DNA in the nucleus by Messenger RNA undergoing transcription and then translation to provide living cells with the ability to form tissue and life. The immense numbers involved, the self-correction systems, such as alternative splicing, strongly suggest that this one-way system must be infallible. Messenger RNA has no nuclear access signal, does not have a reverse transcriptase enzyme and possesses no integrase enzyme. The chance it could re-enter the nucleus is nil. Therefore, cancer suppression must be coded for by undetected genes or genes that may be traceable from the remnants of genes scrambled and dispersed to form the many introns contained within the DNA sequences. The word 'mutation' is now obsolete! The hunt is on. Early research conducted here concluded that the investigation must devolve into two approaches to conquer this disease.

'The primary procedure to achieve prevention required much diversity of thought on advanced genetic modification through manipulating information transfer, a lengthy computerised operation of a process of elimination and deduction to find the genes hidden in the vast and seemingly non-coding ninety-eight per cent of DNA. Unsurprisingly to our creationist movement, the universe, atom, and DNA molecule all mysteriously consist predominantly of this misunderstood energised space. On close examination of this wilderness, we find the behaviour of shadow enhancers influences the principle enhancer's control of genes from a great distance – as much as 50,000 base pairs distant. Furthermore, these principle enhancers themselves can be as far as 10,000 base pairs from their target gene. The realm of classical physics again capitulates to the quantum world of instant data communication via 'entanglement'. Quantum computers, still in their infancy but infinitely more potent than their binary counterparts, use the dynamism of probability and superposition to experience entanglement to enter a very different world for our scientists to translate into reality. It became evident that rectifying the core problem with CRISPR or TALEN cutting tools that might fundamentally damage the structure of DNA is not possible in this instance. So, we handed the task of finding principle enhancers with no genes to catalyse to the guys at Quantum Springs.

'Cancer cells ignore, hide from, and don't receive the instruction to stop dividing and die – known as apoptosis. Programmed cell death does not apply to them due to incorrect information provided by incomplete protein presence at birth. Not before long, news from New Zealand begins to materialise. Incredible sequences emerged compatible with the remnants of code contained in the so-called useless introns. These catalysed genes carry signals and information to code for the necessary proteins to supplement and dwarf existing DNA repair and cancer-killing cells. As a result, tumour suppressors attain 100 per cent protection with no interference from the natural cell cycle. We still have the utmost confidence in DNA's ability to rectify copying mistakes at transcription. I call on every person to herald the planet's supreme scientists and congratulate them on eradicating cancer cells before their birth. People of the world, on their behalf, I give you the all-conquering "Intron Repair Vaccine".'

Scenes from an ecstatic species joined the celebrating citizens in Hera Hera. The many wall screens around the city's plazas showed colourful fireworks displays from around the globe.

Mark raised his arms to gesture a moment's pause. The crowds in the city instinctively paid attention and, in reverence, quieted their fanfare.

'We can reassure sufferers of the disease that the vaccine will stop their cancer progression in its tracks. Targeted by this new method of therapy to clear the remaining cancer damage from their body will be the lymphocytes – white blood cells; NK, natural killers in the immune system; T, thymus – adaptive immune response; and B, bone marrow –antibody promotors. So, on this night, we can all celebrate, glasses in hand, and let the giant pharmaceutical corporations produce the billions of doses now and in the future.'

A scene of pure drama encouraged the jubilant merrymaking crowds to increase the cacophony in the night air. Mark descended from the podium in his usual theatrical style. Once out of the public domain, he rejoined his long-time friends and colleagues for a more reserved round of drinks followed by dinner. The following morning the twelve former motor dealers sat together before a full breakfast of Senegal fresh fruit with bacon and eggs, cheerfully enjoying each other's company.

'Your speech has been well received in Armana,' Johnny said, cheerfully smiling with a wink of his eye. 'Not the easiest lot to please,' he added. 'You're back off to London in a couple of days, Mark, I believe?'

'Yes, that's right. Absolutely no public announcements until we've had a full board meeting back at Lambeth Cross HQ. I will reluctantly leave you and the boys to continue to Silvanus to spend time with Professor Lovall and his army of geneticists. Just be careful, and I know I can rely on your discretion.'

'I think we all agree with that – we owe the professor a great deal for our increased longevity. When we wake in the morning in full health to acknowledge that each new day is a bonus, we can't thank him and his team enough,' added Johnny.

Hans the German rejoined proudly, surveying his friends, 'I am incredibly grateful that all of us here have retained through these long years our sense of humour.' His countenance, however, transposed from benign cordiality to a serious façade. 'Nevertheless, I am happy to know we all still possess the steel nerve and conviction to guide the movement safely into the future. Now that cancer is behind us, I believe the excellent professor is lobbying for Hera Hera to concentrate on time travel. I would appreciate a detailed report on his views and progress on your return.'

After several good days in the company of the world's great clinicians and scientists, who enjoyed a good party, it was time to move on to Silvanus. The superexpress maglev screamed down beneath the west coast of Africa and then under the Atlantic to make its way to the volcanic island of Boa Vista.

The globe's finest architects and constructors combined to build Silvanus, the modern city for genetics and age reversal. As with Hera Hera, they provided every facility for a comfortable stay. Above and below the surface, the metropolis replaced the now obsolete airport and its ruined old host village Rabil.

The senior members of the movement aboard their mini maglevs were subject to strict security control on entering the leading tunnel. The few other passengers were free to travel on to the island's small resort town Sai Rei, and the express continued to Geras off the coast of Brazil. The streetwise party shared an uneasiness as they journeyed up the escalator to encounter more identity checks on entering the perimeter of the thoroughfare. However, Professor Lovall, accompanied by a substantial welcome committee, made them feel more at ease as they arrived at their sumptuous accommodation.

Once checked in, Billy, Miles, Johnny, Hans, Marlon, Jack, Benny, Ron, and Barbara assembled at the professor's invitation for a personally conducted tour of the city. Comfortably seated in the glass-roofed maglev minibus, everyone paid attention to the tour guide on the mike upfront. Then, as the vehicle smoothly progressed to jogging speed, the guide began to describe this amazing place.

'Good afternoon. My name is Ingrid, and on behalf of the scientific community here, I would like to welcome you to our paradise city of research and discovery. We are effectively an island within an island here. A comprehensive desalination plant provides all the water that our local environment needs. Genetics and age-reversal requirements dictate that this facility must have an abundance of water and plenty of fresh water for personal consumption.

'The planners divided the city into six suburbs at its inception, each with its specialised agenda. We first enter through a low-arched bridge into a controlled forest area of beema bamboo groves and peepal trees. These enclose the high-tech laboratories and residential buildings built in a neo-Roman colonial style to study stem cell exhaustion exclusively. Next, we pass the cultivated lawns and leisure facilities to enter a suburb dense with Amazonian trees. Please observe the Georgian offices and houses with their sash windows facing west through the fringe of tamarind, sea grapes and coconut palms out to the Atlantic. The intensive study of altered intercellular communication, deregulated nutrient sensing, and genomic instability – also known as DNA repair – occurs here. Then, moving back into the jungle through the tropical park, you can see the tinted windows below the single-storey laboratories' solar-panelled roofs for dedicated research into telomere attrition and epigenetic alterations. Investigation into proteostasis decline and cellular senescence occurs at our next destination, concealed as you can now see by a vast array of tropical flowers and fauna. Finally, we pass through the last of our beautiful oxygen-producing forests to discover the large complex in which we seek the answer to mitochondrial dysfunction.' At the terminus, Ingrid politely informed the company that she was not permitted to take questions. She cheerfully exited with the well-worn phrase, 'Have a nice day!'

A mirrored skyscraper was towering above the forest in the civic centre. The interconnecting hub housed hundreds of state-of-the-art binary computers to assimilate and analyse the results from the surrounding suburbs. The very top medical scientists of the world were formed into small groups of multidisciplinary team meeting boards. These were used to decide on completed research for an encrypted submission to Professor Lovall at Geras so he could prepare his official announcements. However, they were shrouded in secrecy and unapproachable even by the movement's representatives. It cannot be denied that this detached attitude is symptomatic of the medical profession.

'Yes, I know when you're lying in a hospital bed, you become well aware of who's in control, from the most menial nurse upwards,' beamed Ron.

However, Billy, Johnny and Hans were still uneasy about this and determined to discuss it with the professor. Nevertheless, the suburb administrators made the deans and heads of departments readily available to all the touring parties for formal and relaxed discussion. Hence, the need for intense security was carried out in the main by a camera backed up by a small army of guardians to guarantee safe conditions for work. The people were much indebted for their increased longevity and would never underestimate the wonderful achievements made at Silvanus. During their two-week stay, everyone felt they had familiarised themselves with the activities and resolve of the scientists assembled from far and wide. Each suburb acted independently to funnel its findings to the central tower. Professor Lovall and his team were instantly privy to all the latest information.

Though not dark yet, the anticipated arrival of the professor and his small band of devoted followers did not disappoint. They alighted the mini maglevs some 200 yards from the remote Chapel of our Lady Fatima to lead a torchlight procession a few miles north of Sal Rei resort. In formal red waist-level cloaks over air force, blue attire gave the event the importance it deserved.

Unfortunately, the little church could accommodate only a few invited dignitaries. The crowd outside, and for that matter, the world, had to witness the event via giant streaming picture TV. Even so, the sight of the cavalcade climbing the long stairway up to the chapel overlooking the swirling Atlantic betrayed a dignified charm. The professor rarely made long speeches, and this was no exception. With just enough aplomb, he proclaimed to those present and the entire world that the community at Silvanus had perfected the procedure for a further fifty years of life – to the astonishment of *Homo sapiens*, now the only known species in the universe to control its genome and possibly live for 200 years. 'We can roll out the treatment plan immediately to all hospitals' were his last words. The cheering people made way for his disciples to descend the steps of the stairway to reboard the waiting maglev express to Geras.

The aircraft's demise resulted in there being only one way in and out of Silvanus. This actuality rendered security operations easy to handle by the authorities. In comparison, Geras was remote and impossible to visit without stringent documentation. The movement and the world senate leaders had persuaded the Brazilian leaders to compulsorily purchase all the hotels, municipal buildings (including the hospital), and private properties back in 2056. The offer of extended life, accompanied by the senate's standard financial package and membership, was a considerable incentive.

They assembled a municipality at the city of Geras, situated on the beautiful volcanic island of Fernando de Noronha, 300 miles off the coast of Brazil. This is serviced by a small branch tunnel off the Dakar–Natal maglev Atlantic expressway. An unmanned mini maglev train brought food and drinks the fertile island could not produce every week. The supply ships began to offload the plant, equipment and raw materials to convert the airport and existing buildings (tastefully) into a small metropolis to fulfil the specifications laid down by Professor Lovall and his genetic engineers. The designers located various sports facilities and what looked like playgrounds intended for children aged ten years or less under a canopy of tropical trees invisible from above.

No adult activity was detectable, as all walkways and roads were either underground or roofed. The world-class geneticists living here, supported by teachers and psychiatrists, were more than happy to remain undisturbed in this reclusive paradise to complete their genetic mission. To protect their anonymity, they and their leader, Professor Lovall, were satisfied to let the ambitious science community in Silvanus receive all the acclaim. The professor insisted that only two of his old friends would visit the island in keeping with these measures.

After much discussion, the group decided that Miles Beaumaris and Jack Diamond should continue to Geras. The rest of the ensemble grudgingly agreed to return to Lambeth Cross and wished the two well.

Jack and Miles boarded the mini maglev in good time to merge onto the Dakar express. Once aboard the main train, they were strapped down behind a long series of enclosed freight carriages with a green cross on each. The inscription below each cross, 'Fragile Genetic Material (security immune)', attracted their curiosity. Both were aware of the high-security CCTV following their every move. They took care not to investigate. On arrival at Geras, the maglev tractor unit pulled the carriages into the entry tunnel and disappeared into the darkness.

A short time later, they manoeuvred the mini maglev through the tunnel in a state of apprehension. However, their mood changed once again when the affable professor heartily welcomed them to his tropical home.

'Please be at ease while you are my guests. There's no need for formalities once you are here. I must apologise for not meeting all of you in Silvanus, but these critical years demand a great deal of discretion and caution. I hope you will accept my hospitality and stay at my Atlantic villa for the duration of your visit.'

The large house stood prominently 100 feet above the sea, overlooking a half-mile-long silver sand beach from the balcony front elevation. The view from the rear comprised the complete panorama of the forest that was host to Geras.

'Close friends, my trusted colleagues and their wives are all very much aware that this luxurious dwelling is now the nucleus of far-reaching genetic research. Nevertheless, we here are a little different from anyone else as far as our work is concerned. Our private computer network linked in with Franklin Town is unable to be hacked. We process the worldwide research results to perfect, test, and authorise clinical trials. The only other city granted this shroud of secret protection is Quantum Springs. Of course, we have all the latest technology to be instantly in touch with all the worldwide networks,' the professor enthused. 'The world senate, ever grateful for our accomplishments, readily endorse this mode of practice.'

Miles and Jack familiarised themselves with each room equipped with wall screens, some with banks of computer terminals mainly in operation. Close-circuit images from the laboratory's recreation areas added to the already tight security across the island.

The following day the professor joined the two men on the sun terrace after an exceptionally splendid breakfast. The unspoilt beach below, bathed in the tropical sun beside a blue Atlantic Sea, invited them for a morning stroll towards the rock at the end of the bay. After some small talk, several high-ranking colleagues arrived to accompany them for a walk along the beach. The professor intended to prepare Miles and Jack for the crucial days ahead.

As is usually the case with experienced people, the conversation was purposeful and searching. The entourage explained that the entire planned programme might contain some unpleasant experiences in such surroundings on the seashore. Miles and Jack were hard men to shock and capable of insisting, whatever the circumstances; they had to report the progress at Geras to date in private to Lambeth Cross.

'Although time is not of the essence, we expect a celestial occurrence of some magnitude in the near future,' Jack calmly pointed out.

'Very well, if Graham, Rosalyn and Matron Dorothy would conduct our welcome visitors to the old hospital, we will start there.' The professor led the way off the beach to board the mini maglevs to the town centre.

The term 'old' rarely applies to anything connected with our cities of learning, and the hospital was no exception. The double-door entrance central to the long two-storey building was discreet and in keeping with the city's surroundings. Inside, however, a spacious, brightly lit foyer laid out in polished marble surrounded by lift doors graced the reception area. Below ground was a further ten storeys. Matron Dorothy raised her parasol to attract everyone's attention.

'Our work here starts in the laboratories where in vitro fertilisation is carried out to perform implantation and conception. We begin with a visit to basement floors ten, nine and eight, termed the Ecto Genesis Wards. Professor Lovall will enlighten you with precise details later in your stay.'

The automatic double safety doors opened to admit Matron and the party into the 'The First Trimester ward'. There, stretched out in neat rows in an area the size of a football pitch, hundreds of glass-topped pods that resembled mangers, each mounted on a four-foot column, were visible in the restricted light. At the end of these growth pods, a computer monitor aptly called the IOG (Intelligent Obstetrician Guard) optimised the environment within to develop human cell clusters into embryos to become foetuses and culminate in the birth of healthy human babies. Matron Dorothy relished her role and prepared to conduct proceedings and elaborate.

'Welcome to our extra-uterine life-support system or artificial uterus, more commonly referred to here as the Exowomb. As at the beginning of the universe, there is darkness in these pods. Nothing is visible from the small cluster of cells formed four or five days after fertilisation. However, if we carefully observe the IOG screen, a great deal of activity emanates from the epiblast cells once placed in the artificial uterus. The transmission of critical data throughout this cluster and, to a lesser extent, the hypoblast gives both the knowledge to create specialised tasks to perform. After a short period, we register an incredible DNA data storage capacity of 200 million megabytes. Look around the ward, and you will notice this unbelievable exchange of signals and data to activate or suppress genes taking place simultaneously among our newest arrivals. Please don't ask me where this acquired intelligence comes from because I don't know. We have begged Quantum Springs to link into our system, but they flatly refuse. They probably rightly insist on the grounds of world safety that their machine is to remain isolated. The programmers will only input questions, and the answer to our problem always comes back as "Access to this information is denied".'

Miles and Jack were astonished by the non-biological miraculous information transfer that forms the beginnings of life. It would appear to an independent, knowledgeable observer that the gift of intelligent information to the embryo is life.

Matron continued: 'As we progress through the wards, let me explain the advantages of these artificial wombs. Firstly, we do not expose the embryos to disease or immune reactions in this environment. The observable amniotic tank serves as a cushion for the growing foetus and facilitates the exchange of nutrients, water and biochemical products. Furthermore, efficient oxygenation and carbon dioxide flow through the baby's placenta in the umbilical cord. Waste disposal through dialysis enhances the nutrition supply, increasing hormonal stability.'

Miles and Jack followed Matron, Graham and Rosalyn obediently to floors seven, six and five through the doors into the second-trimester wards. The electricians illuminated the floors with tiny blue and red LED lights that ran between the pods. The third and last round took the two men to the third-trimester wards on floors four, three and two. Overall, these wards were still in darkness, but individual lights appeared softly above the pods. In these cases, wondrous little eyes opened and closed as each child responded to light and sound. At twenty weeks, a five-inch foetus surrounded by darkness was discernible with a mouth, fingers, toes, eyes, and semi-transparent skin. The skull needed not to be soft as there was no painful journey through Mum's birth canal.

As the light above slowly increased and the amniotic fluids drained away, the infant's lungs were mature and ready to function. Across the room, maternity nurses summoned by the IOG central monitor sat by their charges as the light above increased past dawn. The glass canopies, like aircraft cockpits, gently opened to deliver their precious content to the waiting world. This unforgettable and moving experience took Miles and Jack by surprise as they reflected on the verse:

Jeremiah 1:5: 'Before I formed you in the womb, I knew you. Before you were born, I set you apart.'

Graham and Rosalyn proudly led a tour of all the facilities over the next several days. The joyous noise of children emanates from the first-class play areas under the tropical canopies. Games, all played outdoors, supplemented the primary school curriculum, commencing at the early age of three and a half years. Supervised art classes were free to roam the island to draw and paint. The most talented music teachers could foster their young students to the highest grades with every modern assistance. The happiness was infectious and spread into the classrooms, where everyone competed in formal subjects. The movement's two representatives were delighted that sporting and academic standards were of the highest level. At the age of nine, the schoolchildren comfortably passed the Common Entrance Exam to the professor's Yorkshire boarding school.

'Before enrolment, the graduating candidates will spend summer camp to experience short-haul space flights and exciting challenges at Cosmos City,' Graham elucidated. 'It has been the tradition here for the last twenty years.'

Miles and Jack looked at each other, eyes wide open in disbelief, and Miles stammered, 'Are you telling us the Exowomb has been operating successfully for a fifth of a century?'

Rosalyn stepped in and calmly replied, 'Basically, yes. In the early days, male sperm and female eggs were obtained from selected donors and used without their knowledge for fertilisation in the labs at Franklin. One cannot call it a clinical trial, but in a way, I suppose it was. These early offspring have been graduating from Franklin these last two years. Now, of course, our university. I am happy to say they remain within our family to work successfully in the five cities dedicated to scientific research and space exploration at Cosmos. Scientific progress always determines a change in direction, and we enthusiastically undertook new procedures seventeen years ago. The Exowomb is now of a totally new dimension. Professor Lovall has convened a full briefing for tomorrow afternoon.'

For a few days now, Professor Lovall had been turning over in his mind just how much to enlighten his two visitors with the scientific advances there. As they toured the city, their questions became more numerous and direct. Explanation of nuclear DNA analysis, the genetic instruction mechanisms and the chromosome scaffold for gene expression replication had become repetitive. Miles and Jack were no fools and were content that the professor's scientists from the world over were all working within the realm of the Twenty-First-Century movement and its objectives. Nevertheless, the success of the Exowomb was a surprise. They were astonished that the Professor had kept it under wraps for so long and immediately intended to launch an investigation.

Professor Lovall entered the conference room surrounded by his entourage with his usual air of authority. The sunlight streamed through the open regency windows, giving the early afternoon a tropical coastal freshness. 'Good afternoon, my two good friends. Please make yourselves comfortable. You may first find the presence of so many of my staff overwhelming. They are here to answer as many of your questions as possible. There will be a lot for you to take in during our long discourse today. You will, of course, remember that we were able to administer treatment for age reversal at Franklin town due to detailed research. However, in tandem with age reversal, procedures for in vitro fertilisation began to be closely examined in those early days. Transferring facilities to Silvana and Geras accelerated our progress in this respect. The ethical difficulties of dealing with surrogate mothers and emotional attitudes to genetic modifications inevitably forced us to conceive the Exowomb here at Geras. Our perfection of IVF in the humble petri dish produced the totipotent zygote cell to be placed in the human uterus and advance from embryo to childbirth, creating *Homo sapiens*, each with unique characteristics in the intended natural way by our designer.

'However, when the first Exowomb models became available, replication of the IVF method of embryo production became problematic. The information transfer to the hypoblast and epiblast clusters to support the epiblast and form the bilaminar embryonic disc appeared to be breaking down. The signals to pattern the epiblast showed signs of weakness on the IOG monitor, as their power to accumulate mystical instructions for embryo production seemed to fade. A thousand scientists worked to improve the Exowomb and the IVF methods to no avail. Intelligence and consciousness have developed and seemed to be gathering pace for the last 5,000 years. It would appear that the only way to produce a unique person was with the human body. Someone provided humanity with the same anatomy to reproduce for 10,000 generations.

'The breakthrough came from a team led by Miss Ju Jie while continuing their experimentation. She now advanced the research into cryptomnesia and pseudogenes for memory and consciousness lost in junk DNA. They also identified the relevant fragments from introns and selected five and three non-coding regions. Her team subjected many donor DNA specimens to rigorous rehydration and purification for future use in capsules and vials. With these in hand, she succeeded in implanting two gametes, one sperm and one egg, each with an identical set of chromosomes, to produce a 100 per cent compatible copy of the donor DNA to implant the vacant zygote cell ready for division in the extra-uterine life support system – the Exowomb. After many years of exhaustive endeavour, her scientists witnessed the IOG slowly spring to life in awe. The dynamic electrical data signals across the hypoblast and the epiblast were every bit as active as they would be in the human uterus.

'Subsequently, many more scientists joined her team to follow through with her discovery. It became certain that new unique humans are not viable through the Exowomb or any procedures other than natural birth. What became evident to us is that an individual's DNA is designed for transition to a new embryo to mature for that person's continued life and, by implication, ad infinitum. These two passages emphasise the uniqueness of God's creation of each person's DNA.'

Professor Lovall then quoted for the sake of Lambeth Cross:

"Corinthians 11:12: "For as the woman originates from the man, so also the man has his birth through the woman; and all things originate from God."

'Quran 38:72: "When I design him and blow into him from My spirit, you shall fall prostrate before him."'

An uncanny silence descended on the room as Professor Lovall handed over to Dr Jie. The magnitude of her findings floored Miles and Jack. So, Dr Jie, a compassionate lady of Chinese descent, got ready to speak. As she arose, the attendees broke into spontaneous applause. She politely gestured for quiet with a cultured and well-mannered air.

'Ladies and gentlemen, we thank the professor for his brief outline of events. We decided early that the reborn's future must be lived in the universe above us, not here on Earth. The Exowomb has been in the business of resurrection for seventeen years now. The reborn are all graduating from the nursery here to a schooled education finishing with the university at Franklin. Thanks to the genetics of consciousness and memory – again here at Geras – they have total recall of their previous life or lives, which unfolds simultaneously with every current second of their latest ageing process while experiencing contemporary events in the usual way. We are all unconscious and remember nothing during the 'big sleep', safe in the knowledge that our individual DNA will be available for further rebirth in the Exowombs of the future. In other words, when nine years old, they can remember all their previous lives up to that moment and not beyond.

Happily, this continues through their long life into old age and then passes away. Like the atom, an individual's original DNA is indestructible.'

Dr Jie turned on her heels to look straight at Miles and Jack. A few seconds later, she included everyone in the room as a lighthouse would cast its beam.

'Broadly speaking, without going into too much scientific detail, we have successfully resurrected many individuals where 100 per cent DNA is available. All embryonic tissue originates from the epiblast. The epiblast cluster uses its unknown source of immense intelligence to create embryonic tissue and most organs. With the process of rebirth underway, my team has turned its attention to finding our ancestors' 100 per cent DNA specimens to be fused in the Exowomb. The incredible advances in recent years at Silvanus involving the reconstruction of our reborn parents' DNA have at last proved successful.

'A centimorgan is a unit that expresses the relative distance between genes on a chromosome. Quantum Springs provides the new AI computer-designed cutting-edge editing tools to perform reverse autosomal DNA procedures. Our starting point was searching for rejoining markers that separated during crossover in a single generation. Identifying which parent a segment of DNA comes from enables the reconstruction. The relatively new enzyme reverse transcriptase, properly engineered, can explore and copy mitochondrial DNA, progress towards the nucleus and prepare to re-transcript both male and female fragments.

'Similarly, we applied the process of elimination used by Mr Sherlock Holmes using the latest qubit tech to find a parent's 100 per cent DNA makeup. Well aware that significant though this is, the goal of accurately copying a person's complete blueprint is precisely that. Understanding how the signals originate in the epiblast to control the 100 billion neurons in one human brain is beyond our comprehension. Nevertheless, after matching hundreds of living parents' DNA with the results of our reverse technology calculations of their offspring, we are now confident. We have 100 per cent accuracy for each parent DNA and complete genome. Therefore, I repeat that the creation of an original unique individual-character life form remains firmly in the dominion of God.

'Following on from this accomplishment, our genetic engineers are now reconstructing 100 per cent DNA molecules for the parents' parents. Our calculations show that using these established formulas to move up the family tree generation by generation is now a reality. We can resurrect any person genetically connected to that genealogical tree. It will include the many unfortunates massacred in such acts as war, starvation, plague, and more who left a mother and offspring for us to regenerate their DNA. We can calculate their blueprint to discover the sequence of the remaining ill-fated souls. In line with this approach, ancient DNA samples prove extremely useful for validating results. Mark's previous reference to Ezekiel and the valley of the dry bones inspires us to search for archaeological remains of whole lost armies. A small army of DNA investigators across the globe is pursuing suitable specimens as we speak. We are establishing vast DNA libraries across the planet. There is much work to do. I must bid farewell and fulfil my destiny for humanity's role in the universe.'

Miles and Jack were astonished as Dr Jie departed and felt no need to ask questions. Professor Lovall rose to continue.

'The implications of this reverse step-ladder approach aligned with new sequences to restore previous generations' lives are immense. So, all our reborn *Homo sapiens* must take their memories of Mother Earth out into the universe. Copernicus might have been wrong after all, and our planet could be the centre of God's creation. The significance of our achievements is that *Homo sapiens* – us – will not now need to evolve into another species. With generations of human endeavour, the experience of good and evil, intelligence and consciousness are at scientists' disposal. God's intentions for us are becoming more apparent. The torment and euphoria endured over the past for the fundamental gift of free will have prepared us. The realisation that the solution to the ultraviolet catastrophe heralded the transition from a world of classical physics to cross the formidable bridge into the realm of quantum mechanics. Science continues to bewilder us. Our matron explains on the Trimester wards that the information transfer to the epiblast and hypoblast cell clusters is unknowable. However, we at Geras now understand that Quantum Entanglement makes the transfer of data outstrip the speed of light and is instantaneous from anywhere, disregarding distance and time. This new science reinforces our belief in God's design and control for our function and purpose.'

There was no need to hold back any information regarding progress. The professor and his team explained thoroughly that three space stations of considerable size are already present in the solar system. Among other notable features, they were each equipped with two Exowombs.

Everyone looked forward to this year's passing-out parade at Cosmos in a month when the two intended to meet once more. Miles and Jack felt they were now up to date with much information. Both were happy to return to London.

The assembled leaders of the movement back at Lambeth Cross were absorbed but not in the least bit surprised with what Miles and Jack had to report. Mark and Simon were under no illusion to treat the transition to rebirth with the utmost discretion. As the Elders of the world senate committees approached the end of life, they were more than ready to accept an invitation for rebirth in the Exowomb for a future life in the universe. No less willing, the present company of twelve leaders were waiting for their time to come. Professor Lovall arose to clarify his urgent request for the day's meeting, addressing the celebrated ensemble. The now ageing entourage fixed their attention on the wall screen and listened carefully to the professors' words.

'Time and time again, research at the three cities under my directorship has thrown up the as yet not understood undiscovered space within the atom, DNA and particularly now the universe. All three seem to have ninety-six per cent vacuous space without explanation but similar design. The universe consists of seventy per cent dark energy, twenty-two per cent dark matter, 3.6 per cent galactic gas and only 0.4 per cent stars and planets. To cap it all, eighty-four per cent of the matter in the universe does not absorb or emit light. So, it's not been detected yet. We assume after 13 billion years of existence that it's stable.

'The age of science is generally understood to have originated during the eighteenth century through discoveries made by 'natural philosophers, as they were then known. Today it is understood that the vacuum or empty space in the universe is in its lowest energy state with nothing there. Meanwhile, the Higgs Boson is supposed to give everything its mass. However, recent calculations show that the empty space in the universe may not be in its lowest energy state. That would mean our universe may not be a stable entity and could be in a false vacuum. Therefore, a high-energy event could knock it to a lower energy state to collapse and renew itself as the 'reverse cone' of antimatter in the Big Bang. This episode could even explain the creation of the universe. Is it far-fetched? We'll soon find out.

'My colleagues working at the Ice Cube Neutrino Telescope at the South Pole informed me yesterday of a significant increase in activity within their facility. The neutrino is useful because it has a neutral electrical charge, rarely interacts with matter, and travels straight from its source. Another handy attribute this microscopic particle has is the advantage of practically zero mass, which can outpace light through any environment other than a vacuum. Consider this:

Hebrews 11:3: "By faith, we understand that the worlds were framed by the word of God so that the things which are seen were not made of things which are visible."

'The sophisticated digital optical modules buried up to 1,500 metres deep in the Antarctic ice detect the presence of incoming neutrinos. The Cherenkov blue comet tails race across the computer screens to give us notice that the super red giant Betelgeuse went supernova sometime in the early seventeenth century. Our calculations confirm that the light from this cataclysmic explosion will be with us in seventeen days. We must immediately advise the world to take the opportunity to witness the most incredible light show ever and inform them that it is too far away to cause us any harm. However, we must pray to our all-knowing creator not to employ this gigantic burst of cosmic energy to destabilise his current universe so that we can continue our honest endeavours in his name.'

9
1964 Chevrolet Super Nova

(Of Fibreglass Prototype body construction in Fire Frost Silver)

The stars began to fade on the morning of the seventeenth day before dawn. In what should have been the darkest hour, the night sky lit up with silvery magnesium brightness. The strangeness of no heat and terrifying sound contrast that should partner such an event held the upturned faces in awe. There was no noise. The incandescence above appeared to gel into a kind of luminous white inkblot to radiate an even phosphorescence around the planet. The stars of the night were, as in daylight, invisible. At sunrise, our sun faced new competition and appeared a little faint. Although a surreal event, few people observing from the surface felt threatened but fortified in their refound faith.

The uncountable octillion octillions of neutrinos passed straight through the solar system out into the cosmos. Their source on this occasion was the collapsed core of the red supergiant Betelgeuse, 950 times larger than our sun, into a ball of neutrons just five miles in diameter: a neutron star. The electromagnetic waves, including visible light, are slowed by the chaos of the explosion, producing dense and turbulent gases light-years across. Such an event so unimaginably gargantuan should destabilise its galaxy, but it doesn't.

The sophisticated modern neutrino telescopes briefly captured only a handful of these particles in past observations. The recent event afforded intense study of the most abundant particle in the universe. In just seventeen days, the analytical minds of our species worked out its miraculous properties and functionality. The ability of this invisible entity (the neutrino) with practically no rest mass to travel through everything to anywhere is key to its purpose.

Just like the living cell is programmed to die in the human cell cycle, stars in the cosmos have the same destiny to fulfil their purpose to stabilise the universe. However, an explosion half the size of the solar system has to have its gravitational energy dispersed not to destroy its host. The neutrino is the carrier entrusted with the job.

At first, the interruption of the day's and night's normal illumination gave rise to fear of the universe's stability. As the days passed, this light from the heavens, while being enjoyed by the billions of Twenty-First-Century Church members as the prospect of divine salvation, threw the more enlightened leadership into God-fearing trepidation. After a month, changes in the celestial vision demand further attention. The silver-white shroud began to shrink.

The fireball, still visible in daylight, acquired a majestic opaque blue radiance of unparalleled beauty at night. Silence reigned at Lambeth Cross as events began to unfold. Over time the fireball started to diminish to become no bigger than a pinhead of not much consequence in the night sky. Although astronomers past and present are well aware of the dying stages, a super red giant undergoes first-hand observation that must confirm the science. Betelgeuse was one of the two brightest stars in the Orion constellation on a spiral arm of our Milky Way galaxy, which tests our theories to the limit.

The Ice Cube Telescope staff reported a revived surge of neutrinos. Professor Lovall confirmed the pinprick of remaining light produced by another neutron star in a gravitational spin of incalculable speed to orbit Betelgeuse.

His voice boomed across from Geras on the wall screen at Lambeth, 'We must expect a release of explosive energy and distortion. It may catalyse a descent into the hypothetical second vacuum, a lower energy state. It is possible our galaxies could begin to collide and start a contraction of the universe.'

The founder members of the church in the conference room at Lambeth, drinks to hand, gestured to Mark and Simon to make some sort of reply to the scientist. Mark looked around the room, surveying his twenty or so friends with a gentle smile. TV engineers and camera operators jostled around him to produce a commanding position at the elevated desk at the front of the room. He chose his moment to reply, as Sancho Panza would, to remind his erstwhile boss Don Quixote of prudent rationality. Speaking with an air of authority and wisdom, Mark broadcast the last address of his first life to the worldwide community.

'Have faith there are many references handed down to us that the cosmic horizon will, in fact, continue to recede and carry the stars and planets with it. The undiscovered dark energy will continue to grow as it is designed to do and must play a role in the self-repair system to preserve the entity. The stellar death we have witnessed over the past few weeks fuels the star nurseries of the universe – the ejection of all chemical elements showers the surrounding vacuum with a glittering nebula. Let us consider.

Joel 2:30: "And I will show wonders in the heavens and in the Earth, blood and fire, and pillars of smoke."

'At this time, quantum mechanics is happy to dance with classical physics and must play the role together in a self-repair system to preserve the whole structured order. The small amount of visible light we see now emits from the two dark glossy shadow neutron orbs helpless in their accelerated spin towards one another. Super-gravitational energy is clutching them in a vice-like grip towards total collapse. Their eternal union is instrumental in the cycles of heaven to regenerate that part of our galaxy. The light on Orion's left shoulder will flicker and die out. The celebration of the moment of initial fusion will consist of a final fireball ejection of the elements heavier than iron, gold, silver, uranium, platinum and many others to complete the Periodic Table. The spinning disc will begin to form an event horizon of orange around the darkness within. For one second, expect to observe a fantastic beam of energy and light, a gamma-ray burst that gathers pace way out in the universe, a light to guide us into the future and fulfil our destiny in the many years to come.

'Isaiah 60:1: "Arise; shine; For your light has come! And the glory of the LORD is risen upon you.

'John 8:12: "Then Jesus spoke to them again, saying, 'I am the light of the world he who follows Me shall not walk in darkness, but have the light of life.'

Events unfolded just as Mark said they would, except that weak gamma-repeated flares preceded the six-minute gamma-ray burst. Subsequently, all the local matter and light disappeared into the singularity of the newly formed black hole, never to be seen again.

Safe in the knowledge of these recent events and the twelve leaders of the movement's interpretation of a self-repairing universe, the enormous global corporations undertook the construction of interstellar spacecraft on an unprecedented scale. Lambeth Cross had long before decreed that a sustainable population of five billion unique and naturally born earthlings would be most prudent to protect the home planet Earth. The declining birth rate achieved this in good time. Meanwhile, the quantum computers aboard the many space stations orbiting Mars employed the 'magnetic field concept' to restore its atmosphere lost due to the convection of its magnetic field shut down four billion years before. Self-replicating robots controlled from above proliferated across the planet to mine carbon-bearing minerals, build nuclear power plants, and factories to pump chlorofluorocarbons and fabricate billions of tons of gases to establish a temporary greenhouse effect. The pioneers introduced oxygen-producing cyanobacteria to raise temperatures and facilitate the start of photosynthesis. Microbes and other bacteria naturally consume the toxic perchlorate from the soil. The ice caps began to thaw, and an enormous army of mechanised agricultural machines cleaned the land. Inexhaustible amounts of fertiliser below were available for the robots to mine. Deeper down under these excavations, they pumped the water trapped in the crust, encouraged by the newfound warmth, back to the surface.

In less time than anticipated, the quantum computers had constructed a safe atmosphere for the Humartians to establish permanent self-sufficient settlements on the planet. The super-mechanised agriculture farms provided more than enough healthy food to sustain a projected population of one billion reborn souls. The thermodynamic adjustments previously made removed high-altitude dust to make way for an exquisite silver-blue dawn. The new environment produces butterscotch clouds on a vivid blue-violet sky during the daytime, but as sunset approached, the horizon returned to silver-blue.

The new semi-subterranean cities interconnected with the latest maglev transport complemented the accompanying rural fields and evergreen forests that resembled Argyle in western Scotland. Though a much smaller planet than Earth, it afforded oceans, lakes and rivers to accommodate teeming marine life. The preparations for all the descendants of the Exowombs on Earth made them ready for the exodus to Mars. Livestock and the harvest awaited their arrival. No Exowomb remained on Earth. Schools and universities surrounded the giant hospital complexes incorporating extensive Exowomb facilities in every town and city on the rejuvenated planet. The Humartians celebrated the reborn in every ward as the population rapidly increased to the desired target, and life was good there, as they worked and played among old friends and new.

The enormous spacecraft and space stations were now not needed after the final migration. They pulled out of orbit to cross the solar system with their technicians and quantum systems to terraform planet Venus next with the object of settling an estimated six billion reborn.

The quaint Staffordshire church always remained a place of worship confined to its local parishioners – it had never featured in the movement's viral success. However, all twelve founder members agreed it would be perfect as a memorial to themselves and their efforts. The sun illuminated this English pastoral setting. The graveyards had long been abandoned; the occupants' DNA was being transferred to newly established libraries to be processed in the innumerable extra-terrestrial Exowombs. These former resting places of the dead and the spacious car park now housed a collection of classic motor vehicles. The twelve concluded that the star car in the exhibition room should be on an Egyptian plinth to commemorate the cosmic explosion of Betelgeuse that confirmed the universe's stability. Billy, calabash pipe in hand, had searched the world over to find the car that now stood proudly beneath a bank of spotlights on its dais. He had persuaded a Chinese collector to donate the 1964 Chevrolet Super Nova with its original fibreglass prototype body finished in Fire Frost Silver. Standing proud, she overlooked the small pathway leading to the church. Once inside the building, visitors could experience the fourteenth-century interior carefully merged with the twenty-first. The exhibits on view did not deify anyone. Still, they conveyed a sense that intelligent streetwise executives had every bit as much of a right, if not more, to govern the people peacefully.

The giant wall screen on the altar relaying the daily activities aboard the caravan of spacecraft five light-years away in the cosmos seemed of most interest to the visitors. The subtitles streaming at the bottom of the screen informed those present that one billion DNA samples were available, and on their way to start a new population. One could see the accoutrements of everyday life were not much different from those on Earth. All the necessities for adult life on the destination exoplanet Luyten B were available. Midwives busy in the many Exowombs delivered the children into excellent facilities for sports and thirteen years of education. The twelve founding members were reborn on Mars to expedite their graduation and coordinate their arrival as young adults. The pictures of the giant space probe entering the constellation Canis Major were stunning on the church screen. The watching visitors were astonished to learn that Luyten B (Gliese 273B) was a super-earth three times larger than Earth, with room for twenty-two billion reborn *Homo sapiens*. Travelling close to the speed of light, everyone aboard would be thirteen years older on arrival. An event to be witnessed in the little church some seven years hence.

www.ingramcontent.com/pod-product-compliance
Lightning Source LLC
Chambersburg PA
CBHW051146190726
48290CB00006B/2014